PASSIONATE VISIONS

PASSIONATE VISIONS

By

Barbara Rothe

Cover design by Jessica Boatwright

Copyright © 1999 by Barbara Rothe

All rights reserved. No part of this book may be reproduced, stored in a retrieval system, or transmitted by any means, electronic, mechanical, photocopying, recording, or otherwise, without written permission from the author.

ISBN 1-58500-768-4

1stBooks - rev. 02/14/00

ABOUT THE BOOK

Two 20 year old cousins meet at a family reunion and share the joy, humor, and wonderment of their first exhilarating loves. Andrea is a New York City nursing student and Muffy is her effervescent Houston soul-mate. But Andrea finds Muffy caught in the vicious cycle of an eating disorder and, defying parents, Andrea daringly helps Muffy confront the disease.

Following only a few years after her father's death, Andrea unexpectedly experiences tragedy beyond belief. She faces the enormity of this challenge with an inspirational courage and faith bringing <u>PASSIONATE</u> <u>VISIONS</u> to a mystical, uplifting close!

DEDICATION

For families everywhere

Chapter One

After dinner Andrea ran upstairs to the third floor of Tillman Hall, the red brick dorm at Piedmont Hills School. The Macpherson reunion had been held here every summer for the last twenty years. She pushed open the swinging oak door and ran into the bathroom. She heard someone retch, then gag in another cubicle in the row of bathroom stalls. Tiptoeing slowly down the white tiled bathroom floor, she stopped instantly, recognizing her cousin's red ballet shoes beneath the closed door. *Oh no.* Andrea felt her heart pound in her chest.

"Muffy, is that you?"

"Go away, Andrea. I don't want you to see me."

"I'm not going away. I think I know what you're doing. I've seen it in the hospital. We need to talk."

"No. Go away!" Muffy said.

Andrea heard her cry. She went into the next stall, bent over and put her head under the separating wall and looked up aghast. "Open your door I can help you. Please," Andrea begged. "Please!"

Muffy unlocked her door, but stood behind it. Andrea waited for her to come out.

"Andrea, no one must see me like this. Momma would die if she knew."

"Yeah, and you'll die if you don't get some help! I thought you were awfully thin." Andrea held out her hand to her cousin. "Please come out."

"Why are you so strong?" Muffy said in a loud angry voice.

"I don't know," Andrea said.

"Why?" Muffy screamed, and stepped out.

Andrea gasped as she saw her favorite cousin. Tears slipped from her red-rimmed eyes, saliva and vomitus were about her mouth. Her heavy blond locks hung by her swollen distorted face with strings of hair turned dark, and stuck in puke on her cheeks.

"Answer me. I've got to be strong to stop this."

Andrea stared in horror at her.

"Answer me!" Muffy's eyes wide, she screamed at her again.

Andrea shuddered. "I don't know."

"Answer me, for God's sake! I need what you have." She stamped her foot. "Talk!"

"I don't know." Andrea frowned. "It probably has to do with my father's death. Now, will you let me help you?" She held out her arms to Muffy, but Andrea saw her cousin step back.

"Why didn't you tell me that before?" Muffy's eyes squinted at her in distrust.

"Tell you what?"

"Why you're strong?"

"I'm not. I just answered 'cause you *shrieked* at me, *talk!* And because, I want to help you. Please Muffy," Andrea begged. "I promise I won't tell Aunt Elizabeth. Why on earth would I tell your mother?"

"You've always been so happy and confident," Muffy said. "I remember Momma cried when Uncle Paul died. They talked about your father's sudden heart attack, and how poor you and Aunt Marie would be because he had no life insurance."

Andrea held Muffy's blue eyes. She spoke softly. "Please just tell me about it."

"If Momma finds out, she'll punish me in her way. I have to be *very* careful."

"I promised. Come on, let's go to our secret hiding spot." Andrea took Muffy by her arm to the row of white porcelain sinks across the large bathroom. "Now, wash your face and hands with me."

Andrea watched Muffy out of the edges of her eyes as she washed her own hands. Though they were both five feet eight, Andrea looked so much bigger than her cousin. Then she looked at her own reflection in the mirror. Her serious sea-green eyes stared back at her. Her dirty-blond hair looked even darker next to Muffy's golden waves.

Muffy peeked over at her above the wet paper towel still at her face. Her eyes crinkled. "I've got a six pack of Schlitz hidden under my bed." Muffy tossed the towel into the trash basket, bolted out the door and down the hall to their shared weekend dorm room.

Andrea dashed behind her, watching Muffy's thin legs. "You're looking great in your red plaid pedal-pushers and matching Capezio's."

Muffy yelled back over her shoulder. "Hope our cousins will still be in the dining room with the others, and won't see us. I'll hide the beer in my big swim bag.

"I have to be careful, because Momma searches and examines *everything*." Muffy whispered harshly as she and Andrea ran back down stairs, and out the white double entry doors, and by the stone benches where the older family members visited after dinner. They skipped down one of the two curved stairways that led to the imposing entrance, skirted past the scrolled brick marker, *Piedmont School For Boys. Established 1835,* and out across the rolling green lawns. They caught hands and capered by the red brick Science Lab toward the pool set in a valley beneath spectacular wooded hills. The shining yellow sun had almost finished its long lazy slide down the blue August sky, in front of the gently swaying oaks and maples of the Piedmont forests of North Carolina.

"Away at University of Texas is easier for me, but once I caught Momma searching my dorm room, when she came earlier than she told me." Muffy sighed. "I walked in from class and found her reading my mail."

Andrea stared at her wide-eyed as they passed the pool. "Are you serious?"

They sat down on a towel behind a small thicket of blooming pink oleander bushes, nestled next to a garden marked with rows of tall tasseled summer corn. The air smelled of freshly cut grass, and the crickets sang in the warmth of the early evening. It's where they had talked surreptitiously every summer for as long as Andrea could remember.

Occasionally, over the years, Muffy would be unable to come if she were on vacation with her family in Greece or Europe. Andrea, too, had missed several reunions. She hadn't been able to get off from her summer waitressing jobs on Cape Cod, or Mother had said they just couldn't spend the money. Her sisters and mother had only come together once in the seven years since her father had died.

But this year Andrea had wanted to see Muffy so badly that she'd saved some of her weekly school meal allowance, and some of her baby-sitting money to be able to pay for the Greyhound bus fare. Muffy had picked her up in Charlotte, and driven her to the reunion in her family's big white Cadillac.

"Yes," Muffy said. Her knees touched Andrea's as they sat Indian-style and looked at each other. Muffy's bright aqua blouse brought out the deep blue of her concerned eyes. She frowned. "She reads my letters, smells my clothes, and interrogates my friends and their mothers about what I do, say, and think. She doesn't trust me, and it's such a pain." Muffy looked directly at her. "Actually I'm a pretty good kid. I try to please her, but it's never enough." Muffy pulled a bottle of beer from her bag, opened it and handed it to Andrea. She opened her own, and Andrea watched her take long deep swallows till the bottle was half empty.

Andrea sipped her beer. "Why didn't you tell me this before?"

"I didn't know that Momma snooped, or how much for a long time. I went to the University of Texas, her first choice, not mine, and I even joined Pi Beta Phi, the sorority that she was in when she was there. Most of my *real* friends joined Kappa Alpha Theta, but I can live with that. I wish now I'd at least gone to Virginia, my first choice, so she couldn't drive up from Houston in three hours and walk in on me at any time."

"I bet Aunt Marie doesn't do that to you," Muffy said.

"She's strict like Aunt Elizabeth, but she's always at work in the hospital. When I was in high school and before I had my driver's license, I'd wanted her to drive me shopping, but she never could." Andrea looked down at her plain white shirt and navy pedal-pushers. "Now, I'd be happy if we could just go to a movie together."

"She trusts you."

"Mother laid down three rules--no smoking, drinking, or boys in the house when she wasn't home. She worked the evening nursing shift to earn twenty dollars more every month."

"You're lucky," Muffy said as she lit her Pall Mall.

"I am, but I'm sure no goody-two-shoes. I simply couldn't break her rules too much, when I watched her work so hard for me." Andrea thought of her mother's tiny bedroom in their attached house compared to Aunt Elizabeth's elegant master suite in her enormous River Oaks Southern Colonial, where Andrea had visited Muffy many summers before her father had died. She'd only visited once since then, and her aunt and uncle had paid for her trip.

Andrea lit her own Camel and carefully studied Muffy, her thick blond hair already back to its perfect pageboy which framed large round eyes and deep dimples on each lovely cheek. "How long has this been going on?"

Muffy looked down at the green towel. "Since I went to college."

Andrea paused and stared at her. "Tell me the truth," she whispered in a low voice.

#

Muffy took a drag from her cigarette and exhaled slowly looking at her towel. She looked up directly at Andrea, took a deep breath, then looked down again at her towel. "All right," she sighed. "The spring of my junior year at Houston Episcopal Day School. It was gradual, and on and off at first. I remember that first I wanted to stay a little kid and have fun--come to reunions and play with you and all my cousins. Then I wanted to grow up as fast as possible and I got sort of scared. You're twenty next month, a senior nursing student in New York and I'm twenty-one, a senior at UT. That time is forever behind us."

Andrea frowned. "How many times a day?"

Muffy looked up innocently. "What do you mean?"

Andrea looked at her directly. "You know what I mean and I want the truth."

Muffy looked at Andrea's half-full beer bottle, then reached into her bag and flipped off the top of another beer with her opener. She turned to the nearby giant Magnolia trees in the darkening sky. She heard the shouts and shrieks of her younger cousins playing in the lighted pool. She'd always loved this campus. She'd wished she'd been a boy, so she could have been a student here, like her two older brothers.

She felt Andrea's gaze and knew she waited. Tears welled in her eyes, and slowly slipped down her face. She bent her head low over her crossed ankles, her long flaxen hair falling to the sides of her face, shielding herself from Andrea and the whole world. "This summer," her voice barely audible, "five or six times a day. It's been real bad, but at school it's better--maybe just two or three, and on good days, only once." She put her elbows on her knees and covered her eyes and face with her hands, as if to keep Andrea from getting closer.

She felt Andrea's arms around her. Muffy crumpled over and cried out loud, her shoulders shaking in spasms.

Andrea whispered in her ear. "Do you take laxatives?"

She wished Andrea would shut up and go away. She listened to her heart beating in her chest. After long moments of silence, "Yes," she murmured quietly, but she felt an immediate sense of relief wash over her. It had been so long, so tight, a silent secret of guilt. She lowered her head further wishing she could be swallowed up in the rows of sweet smelling corn where she sat.

"Don't," Andrea said. "Promise me, you won't do that."

"Muffy, where are you?" Then a second time she heard her mother shout louder. Muffy cried harder. "I want you to come now, and talk with Aunt Mary Anna."

Frightened, she felt goose flesh rising on her arms. Muffy looked up at Andrea. Their eyes met, and they smiled. "Ictaminigoalagosectobingolady, yoo hoo!" they whispered together, and Muffy nodded her head in their secret signal of long ago--established at this spot, at this reunion, when she was five, and Andrea four.

Muffy quietly picked up her bag, and Andrea lifted their towel. Wordlessly, they crept quickly on their hands and knees over the damp green grass, and into the very middle of the rows of corn. Only when they were safely nested did Muffy smile at her. "One more time--may it work." Muffy had said it this time, and grinned with Andrea, as her mother's voice grew more distant and then stopped.

Like many times before, they lay their towel against three corn stalks, and broke them down. They spread their towel on top, lay down on their stomachs, and cuddled quietly next to each other. They each opened another beer. "Do you think it's safe now?" Muffy whispered.

"Yes," Andrea said softly, and they lit their cigarettes.

"Remember the year we'd both started smoking, then we came here that summer and measured out this very spot--in line with the pool house, so they couldn't see our smoke? Did Aunt Marie ever find out you smoked in high school?"

"I told her after I started--that first summer I waitressed on the Cape and made so much money."

"You told her?" Muffy asked incredulously.

"Yeah. I got rocks in my head, but I did."

"What'd she do?"

"Yelled a furious long lecture, but ended, *don't you dare smoke in public. You need an excellent reputation to get a scholarship. If you must smoke, at least wait until you've graduated from high school.* So, I smoked in private, and with just a couple of friends who swore not to tell. She smiled at Muffy. "And then of course, I tried to keep her from smelling it."

Muffy smiled into Andrea's serious trusting face and took her hand. "I'm so glad you're here. I'd've been miserable if you hadn't come. You can't imagine how awful the drive was this year, all the way from Texas. If Billy and John Taylor hadn't come, I don't think I could have done it."

"Do your brothers know you're sick?" Andrea asked.

"No, I've told nobody except you, but John Taylor knows. Like you just now, he heard me once at home, but we haven't talked about it." Muffy sighed deeply. "I think he understands, because he wanted to be a doctor, but after college my parents pressured him to follow Billy into Daddy's oil business." She hesitated. "But, what am I going to do?" she wailed.

"Get well." Andrea said firmly.

"But how?" Her voice, desperate.

"I don't know exactly . . . but, I'm going to find out at nursing school, and write you. I've only seen one hospital patient with your condition, which I think is relatively new. I think it was called bulimia or maybe it was anorexia. Anyway this patient wore sunglasses all the time, because she didn't want to get close to us, but she did get well and went home. First thing the doctors wrote in big red letters in her chart was NO LAXATIVES, EVEN IF REQUESTED BY THE PATIENT. You must promise me you'll do the same."

"All right, but remember--only write me at college, or Momma will read it. You know I'd like to wear sunglasses all the time, too. I do as much as I can." Muffy paused and looked away from Andrea. "But how did she stop . . . ah, the up-chucking?"

"I honestly don't know. She saw a psychiatrist everyday, and the only thing I remember in the nursing conferences was that she learned why she was doing it and slowly improved in the hospital--in a different environment from her home."

"Why was she doing it?"

Andrea thought of the patient for a moment. She had been Andrea's age and had made Andrea so sad. And now, to think of her dearest cousin sick with the same disorder. "I think they said she felt scared and totally controlled by everything in her life."

"But that's exactly how I feel, but not by everything--just by Momma. But psychiatrist? Momma would die if I said I wanted to see a psychiatrist. She'd say, *how embarrassing. What would my friend Ella Louise say?*"

"Muffy, this patient was in the psychiatric wing of our hospital. That's what you're going to need to get well. You've established a pattern over four years."

Muffy shook her head slowly. "Never." She sighed deeply. "Momma would never allow it."

Andrea watched her closely. "Well, maybe you'll have to do it anyway."

Muffy looked down at her beer and shook her head. "She'd kill me."

"But maybe this disease will kill you." Andrea's voice rose. "Have you thought about that?"

Muffy turned her face to look at Andrea. Her forehead wrinkled and her baby-blue eyes grew wide. "It can't, can it, Andrea?"

She looked at her directly, then took her hand. "Honestly, I think it can, but Muffy, I saw this one patient get well and leave the hospital, and if she can do it, so can you. There's so little known about this new syndrome. I'll go to my instructors, and to the medical library, and see what I can learn. I promise. I'll send you all the literature that I can find."

"Oh, Andrea, thank you. I knew you'd know how to help me. I had planned to ask your help, but you faked me out and found me at it. I know you won't tell anybody. If only I were strong like you. I'm so ashamed that I can't stop. Sometimes I feel so dirty that I shower and shower, brush my teeth over and over, floss repeatedly, but I still feel filthy. Then I hate myself."

"Well, I don't hate you. You're more fun than anyone I've ever met. You've always been my best friend and cousin. And Muffy . . ." Muffy felt her hand tighten, "I have a friend, a doctor, and he may be able to help us too."

"A doctor, a boyfriend? How old is he?"

"He's six years older than I am. His name is Tom Scofield. He's *wonderful.* And, he knows *everything.* I can't wait for you to meet him. You'll love him, too--everyone will!"

"Wow! When did you meet him? Where?"

"Last week. We were in the OR. I was the student scrub nurse. He pulled down his mask after the case. I was right there looking up at him and I just fell head over heels in love--just like that!" Andrea rolled over onto her back and looked at the puffy white clouds passing across the darkening sky.

"Like in that movie, *Indiscreet* with Ingrid Bergman and Gary Grant. Remember, he walked through her front door and she stood there with cold cream all over her face? Oh, how romantic. Love at first sight."

"It is!" Andrea said gleefully and rolled back over onto her stomach and looked directly into Muffy's eyes. "But first I'd listened to him. He's an intern. He had answered questions and talked intently for three hours with the chief surgeon. I wondered all the time what he looked like. I loved the sound of his deep voice. It's very sexy. I think I fell in love with his serious voice first."

"Oh, Andrea, you're so funny." They tittered and laughed together on their towel and opened up their last beers. "Do you think he likes you?" Muffy asked. "Have you gone out with him?"

"He asked me later that day in the OR, if I'd eat with him in the cafeteria, but I was on split shifts. That means you work seven to eleven in the morning and then seven to eleven at night. He couldn't get off to eat until after seven. He didn't say anything about asking me again, but I'll just *die* if he doesn't!"

"What does he look like?"

"When he pulled down his mask, his whole face broke into a giant smile. Every muscle in his face must work when he smiles. He has wonderful, big, defined lips and they just burst apart over beautiful white teeth. The insides of his eyes are very dark, almost black, and I swear they grinned, too. Even his ears wiggled."

"Wow! No wonder you have such an *enormous* crush."

"And," she rushed on, "under his scrub cap there was a crop of very thick, dark, brown hair, but at his temples it had the most adorable silver threads woven into it."

Muffy gasped. "Are you kidding? He's prematurely gray?"

Andrea grinned at her. "Isn't that sophisticated?" She took a sip of beer. "But now, Muffy, how about you? How's Bucky? What's it like to be pinned? Is it better than going steady?"

"A hundred times! Momma wants us to have our engagement party this Christmas, and then I can marry the week after we graduate from UT. Bucky'll work for Daddy in his office like Billy and John Taylor. You know, he's a trust baby."

Andrea frowned and turned to look at her. "A what?"

"A trust baby."

Andrea giggled. "I've never heard of such a thing."

"Oh, you old Yankee. It's when some boy has inherited wealth, so much so that he can live on the interest from his capital. He doesn't really *have* to work, but most do anyway--at least a little bit."

"Wow! Then you'll be rich."

"Muffy!" The voice was high pitched and loud.

Andrea saw Muffy's head jerk up, and her body twitch on their towel. Andrea put her arm over Muffy's shoulders, and wished desperately that she could say something helpful or even funny to relieve Muffy's discomfort. Instead she gently rubbed her back in circles.

"Muffy!" Andrea heard Aunt Elizabeth's commanding voice again from somewhere nearby in the darkening quiet of the campus. "I know you're somewhere around this pool, and if you aren't in the dorm in fifteen minutes you'll be in serious trouble. Do you *hear* me?"

Chapter Two

At the final reunion breakfast on Sunday, Andrea watched her stooped, six foot three, great Uncle John Taylor stand and say the Blessing and closing words of the Macpherson reunion. As he rested his fragile fingers on the back of his dining room chair, his snow white hair fell forward on his forehead, over his bowed head.

"God, we thank thee for this beautiful August weekend, for this opportunity for our family to come together from all parts of this great nation. We thank you for our country, our freedoms, our Republican leaders. We would ask that You strengthen this family--its babies, children, aged members, and all those many in-between. Make this family a circle of strength, love, and acceptance as each birth and marriage increases our joy of sharing. Make us remindful that each crisis faced together as a family strengthens us all. Amen.

"Would my remaining sisters stand with me now to be acknowledged?" Frail great Aunt Jessica Louisa stood, leaning heavily on her cane, with Ollie Elizabeth and Mary Anna next to her. The three aged widows smiled, and graciously, humbly acknowledged the applause given them.

Andrea loved the theme of his final family prayer. It made her feel that she had a big family, not just her mother and two married sisters. As she sat down next to Muffy and her family, she looked around the dining room she loved.

The assembled Macphersons ate in one corner of the baronial dining room--at nine, dark pine, rectangular tables of eight. Each person went through the cafeteria line and brought his or her plate to the tables, with some family members assisting their parents as well as the little children with their trays. The school let them employ the school kitchen and housekeeping staff for their weekend use. One Macpherson cousin or another was always a student here, and currently, one of her uncles was assistant head master, and her Virginia cousin, John Mark, worked in administration.

Tudor beams scaled the beige walls that rose in gothic proportions and showed off the claret red, golden yellow, and bright blue stained-glass windows, trimmed with dark oak wood. Sheaves of horizontal sunshine filtered through the windows, and bathed the small corner where she sat.

Andrea smelled the aroma of the traditional closing breakfast of salty Virginia ham brought by the Virginia contingent, sausage contributed by the Ohio group, grits smothered in cheese, eggs, hash brown potatoes, and cinnamon buns added by the local North Carolinian relatives. The red and black squares in the plaid carpet were intertwined with a thin yellow stripe. Andrea treasured the masculine room in this venerable old school of erudition--*for America's young Sons of the South* she read when the school catalog arrived every year. It was sent annually to her mother, although she had no Southern sons.

Andrea watched how and what Muffy ate, as she had at all their meals since she had found her in the bathroom Friday evening. Andrea secretly studied her figure, her teeth, and tried to stay with her right after they shared their meals in the hopes of distracting Muffy from running to the bathroom.

After breakfast, everyone walked slowly back to the big foyer of the school dorm where all the Macphersons had slept for the weekend. The double paneled doors were pushed back into the walls, and the huge room filled with Macpherson relatives as they poured over the photographs that had been placed on the hall tables. The photos had been taken at the Saturday evening cocktail party and formal dinner where all the women dressed up and the older Macpherson men wore gray, black and maroon plaid kilts and knee high gray socks.

Andrea looked around and felt alone again. Her relatives selected and signed up to have photos sent to them. They hugged and said good-byes for another year. She wished her mother, sisters and father could be with her. She always missed them here, where she remembered them all together when she was a child. They had made the exciting car trip South every summer to see her mother's family.

Andrea briefly scanned the photos.

"Aren't you going to buy some photos for Aunt Marie?" Andrea heard Muffy's voice behind her.

Andrea turned around. "I'm not sure yet--which one to get."

Muffy rushed on, "But I must run now and help Mama finish our packing and load the car. She said to tell you to meet us in 15 minutes at the driveway in front of the dorm.

"I'll be there," Andrea said looking over to the staircase to check that her small suitcase was where she had left it. She looked back at the photograph where she was pictured with Muffy's parents, Aunt Elizabeth and Uncle Orville, and with Muffy's older brothers, John Taylor and Billy. Mother would want to know every detail of the reunion and she would tell her everything, except about Muffy. Andrea had wanted to buy a photo for her mother--of everyone assembled Saturday night--her mothers' brothers, her three older aunts and uncle, and then her favorite sister, Aunt Elizabeth, who looked so glamorous, next to big Uncle Orville. But she didn't. There was never enough money and she knew her mother wouldn't approve that extravagance. She'd just tell her, and she must remember about the new Ohio baby added to Cousin Gee's genealogical tree.

There was only time to whisper with Muffy in the back seat of their Cadillac as the Davidson family drove her to the Greyhound bus stop in Charlotte. Uncle Orville turned the radio from the song "Thank Heaven for Little Girls," to the news. "The Russian SputnikIII launched into space--" then Muffy giggled in her ear again.

In the Greyhound station, Aunt Elizabeth said to Andrea, "Would you like to visit us right after Christmas during the holidays? It would be such fun and we might have some exciting times next Christmas at our house," she said with a smile and glance at Muffy.

"Oh, Aunt Elizabeth, thank you. I'd love to. That is, if nursing school vacation is long enough for the bus trip. I don't remember how many vacation days we get this year."

"Oh, we'd have you fly to Houston, like last time." Her aunt looked about the station. You couldn't take a . . . a bus. This will be our Christmas gift for you. I'll write my dear sister."

"Oh, thank you, Aunt Elizabeth." But Andrea had heard something different in her aunt's voice. It made her flush with embarrassment. She looked at the elegantly dressed Davidson family, as if for the first time, standing in the Greyhound bus station. They looked out of place. Why, we're worlds apart, Andrea thought in surprise, even though we are in a big, loving family. Why haven't I ever thought of this before?

"Come now, my little Miss Muffin," her Uncle Orville said to Muffy, "say good-bye to my little dumplin."

"Come on now, my darling blond cuz. Give me a hug," John Taylor said.

"Y'all come now, Andrea. I'll take you to our friend's annual Christmas bash. My friends will love your sea-green eyes, even though you're a Yankee."

"Stop horsing around, Billy," Uncle Orville said, " and don't you go insulting any Macphersons, especially my little dumplin." Uncle Orville's arms wrapped her to his immense chest, where she'd always felt warm, safe, and protected. She heard his deep voice bellow out, and his chest heave as he laughed, "Good-bye, my little dumplin. We'll see you at Christmas. Tell that wonderful mother of yours, and your sisters, hello for us."

She hugged them all good-bye, and with tears in her eyes she whispered fiercely into Muffy's ear, "Remember your promise and I'll write as soon as I can."

Andrea boarded the eleven o'clock bus and took out her nursing school text book, but she rested her head back on the vinyl brown seat and looked out the window. They traveled on a long winding road through the Piedmont's southwest corner.

The bus drove by little towns where bungalows lined the streets, and on this serene Sunday afternoon, people sat visiting on front porches. Homesteaders, artisans, and religious believers had settled here, leaving a heritage of arts and architecture. They passed sweeping hillsides surrounded by enormous old Magnolia trees.

Soon they entered the northeast which formerly was North Carolina's wealthiest area. Andrea watched splendid homes of the mid-nineteenth century--Greek revivals with columned porches, and the later Italinate houses with arched tracery windows, ornate roof brackets, and distinctive moldings. She leaned closer to the window and caught glimpses of the reverse painted doorway surrounds with simulated stained glass sidelights.

Andrea yawned and closed her eyes. She thought of her father and her family--back to the spring evening that they had all walked across the street together to Pelham Memorial High School for the Girl Scouts Court of Awards. Mother had been given her five year pin as Girl Scout leader. Her older sisters sat with their troops and were called up to receive badges and pins.

She sat with her Daddy in the balcony seats high above the big gymnasium. There was a round, black bar in front of where they sat in the first row. Andrea had to look under or over the top of it. She saw on the gym floor all the groups of Scouts dressed in green, and Brownies dressed in brown, as they had marched to their positions. They sat in rectangular sections, according to their troop number and rank. All of a sudden Andrea started to cry. She felt her Daddy's arm over her shoulder.

"Why are you crying?"

She cried harder.

"Andrea, please answer me. We'll have to go home if you can't stop crying." Her father said and handed her his handkerchief.

Andrea blew into his white handkerchief. "Daddy, do you see that one little girl there--the one on the edge of the last row down there?" She pointed even though her mother kept telling her not to point. But Mother couldn't see her now.

"You mean the little Negro girl?"

"Yes," she cried.

"Why are you crying about her?"

"Because she's the *only one* . . . *alone,* in the whole gym. I've looked everywhere. I don't even see her parents sitting anywhere around down there or up here where we are."

Daddy pulled her up onto his big comfortable lap, and held his arms around her. "I'm sure her parents are probably here, but you can't see them because it's crowded." He said nothing for awhile.

"Andrea, what you feel is compassion. I think you were born with it. Let's you and I go home now." At the door of the gymnasium, Daddy had picked her up, and carried her down the long basement hall and out the door of the high school. He crossed the street, and put her down on the third step that led up to their front door. He sat down next to her. "Andrea, do you think you understand what compassion is?"

She looked up at him. "Is it sad?"

"Yes, but it's more than that. It's a feeling of love, tenderness, and empathy for someone, because you understand their situation or circumstance. Is this clear? And have you felt this way about anybody or anything else?"

"Well, it makes me sad when the kids at school throw stones at the twins."

"Twins?"

"The Goldbergs--Anthony and Anna, who live down on Nyack Avenue, closer to the train station. And the children at school don't like Carolyn Cohen either. She stole penny candy at Lauracelli's drug store. Her mother found out, and made her eat candy, nothing else, for a whole week for punishment, and her face got full of pimples, and she cried a lot in class. I took her some crackers from our kitchen, but I didn't dare tell mother."

"Sometimes people are frightened and mean to other people, because they are different. Do you understand?"

She looked at her daddy. "I think so."

"Andrea, you're only seven, but I've heard you say that you want to be a nurse when you grow up--like your mother was before we were married. I think you would be a very good nurse, because you have compassion."

"Do I get a degree?"

Her father threw back his wonderful bald head and laughed out loud. "You have heard me say that already?"

"You said that to Roddy and another time to Theweeze."

"Yes," he had answered. "And, you must get a degree if you decide to become a nurse. Have you practiced your older sister's name lately? *Lou*ise, not *The*weeze."

"I forgot." She sighed.

"Well, let's do it three times together now, and then, it's time for you to be in bed."

"Daddy, do you think I could go with you soon, down to your office on Canal Street? I love to type a letter to mother in your office and play on all your machines--especially the typesetting and adding machines. I love to stop at the Automat on our way back to Grand Central Station. It's such fun to see all the glass cages spin around with sandwiches, pies, and cakes, and then put in the coins to open them up." She caught her breath. "And Daddy, can we stop next to the Oyster Bar in Grand Central, where you get in one corner and talk to me, and I can hear you way across at the hole in the other corner?"

Chapter Three

A few weeks later Andrea walked in her student uniform through the long, white tunnel that led from the hospital to the basement of her nursing school dorm. She couldn't wait to shower and get ready for her second date with Tom. It had been a whole week since she had even seen him in the halls or cafeteria. The interns lived in separate rooms on the top floor of the hospital. She knew from friends that it was a row of very small rooms, sparsely furnished, and not very plush. Even so, she thought, it would be exciting to visit the twenty-third floor.

Andrea darted up the stairs to the lobby to check her mail. She smiled to see Muffy's handwriting on her familiar note paper.

Andrea walked out the double glass entry doors of the nurse's residence to see what the weather was like. She opened Muffy's letter and frowned deeply as she scanned her brief note.

September 15

Dear Andrea,

Have you been out with your dream boat yet? Is he still wonderful?

I've been waiting to hear from you After the reunion I was better for awhile, but last week Momma wanted me to go to so many parties with Bucky and all our friends, and hers, too--before we started our senior semester at UT. I really felt awful and on the weekend I must have done it, you know, at least 8 times. It made me feel really bad and even weak.

I was so glad to get back to the sorority house Sunday night.

And I'm sure I'll be better now that Bucky and I are here at school. He is so dreamy.

Please write me all your news. I am dying to hear from you.

Love,
Muffy

Andrea shook her head and sighed as she put Muffy's letter back in the envelope. But now she had to decide what to wear. She'd need a sweater for later, on this rather cool autumn evening. She took a deep breath and felt a twinge of nostalgia as she did every autumn when school commenced and spelled the end of happy-go-lucky summer work days. But nursing school went straight through the summers.

She took the elevator to her fifth floor. The first five floors were students' dorm rooms. The fifteen floors above were faculty offices, classes, nutrition and science labs, and nursing arts rooms.

She remembered her first visit to the Dean's office in her fourth week of school. None of her classmates had been called in, and she'd been nervous. The Dean sat so straight in her chair. She didn't wear a nurse's uniform as Andrea had expected but instead a severe navy blue suit with a tailored white blouse, almost like she was in the Navy. Her black hair was pulled back tightly into a chignon, every hair in place.

"Miss Deck, I've called you to my office to inquire why two nights a week you've signed out to Hunter College? As you know, there are no curfew restrictions here, but we do require you to sign in and out in the event we need to reach you. At New York University-Lexington Avenue School of Nursing we consider you adults and responsible for your own hours, but I find it highly unusual to see where you're going."

Andrea sat in the chair in front of the Dean's desk, her hands clasped tightly together. "Dean Lyman, I've enrolled to take a college course in English Literature. It meets two evenings a week."

"Is nursing not challenging enough for you, Miss Deck?" The Dean had stared so hard at her that she found her eyes glued to hers in fright.

"No, I take the English course because I must get my liberal arts degree."

The dean's perfectly etched eyebrows arched high on her face. "You choose to do this now and not wait until you graduate, Miss Deck?"

"Yes, Dean Lyman." Andrea squeezed her hands tighter.

"You wish a liberal arts degree, not a Bachelor of Science degree in nursing?"

"I don't know." She felt like crying. The Dean was so severe.

"Why don't you want a degree in nursing?" Dean Lyman said.

"I promised my father I'd get a degree. We all did."

"And who is all?"

"My older sisters. My father talked about it a lot. Daddy never specified what kind of degree. I assume a liberal arts degree, because at dinner he was always talking about English, history, art, and music."

"Why did you select Hunter?" Dean Lyman said.

"Because I can walk there from this dorm."

"Miss Deck, are you aware that there is a nine month probationary program at The New York University-Lexington Avenue School of Nursing? After this nine month period you will rotate through hospital departments under supervision. If for any reason whatsoever you fall behind in your grades in this initial stage, or if you're late or not functioning to a level of a Lexington Avenue nursing student in the hospital, you will have to cancel your plans of working on your degree *while* you are a student here. Is that clear?"

"Yes, Miss Lyman," Andrea said quickly. She suddenly realized she'd been holding her breath.

"Miss Deck," and she smiled for the first time. Andrea relaxed a little, but felt too scared to smile. "You need to know that you can earn a B. S. degree in nursing from Hunter College. You have only to take one year of psychology, chemistry, and biology in order to obtain that degree. The rest of the courses can be in English, art, and music appreciation or any liberal arts course you wish to take. If you went to school full time *after* you graduated from here, you could earn that degree in two academic years."

"Oh, thank you, Miss Lyman. I didn't know." Andrea smiled happily. "My father would approve of all the liberal arts courses."

"Miss Deck, from your high school record," and Miss Lyman looked down at an open folder on her desk, "I think you have leadership abilities, and those could take you far in a nursing career or in an academic teaching career in nursing."

"No, I just did all those clubs and sports and was president of my class because our high school principal, Miss Quinlin, told me that's what I should do to win a college scholarship. But the scholarship wasn't quite enough for college and that's why I'm here. Many people in Pelham work here or have gone to nursing or medical school here. Some of those people were good friends of my father's. They know my mother who's a nurse at New Rochelle Hospital. I think they were responsible for my winning the scholarship."

"You probably earned that scholarship by your own efforts, and I see you've just been elected president of your class here."

"Yes, Miss Lyman."

"You're quite serious for eighteen."

"I have to be!"

"I see. You keep your grades high, Miss Deck, both in academics here and in the clinical arena when you start in the hospital, and maybe I can talk to the Dean of Women at Hunter College about a scholarship for you some day."

Andrea bounced up out of her chair and shook the Dean's hand, "Oh thank you, Miss Lyman." She saw the Dean's dark eyebrows jump high on her face again, but then she smiled.

"Remember, Miss Deck, I will be watching your progress here in nursing school."

"Yes, Miss Lyman."

But that was two years ago and Andrea had never been called to her office again. Andrea walked from the elevator to the shower room and peeked in. All the shower stalls were taken. She walked back to her small green room with its large window that looked out over busy Lexington Avenue.

She turned on her radio and pulled out her high heeled pumps. On her narrow bed she laid out her new dress with its black scalloped neckline and a full beige skirt with black pique swirled designs on it. It had a wide black waist that made her look thin. She'd just bought it last weekend with her saved-up baby-sitting money.

When in high school at home Andrea had earned 35 cents an hour babysitting, but here her customers even had to pay taxi fare to and from the dorm plus a dollar an hour. Students were in such demand that every time she signed up, she could baby-sit in elegant New York homes. Andrea pocketed the cab fare and walked whenever she could to made even more money.

Before she was ready, the buzzer blared in her room. She picked up the little round ear piece from the wall receiver. "This is Miss Deck," she said as primly instructed on the first day of school.

"Miss Deck, Dr. Scofield is in the lobby for you."

"Thank you," she trembled. She pounded on Gerry's door next to her room, but then remembered Gerry was on evening duty in urology, and wouldn't be back until after eleven.

She ran back to her room and looked once more in the full length mirror she and Gerry had bought and illegally hung on the inside of her closet door. She leaned way over and lifted each breast up and placed it higher in her bra, then smiled as she re-appraised herself in the mirror. Her pageboy just wouldn't go right. She threw her cigarettes into her black pocket book, grabbed her black cardigan sweater, checked the mirror again, put a finger full of Colgate's toothpaste on her tongue, locked her door, and tottered carefully on the slick gray floor to the elevator. She knew she should make Tom wait longer, but she couldn't.

She stepped out of the elevator in the large lobby and saw him stand up from his chair over by the entrance doors.

She caught her breath. He looked so much taller in a navy blue blazer and gray flannel trousers than in his green OR scrubs, but his face looked exactly like the first time she saw it when he lowered his mask. She grinned up at him and then laughed in giggles.

"What's so funny?" his deep voice loud, his face wreathed in smiles. His glimmering eyes were almost black.

Andrea looked around, positive that everyone was staring at them. "I don't know," she struggled. *Damn, I can hardly talk, let alone breathe.*

Tom took her arm and ushered her out the nursing residence front door. She was keenly aware of the pressure of his hand on her arm.

She turned to look up at him. "Where are we going?"

"Out for dinner."

"I know that," she giggled, "but where?"

"To Asti's. It's down on twenty-third. It's a grand restaurant and one of my favorites. Have you ever been there?"

"No."

"We have a reservation for 6:30, then we're going some place else."

"Where?" Andrea asked as she noticed they were heading toward the Lexington Avenue subway.

"Are you always so curious?" He turned his head to smile at her as they walked but Andrea couldn't answer. He was so handsome, aristocratic in a way, but it was his eyes, and then his silver temples, and then his smile. His hair at the back of his neck looked wet from a recent shower. She imagined him standing in the shower.

"You didn't answer my question," Tom said walking more slowly and looking at her.

Andrea stopped and looked up at him. "What? What question?"

"Are you half asleep or don't you listen to all your dates? And are you always so curious?"

"Oh, I'm sorry. Yes . . . no, oh, I don't know." *Oh, please don't let my face flush now.* She quickly put her head down and started walking again.

"Well, I hear you date all the medical students."

"Sure, I do," she teased. "And where did you hear that?"

Andrea turned her face up to look at him again. She grinned, happy to know he'd inquired about her. She didn't tell him eating lunch and dinner with the medical students saved her money for her clothes and train trips home to see her mother and married sisters.

"I heard, too, they go to watch you play basketball at the gym in the medical school dorm."

"They do? Well, I sure didn't know that! We have a great team for never having time to practice, and we're winning in our league now."

"It's your legs."

"What?"

"It's your legs they like to watch."

She felt her face blush and heard him laugh as he looked at her, but she kept her eyes on the street they were crossing.

Operatic music enveloped them as they walked into Asti's. Andrea was enchanted by the restaurant as well as Tom, who seemed so at ease. He knew every aria played and identified which opera it was in. The waiters sang as they worked, and at one point, the manager at the front desk tapped on the metal keys of the cash register with a silver knife. The waiters walked about singing to the patrons. One approached them and sang the most beautiful aria Andrea had ever heard. Tears came to her eyes.

"Who wrote that magnificent song?" Andrea asked. She felt Tom's eyes on her all the time, and finally she met his. His shining eyes were like a midnight sky under his thick, dark hair that fell forward on his brow. "I've never heard such music."

"It's from Puccini's *Tosca*. It's the final aria. Do you like it?"

"Oh, yes." And this time she couldn't take her eyes from his. "How do you know all this? How can you know so much about music when you're an intern?"

"I've always loved music. I used to go in to the Metropolitan from Scarsdale with my parents, and then I took music appreciation at Dartmouth. I was an English major, not a pre-med major, though I knew I'd be a doctor like my father. I knew that, I guess, when I was about five."

"Oh," she said, and no matter how hard she tried to pretend he was just another date, she couldn't. She smiled at him with genuine fascination, something she'd never done before. She'd always been leery of boys, having had no brothers. She tended to joke, tease or be sarcastic, to keep them safely at a distance.

At that moment, she knew without a doubt that she wanted to marry Tom Scofield. But then, he was probably just playing with her. After all, he was worldly, intelligent, sophisticated, handsome and twenty-six. He'd probably had tons of dates, 'gone all the way' many times by now, something she just couldn't bring herself to do--at least not yet. She was just too scared. It went against all the rules she'd ever learned.

"Andrea, you're sweet and very cute."

She felt her face blush, and knew her neck would be flushed and red blotchy looking. *Oh, why didn't I wear a turtle neck?*

"Thank you," she said.

"We have to go now," Tom said getting up and taking the bill. He pulled out her chair as she got up.

"Now, are you going to tell me where we're going?"

"To the opera."

Holy Cow! No one ever took me to the opera.

"But," Tom said as he put his money back in his wallet, "I've spent my entire month's salary on our dinner, so we're going to see Puccini's *La Boheme* free, at the YMCA not far from our hospital."

"Oh, how wonderful. I've never seen it."

They sat on folding wooded chairs on the linoleum floored auditorium where La Boheme was performed on a small elevated stage. Andrea cried at the end of the first act when the music soared. Tom put his arm around her, and kept his hand lightly on her shoulder. She was keenly aware of his hand until she again became mesmerized by the beautiful sad story and music. She cried again when Mimi died at the end.

"Have you seen other operas?" Tom asked her at the intermission.

"I went with the Pelham Junior High group into New York for the Wednesday matinees during the Metropolitan's season, but I didn't go when in Senior High. Did you go from Scarsdale High, too?"

"Until I was shipped off to Andover, because my grades were bad."

"Did you like that?"

"Not at first, but later I loved it, especially the sports, and I did get a great education."

"Did you know the Monroe brothers at Andover?"

"Yes. How do you know them?"

"One dated one of my older sisters, but I used to dance with Jimmy at the Assembly dances."

"You went to Miss Covington's Dancing classes?"

"Yes. Wasn't she a riot clicking her clicker all the time, trying to establish order? But I sure had fun at all those dances at the various Westchester County country clubs. I especially loved the dancing contests."

"So you're a dancer. I guess we'd have met if I'd been younger or you older."

"Perhaps."

"I have to stop briefly at my parents apartment on our walk back to the hospital. I left my surgical text there, and I need it. It'll just take a moment."

They walked to Manhattan House, and Andrea met his parents briefly at the door before they headed back to her dorm.

"It's getting late, but we're not going in," Tom said at her dorm door. I don't want to leave you. I'm going to leave my book at the reception desk, to pick up later, but we're going dancing."

"We are?" she giggled and felt giddy.

"Yes, at the Biltmore."

They jitterbugged and sipped slow gin fizzes until the final dances, when the band played "Stranger in Paradise," "Tender is the Night," and then "Love is a Many Splendered Thing." Andrea could hardly stand. Tom held her in a tight embrace and she slipped both her hands around his neck. When he kissed her at the end of the dance, the band players clapped, and she turned to them, her red face glowing.

"It's time to go," Tom said. "They're packing up their instruments."

They necked all the way home in the taxi, and as Tom's hands slipped down her throat toward her dress neckline, Andrea shifted away from him, but stayed in his embrace. *I'm not petting on our second date, no matter what!* His hands traveled back up her neck and over her hair.

At the lighted front door, Tom kissed her again. "Good-night Andrea." She heard his husky voice filled with emotion. She blinked open her eyes wide, embarrassed to have exposed her emotions that she knew were written across her face.

"I'm off night after tomorrow," Tom said. Can you meet me for dinner? It'll probably have to be in the cafeteria, if I get off really late. I'm on the toughest service right now, Neuro, and I'll be on it for another four weeks."

"Monday? No, I have class at Hunter College."

"You go to Hunter?"

"Yes."

"What time do you finish? I'll pick you up and walk you home," Tom said.

"Meet me at the courtyard, next to the Hunter College Playhouse at 68th, between Lexington and Park. I'll be there at nine. I may have to eat somewhere on the way home or in the hospital cafeteria, because you see after I leave obstetrics at 7, I run to the dorm and change out of my uniform before walking over to class.

"Fine," Tom said staring at her.

"Thank you for a wonderful evening," Andrea said looking up at him. I love to dance, and I loved Asti's and La Boheme. It was so beautiful."

"And so are you." Catching her off guard, Tom kissed her again, but she pushed him gently away. "Stop," she whispered catching her breath, "people are going by us."

She heard his deep care-free laugh, "Oh, they are?"

Chapter Four

Andrea lay on her side on her bed in her dorm room and wrote her letter to Muffy. She consulted the articles that she had strewn around her, then assembled them along with her letter and put them together in the brown manila envelope. She took the letter out again and re-read it for a second time.

Sept. 22

Dear Muffy,

I'm sending you all the information about what we discussed last month. I'm sorry it took so long, but there isn't a whole lot known about this condition. I think this information about bulimia and anorexia will help you. Promise me you'll read every word and try to figure out how to apply this material. Remember to read it *all* very carefully. Write me if you have any questions.

I'm absolutely *dying* to hear from you again. Hope you don't have to work too hard at UT this final year. How's your trust baby?

Do you get to see him everyday? If you do, I'm super jealous, because Tom's 'on' every other night for the whole year so there's barely time to see each other. The night he's 'off,' he has to get some sleep because he can be up all night the next night, when he's on.

He's absolutely groovy. I've had our first official date. Really, it's our second, but the first doesn't count because it was just dinner in the hospital cafeteria. We went to an opera, La Boheme. It was so beautiful, and after the opera we stopped by his parents' apartment near the hospital, and they were there! His father is a doctor, too. He sort of scared me, but his mother is beautiful and seemed kind. Then we went dancing at the Biltmore. And oh, can he dance!

I'm on Obstetrics for three months, and I love it! It's such fun to see the babies born. I can hardly wait to have Tom's. Do I shock you? You can tell I really have it bad. I sure hope he feels the same way. I think he does, because he tried to kiss me on our first cafeteria date, but I wouldn't let him.

I know 'hard to get' is the right way. I told him I had a date when he asked me out a second time. Keeps 'em guessing. Aren't I awful? But then, I wasn't so strong the night we went to dinner and the opera. I think I'll really *die* if he doesn't love me as much as I love him!

I've got to stop and study, or I'll flunk my stupid History of Nursing test tomorrow.

Write soon. I can hardly wait to hear from you!

Love,
Andrea

P. S. Say "hi" to Bucky.

Andrea

#

Muffy was glad her roommate was at class. She sat at her desk in her sorority house room and wrote back to Andrea right away. She stood up and went to her front window to read her letter again.

October 1

Dear Andrea,

Thanks for all the information. I read it all. Every word, I promise you. Some of it applies to me, but certainly not all of it. I'm much better here at UT now. I hope I'll soon be back to normal. School is fun. I love cheerleading, and we are busy hazing the new pledges. It takes a lot of time, but my schedule is fairly light this fall. I had wanted to major in psychology and minor in philosophy, but Momma and Daddy encouraged me to do English, and I'm so glad they did, because it's not too hard.

Bucky is such a hunk. We'll be going to homecoming and I have a wonderful new prom dress to wear. It's a strapless, royal blue satin gown. Momma will bring it from Houston soon. I bought it the day before I drove to UT, but I couldn't bring it with me, because it needed to be altered.

Do you remember meeting Bucky's mother, Aunt Ella Louise, mother's best friend, when you came to Houston last spring on school break? I call her aunt even though she's really not. Well, she told Momma, and Momma told me, that Bucky plans to propose some time this fall. Isn't that exciting? I hope he'll do it after the prom. I can hardly wait!

Tom sounds *divine.* I can't imagine your not being able to see him every day like I see my Snooky. I do hope by now you have him wound round your little finger, like you've had every other boy you've ever dated.

I can't imagine *living* and going to school in New York City so that you could just go to a New York opera. It sounds so casual in your letter, but I think it must be very glamorous. I do so love to go there with Momma and Daddy.

Once when I was little, we stayed in the Junior League Suite at the Waldorf Astoria. That's because of Momma. She's a member and has worked very hard for years in the League. Now she's a Sustainer, so she doesn't work as hard. I've begged Momma and Daddy to take all of us on spring break next year. I'm hoping Momma will let me buy my wedding dress there, so you can come with us!

Thanks again for all the helpful information. But, I promise you, I'm much, much better.

Love,
Muffy

"Momma Momma! I'm so happy to see you! Did you bring my gown?" Muffy called down to her mother as she saw her getting out of the white Cadillac in the circular drive in front of her sorority house. Muffy quickly hid her letter in a coat pocket in her closet, then ran down the stairs to meet her mother. They hugged and went in together, her mother carefully carrying the gown wrapped in white tissue paper over her arms.

"Muffy! I didn't expect you'd be here now!" Her mother was elegantly dressed in a red silk suit with black velvet trim. Her shoulder length blonde hair was worn in a page-boy, just like Muffy's.

"Yes, my class was over as soon as we finished our exam, and it was so easy I finished in thirty minutes. I was just heading out for lunch."

"Oh." Her mother looked disappointed, and Muffy imagined her mother had wanted to look about her room. They walked up the stairs and into Muffy's room. Muffy took her dress from her mother and unwrapped it.

"Momma, it's such a beautiful color. Thank you for bringing it." She hugged her mother.

"I want you to try it on to make sure it fits correctly. It's the perfect color to bring out your beauty--your full blond hair and sparkling blue eyes. You'll be stunning."

"Oh, Momma, I love it." Muffy turned around and around in front of her full length mirror in her beautifully decorated pink and white bedroom. "I think Bucky will love it too."

"You look beautiful," her mother said, "but don't get any thinner or you'll lose your bust line. Bucky will want you to have nice, big, round bosoms."

Muffy's smile faded as she looked down at her shimmering satin gown. She looked in the mirror again and frowned.

"I'll try, Momma, but I'm so excited about homecoming that I can hardly eat. Did Aunt Ella Louise tell you any more?"

"No, dear, she didn't. You must be patient, and not push Bucky."

"Oh, I wouldn't. I love him so much."

Her mother smiled at her. "Now, Muffy, show me what you're going to wear to the football game and then let's eat a little lunch. I must get back to Houston for your father's business dinner at the club. The men are upset and meet tonight about the Supreme Court's decision that schools in Little Rock must integrate."

"Remember dear," her mother said later as she got into her car, "have a wonderful weekend, and don't be disappointed if Bucky doesn't propose. I'm sure he will sometime this fall or winter. Those were Ella Louise's last words to me. And Muffy, I think your indigo blue sweater goes better with your pleated skirt for the football game, rather than the green one you choose."

"But, Momma," she said, her voice almost a whisper. "You didn't say winter last time. You said fall."

"Well, dear, I can't remember exactly every word Ella Louise said. Now you remember to telephone me on Sunday, and tell me every detail of the weekend events. I just loved my homecoming, the fall of my senior year here, right in this same sorority house. That's when your Daddy proposed to me."

Muffy ran right up to the bathroom and put her finger in her mouth and vomited every morsel she'd eaten for lunch. She thought of her mother's words about her bosoms and blue sweater. She leaned heavily on the toilet. She felt weak, and her head spun. She had to stop this. Bucky wouldn't propose if she didn't have any breasts, and mother was right; they were getting small.

She washed her face and brushed her teeth vigorously at the sink. She looked at her watch and decided to take a shower. She had just enough time before her roommate and friends returned from class. She rested for a moment on her bed until all her friends poured into the room. Homecoming weekend was about to start.

#

Tom and Andrea slipped into the first booth in the corner drug store down the street from Hunter College and ordered their dinners.

"What did you learn tonight? What course are you taking?" Tom asked after their orders were taken. His face was serious as he stared at Andrea. He wore an open blue shirt with his khaki trousers. Andrea looked at his temples, fascinated with the silver highlights scattered among his thick dark hair, his eyes an even deeper brown.

"I'm taking Classics this semester, and we're into the Roman Empire." Andrea unfolded her napkin over her pleated plaid skirt.

"What other courses have you taken at Hunter?"

"The first fall I took English Lit, then I took psychology in the spring and summer. After a year of chemistry, I took art appreciation."

"What are you going to major in?"

"Nursing, because I can get a B. S. degree if I take just one more science course--biology. Then the rest of the courses can be whatever I want in liberal arts."

"When will you finish?"

Andrea frowned. "I've no idea. I'm not even sure I can take another course, because my senior year just started, and I have so much evening and night charge duty that I'll be lucky if I can finish and pass this course." She sighed. "I'll probably have to wait now, and complete my course work after I graduate from nursing school next August. Also, I'll have more money for school then."

She felt Tom studying her face. "What does your father do?"

"My father was an editor of a trade magazine in New York City."

"Was?" Tom looked up from buttering his bread.

"Yes, he died when I was thirteen."

"I'm sorry. Tell me how he died." He put his hand over hers on the table.

Andrea stared at him. No friend had ever asked her that in all these years. She put down her fork and hesitated for a moment.

"I walked home from school. It was a beautiful spring day, April 22, a Thursday. Mother met me at the front door, told me Daddy had had a heart attack in Grand Central station and was in an ambulance on his way home. She was very agitated, because our family doctor wouldn't come to the house. It was his afternoon off.

I told her to call Dr. Rezen. I thought of him, because the day before I'd seen him when I had a Girl Scout meeting at his home. Mrs. Rezen was my leader."

"You mean the Dr. Rezen from our hospital?" Tom asked.

"Yes. He and Mrs. Rezen were with us in minutes--only barely before the ambulance siren blared to a stop at our front door. The ambulance attendants wheeled in my father who was sitting up on a stretcher. Dr. Rezen listened to his chest and said that he had to be admitted to the hospital, go into an oxygen tent immediately. I started to go kiss him, but Mrs. Rezen, who stood next to me, placed her hand on my arm and stopped me. I think my father saw that gesture for he looked at me and smiled, and I waved good-bye to him.

"They wheeled Daddy out backwards and down the front path to the ambulance. I stood by the front door and waved to him the whole time. I watched Mother get in Mrs. Rezen's car and Dr. Rezen stepped up into the back of the ambulance.

My older sister, Louise, was away at Connecticut College, where she was a junior. My middle sister, Roddy, was at home. We ate, did our homework, and then I went to bed and waited till mother came into my bedroom to tell me what I already knew. I remember I looked at the luminous green dials on my little alarm clock as I heard her footsteps coming down the hall to my room. It was twelve minutes after two."

"What an enormous shock to see him just a few hours before he died."

"Yes." Andrea looked at him directly. "But that was a long time ago."

There was a long, singularly comfortable silence. Andrea pushed her plate away, then lit a cigarette. She hesitated, then decided to go on.

"Actually, the trauma was worse for my mother. She was all right at first--that is, until she learned there was no life insurance. Then she immediately let our maid go and walked upstairs and got into bed and stayed there day and night for what seemed like forever. I was terrified she was going to die, too. But finally many weeks later when I ran in from school and up to her bedside, a doctor was there with my older sisters and some of our friends with our minister, and that doctor subsequently gave her three electric shock treatments, which enabled her to recover from her shock and fright."

Andrea looked down and sensed Tom's eyes on her. She wondered why she'd told that secret of long ago.

"Wow." Tom said. He slowly started to sip the last of his coffee.

"She's a wonderful mother and a terrific nurse," Andrea said with a slow smile. "All through high school, whenever we went shopping together, people stopped her on the streets, and in the stores, to thank her for taking such good care of them.

"But, Tom," Andrea's brow wrinkled. "I still have to study nursing tonight so I have to get back to the dorm." They stood up and moved out from their booth. Tom put his arms around her right in the middle of the restaurant. Andrea was embarrassed, but didn't ever want to leave his embrace.

They slowly walked down the street, arms wound round each other's waist until they were back at her dorm.

"You're the only friend who's ever asked me about my father," Andrea said at the door. "Thanks."

"I'd like to hear more about him." Tom kissed her forehead. He smiled. "Can you come up to my room?"

Chapter Five

"I don't know. Is it safe up there?" Andrea smiled up at Tom at the front door of her nursing school dorm. Then she quickly shook her head. "But no, I can't tonight. I have to study for a clinical unit quiz in the morning."

"It's probably best," Tom sighed. "Neuro is the worst its been, since I started my internship. I'll call you when I'm next off. . .and awake. It may be awhile." Tom kissed her briefly and was gone.

The phone was ringing when she entered her dorm room.

"Muffy? Why are you crying? I can't understand you? How did you get my number? Are you all right? You've never called before."

"Andrea, Andrea, I'm engaged! Bucky asked me to marry him after the homecoming prom. He was a little drunk, but he did it. I was so afraid he wasn't going to. You must come at Christmas. Momma is going to have a *huge* engagement party. Please say you'll come. We'll be married as soon as I graduate next June, and I want you to be my maid of honor! Remember how we planned our weddings when we were little? Oh, Andrea, I'm so happy."

"I'm excited for you, but how are you feeling? You know, how is your health?"

"I'm pretty good. I got a little better, then I got worse, because I was afraid Bucky wasn't going to propose, but he did and now I know I'll be all right. Everything will be all right because I'll be married to Bucky. How's your Tom?"

"He's wonderful and caring, but has to work so hard that I can't see him much. But then, my school work is harder now, too. I have my first senior charge duty this fall, and it's a lot of responsibility. I have to be so careful not to make any mistakes, and there's always more work than we can possibly do in an eight hour shift. It's hard to explain it all, especially on the phone. I'll try to come at Christmas, but I have to ask mother."

"Oh, you must come. I'm so happy! Good-bye Andrea. I just had to tell you."

"You sound more bubbly ecstatic than ever. I'm thrilled for you, but Muffy, please remember your promise to me and stay well. I'll let you know about Christmas. Good-bye."

#

The next time Tom and Andrea met in the cafeteria, they decided to go to Pelham on the very next Sunday they both had off. Andrea was eager to see her mother and have her meet Tom. She hoped he wouldn't mind that she lived in a tiny attached house and ate dinner in a dining room with a piano, because the living room was too small for it. When they had moved from their big house after her father had died, they had sold so many of their possessions, but mother hadn't been able to part with the piano.

Ten days later Andrea studied her mother who watched Tom eat. Her mother's lined face looked tired above the print blouse that peeked out at her neck above her fitted brown suit. Andrea smiled at her mother who seemed to enjoy Tom as she did. They talked about surgery and hospital cases most of the time. Like in the cafeteria with her nursing school friends or his fellow interns, Tom regaled them about funny incidences relating to the traumatic life of an intern. The entire little dining room came alive with his energy, enthusiasm, and laughter.

"Tom, I've never seen anyone eat so much or enjoy my dinner like you have. It's a pleasure to cook for both of you."

Andrea grinned at her. "You don't have to worry about starving Armenians, Mother."

"Andrea, now stop that." Her mother turned to Tom. "Apparently, I used to say that when Andrea wouldn't eat her vegetables."

"Mrs. Deck, this lamb dinner is delicious. It's my favorite, and I was hungry," Tom said.

"I know how hard you work. At my hospital in New Rochelle, the interns have a very difficult life, and I imagine it's worse at your famous hospital."

"It's fabulous training. I've wanted to be a surgeon since my little brother was seriously injured and then later, died," Tom said.

Andrea gasped, "You didn't tell me that." And right in front of her mother, she reached across the table and put her hand over Tom's.

"It was an automobile accident," he said to both of them. "Billy was hit and run over as he crossed the street on his way home from grammar school. His right leg had to be amputated at the groin. He came home and was sick in bed for months. They could never get the infection controlled in his stump, and he died three months after the accident. If we'd had antibiotics then, he'd have lived, but that was not to be God's plan."

"I'm sorry. Do you have other siblings?" Mother asked.

"Yes I have an older sister, Sandra. She's married. She used to live in the city, but then she moved with her husband, Philip, and their baby to New Hampshire. That's when my parents moved into the city from Scarsdale."

Andrea's mother looked at her watch. "I've enjoyed seeing you both so much, but I must leave for work now. My assistant charge nurse has to attend her young daughter's church play tonight, and I promised I'd take her evening shift. Tom, it's been delightful to meet you. I'm glad you could join us for church and dinner on this beautiful fall Sunday. She turned to Andrea.

"Now dear, you may write Muffy that you can visit her at Christmas, if your school work allows you to go. You must write your Aunt Elizabeth and thank her for her kind invitation, and offer to make your own airline reservations, even though Uncle Orville will probably do it once he learns your schedule."

"I will, mother, and I'll do the dishes and clean up," Andrea said looking at her watch.

"And, Andrea, you look peaked. I want you to get more rest. Tom, I hope you hear me."

"There's no chance of my exhausting her, Mrs. Deck," Tom said smiling, "while I'm on Neurosurgery. Only two more weeks and it's over."

After her mother left, Tom helped Andrea dry the dishes at the kitchen sink. "Why didn't you tell me before about your brother Billy?"

"There wasn't an opportunity."

Andrea turned to look at him. "Do you remember him well?"

"Yes. I played games, cards, and read him stories every afternoon for all those months. Billy was eight; I turned twelve the day after he died, but we were best friends. I'll never forget any of it."

"Now I know why you're serious and asked about my father."

Tom looked at Andrea. His voice was low. "It's not something you ever forget."

Andrea emptied the dishpan. The silence seemed intimately comfortable as she watched the water slide down the drain. She frowned. "But I worry I will. I review memories of Daddy sometimes, before I go to sleep at night."

Tom looked at Andrea. "I've forgotten details, but the feelings--the love, sorrow, joy and the loss of Billy will always be there."

Andrea reached up and hung up the red and white striped dishrag on one of the three, little, wooden sticks that swung out over the sink counter, and Tom put his arms about her, lifted her up, and carried her across his arms into the living room sofa.

He sat down with Andrea on his lap. The sun streamed in the porch door windows and Andrea heard Tony Bennett singing "Because of You" on the little, gray, kitchen radio she used to listen to when she ate dinner alone in the kitchen during her high school years, because her mother worked 3 to midnight at the hospital.

Tom cupped her face in his hands. She wanted him to kiss her. She stared at his full, soft lips wanting, yearning to feel their touch. He took one finger and outlined her face in a circle. She tingled all over. Her shivers rose from her groin and tickled up her bottom. Tom slowly, tenderly rubbed his index finger over her lips, parting them slowly, touching her tongue and then outlining her lips with her own moisture.

"Kiss me," she pleaded. He slowly kissed her, hardly touching her lips. Andrea swooned and pulled him to her tightly, her arms about him.

But Tom gently untangled her from him so he could watch her face.

"You're beautiful." And finally he lowered his lips again, to her searching, aching lips. She trembled and felt abandonment in her waves of passion. She never wanted him to stop. *Take me, take me,* she whispered silently to herself.

Tom raised her long blond hair above her head and looked down at her again. He caressed her neck over and over, lifting her hair to the top of her head and letting it fall. He patted and played with her hair. "You're so beautiful. I can't believe I finally have you in my arms. I've dreamed of this since I saw you in the OR."

"I have, too," she told him. Her body tingled from head to toe, and she knew he knew it, and she wanted him to know how reckless in her abandonment she felt.

Tom cradled her gently in his arms and kissed her ears, her hair, her eyes and her nose. She never experienced such delight. His hands moved down and caressed her breasts over her sweater. He leaned over and rubbed his head into her chest. She rocked him, thinking of his baby brother, Billy, then stroked his hair and head and ears. She fingered her hands through his hair, kissing his gray-tinged temples.

"I love you here, where your dark hair turns white." She heard her voice in shocked surprise.

"I love you everywhere." And Tom slowly unbuttoned the top pearl button of her black sweater and then each button until they were all open. He gently took off her sweater and caressed her smooth, white, goose-fleshed arms, shoulders, and throat with his eyes first and then his lips while he skillfully unclasped her bra behind her, and she knew he had done this many times before. But she didn't care. She didn't want him to stop. She couldn't stop.

He softly cupped and lifted one breast free from the confines of her slip and bra and fingered the light pink areola around her nipple over and over with one finger, watching her face, and she wanted him to see the intense pleasure he gave her for the first time in her life. And then he came to the protruding, darker, rose nipple itself. She sighed as he touched it, and then cried out when she watched him softly rim her swollen nipple with his pink wet tongue.

Her whole body taut, she waited for his next touch. Mesmerized in fascination, she saw his lips suckle onto her nipple, and she screamed with joy and felt a surge of moisture and pleasure so intense she cried again and could feel him hard and wet beneath her.

I love it. I love him. I can't stop!

He released her other bosom and caressed it as the first and then, gently, softly, placed his head between her breasts and groaned a deep howl as she felt him under her, and she exploded with rapture a second time. She had wanted to share her excitement with him, because she knew now she would have to stop as much as she never wanted to.

"Oh," she shrieked and hid her head, "I'm so embarrassed."

"Don't be, Andrea. I love you. It's all right. There's no one like you. You must be mine. We must be one."

"Oh, Tom, I don't know. I only just met you. How can we be here doing this? I can hardly stop, but I must. We just have to."

"Everything will be all right." His voice was gentle and he stroked her hair. "Let's just stay like this for a little while."

When they awoke later, it was dark. Andrea could hardly believe it. "Where did the time go? I wanted to show you Pelham, and where I went to school."

"We'll come again and again," Tom said.

"But we must get back to the hospital now," she said.

Tom nodded.

Andrea stood up, but so did Tom. He embraced and started to caress her again and finally, she pulled away.

"Wait, there's *Once In My Life*," Tom said, listening to the music from the kitchen radio. He took her in his arms and danced Andrea around in the small living room, then skillfully circled the dining room table and into the tiny kitchen, where he stopped on the refrain, *someone I've needed so long.*

Andrea smiled up at him. "Tom, it's late. We must get back to the hospital. Can we leave now?"

Chapter Six

As Tom and Andrea drove back into the city, Tom said in the dark, at the wheel of his father's black Packard, "Tell me your favorite memory of your father."

Andrea was looking at the lights in the windows of the attached houses they passed. She smiled as she heard his voice. *It's like in the OR. I loved his voice before I even knew who he was or what he looked like.* She turned to look at the handsome profile of his face, and then turned back to the window. She remained quiet in her own thoughts. Tom waited. Then she described for Tom her favorite memory of her Daddy sitting at the head of the dining room table, just after dessert, but before her mother rang the little bell for Evelyn to come in and clear the dirty dishes, and take to the kitchen their folded white linen napkins in their plastic napkin rings.

It would be summertime, her favorite time when there was no school to worry about, no remedial reading to go to in the dark basement of Colonial Grammar School. That was the worst thing about school, and gym class was the best--that, and play day, when the whole school was divided into teams that played different games one entire day on the black-topped playground behind the school.

Andrea loved summer when the house looked, felt, and smelled differently. All the living room furniture was covered in white, light blue, and peach slip covers. The brown dining room rug was replaced with a green braided straw carpet that felt scratchy and uneven under her bare feet. Little, round, black metal fans spun around in many rooms, strategically placed on floors or bedroom dressers. Early in the mornings, Mother lowered all the raised shades and windows from the night before and made the house darker and cooler than outside. Then late in the afternoon, just before Daddy walked in the front door from the Pelham railroad station, she opened all the windows again to catch the summer breezes, but the shades remained partially drawn to keep it as cool as possible.

The open windows in the dining room were behind her Daddy and behind Andrea when she sat on Roddy's side of the table. Every month, she switched sides. Her sisters couldn't wait till the end of each month when she was moved, but she'd hoped they were only kidding. She heard the evening summer sounds of children playing hide and seek in the neighborhood, the smell of burned leaf piles along the curb, and often times, the sound of leaves blowing in the big maple, oak, and elm trees in the front and side yards.

"How about a story?" Daddy would say. Andrea looked expectantly at his pale blue eyes, and he had always nodded. She would go to him and climb up into his lap. Her sisters were way too big to do that.

"Wait, Daddy, I have to go to the bathroom, Can I please be excused?" her middle sister Roddy asked one night.

"*May* I please be excused, not *can* I," Mother said.

Roddy said it, and when she came back, Andrea had already explored the silver chain that crossed her Daddy's chest. It went from one vest pocket to the other. At one end was a round flat silver watch where he had already taught her how to tell time. And at the other end was a thin sliver of a silver knife. She always tried to open it, but couldn't because she bit her fingernails.

Her father always told such a good story, and the ending was the best part. Andrea would feel his chest rise and fall. She held her breath, peeked up at his face, and listened expectantly for his voice to continue. He would pause, wait, and then finish the last sentence or two with a flourish--a surprised laugh or cry or frown. His fanciful story was always different and more wonderful than all the books her mother and granny had read to her.

"Did you like that story, Andrea?" he said as he bent his head down to her. She smelled the cigarettes he'd been smoking all day. "Yes, but . . ."

"But what?" he said with a gentle hug.

Andrea looked around the table. Her mother and sisters were looking at them. She cupped her hands, put them around his ear and whispered," I made up a different ending than you did, but please don't tell anybody."

And she watched his face break into a surprised smile, his blue eyes twinkling and wrinkling at the edges beneath his beautiful, shiny bald head. He turned in his chair to the little radio that sat on the radiator cover behind him, and as he turned, he lowered his head and voice. "Was that the first time you made up a different ending? And will you tell it to me later when you're ready for bed and I kiss you good-night?"

"Yes, it was and I will, Daddy," she whispered back.

Tom kept his eyes on the road, but Andrea saw him smiling in the dark car. "Sounds like your father had a crush on you like I do."

"Oh?"

#

Later that week Andrea had selected her simple black dress to wear to the Scofield's. Tom had invited her to join him for dinner at his home with his parents. She smoothed her dress as she sat down at the dining room table, to Dr. Scofield's right. She heard a buzzer and realized Mrs. Scofield must have a maid's bell that she had touched with her foot under the dining room table.

She heard the swinging kitchen door behind her open and a voice say, "Yes, Ma'am?"

"We're ready now, Mammie," Mrs. Scofield smiled. Andrea admired her grace and natural elegant coiffure, her silver shoulder-length hair with a deep wave to one side of her face. Her lovely warm smile embraced Andrea and she felt immediately that Mrs. Scofield somehow understood how Tom's father frightened her.

Dr. Scofield sat erect at the head of the table, but his shoulders slumped slightly over his torso. His head jutted forward so his eye glasses had slipped down his nose. Andrea felt his narrow beady eyes peering at her over his glasses.

Grapefruit nestled in little glass bowls on top of burgundy gold-rimmed china plates. They sat on delicate, intricately designed, lace place mats. Andrea waited until they were all served and Mrs. Scofield picked up her pointed silver fruit spoon at her right. After she did, Andrea asked Tom to pass the little silver sugar bowl.

"My mother always spoiled me when I was little, Mrs. Scofield, and I need sugar on my grapefruit. We frequently had grapefruit for dessert, and sometimes Evelyn warmed them in the oven and put a cherry in the middle. Then, the powdered sugar my mother let me put on mine would melt into the grapefruit and look more like melted snow than a little white snow hill."

"It's interesting you'd remember in such detail, Andrea. Did you often have grapefruit for desert?"

"Yes, because my father was diabetic. He wasn't supposed to eat sweets, but he cheated all the time," Andrea said putting the sugar on her grapefruit.

"Yes, Tom told us you lost your father when you were young."

"Yes, that's true," Andrea smiled at Tom across the table, above the maroon and yellow chrysanthemums clustered in a small silver bowl over an oval mirror. The center piece was reflected in the mirror, and contrasted with the rich flame mahogany table.

"They know so much more about diabetes now," Dr. Scofield said in his deep voice.

"So I'm learning," Andrea said. "Now I understand why my father was in shock so many nights. I use to sleep in the room next to my parents, and frequently I'd get up in the middle of the night and help my mother give Daddy orange juice. He was a terrible diabetic patient." Andrea shook her head and chuckled, "But, he was one terrific father."

Mrs. Scofield smiled at her. "It's nice you have happy memories of your father."

"Oh, I have a lifetime of them." Andrea smiled happily and looked into the open living room behind Tom. She admired the wood trimmed Victorian love seat upholstered in navy velvet and the antique Sheraton desk that faced her. The same blue, beige, and burgundy hues in the draperies and upholstered furniture wound round together in the magnificent Oriental rug.

"And Tom," his father said, "please tell us about your week in the OR." Andrea watched Tom in fascination, but then became confused. In the comfort of his lovely home, he didn't smile, and spoke in a dull monotone. Andrea asked many questions as did his father, but it elicited no change in his expressionless talk. He looked at his plate, at the kitchen door behind her, out the window, and never once at them.

Mrs. Scofield turned to Andrea. "It's good you're a nursing student, and these medical conversations don't bother you at the dining room table. It's something I've grown accustomed to, and my husband can hardly wait to learn of Tommy's exploits in the OR. You see, Andrea, many years ago Harold trained there as well, although now he works uptown at the great rival-- Columbia Presbyterian."

"Oh, I love it!" Andrea cried out. "I'm used to it. After my father died, my mother went to work as a nurse. Her hospital experiences were our main topic of conversation at all our meals during my high school years."

"And that's why you're in nursing today?"

"Well, my scholarship wasn't enough for college, which is really what I wanted to do, but I've taken several courses at Hunter. I'll take more after I graduate next August, so I can get my degree."

"Why, that's wonderful Andrea. You're quite ambitious."

"Not really," she said, turning to smile at Mrs. Scofield. "More a promise to my father."

After coffee and dessert, Andrea walked slowly by family photos lined in frames along the wide window sill that extended from the dining room to the far end of the open living room. As she walked, Andrea looked up and out at New York's towering, lighted buildings against the black sky. Then she studied each photograph.

"Tom," she asked, knowing they were all behind her, "is this your sister, Sandra, with her husband and baby?"

"Yes," he said coming to her side.

"And, this must be your younger brother, Billy, whom you loved so much." Andrea bent over to look closer at the photo. "What a precious face he has, and his eyes . . .Why they are perfectly round, and big trusting, and . . . *innocent*. I can imagine he loved having you play cards and read to him when he was sick."

"There'll never be another Billy," she heard Tom say in a loud, strained voice and she turned quickly to look at him. He put his arm tightly around her shoulders and she froze, thinking he was going to kiss her right there in front of his parents, but he turned with her to face his parents. Andrea was shocked to see their anguished faces, tears in their eyes as they both stared at Tom.

She was terribly confused. Tom was acting so strange . . . severe, like his father. *Weren't they over their son's death of fourteen years ago?* She never cried about her father anymore.

"Oh, I'm so sorry I upset you." Andrea reached out for Mrs. Scofield's arm with her hand. She smiled at Dr. Scofield's wet eyes in his haggard lined face.

He cleared his throat. "Tom, do we have time for a few hands of Bridge?" Dr. Scofield hesitated, then looked at her, "That is, Andrea, if you play?"

"I do, Dr. Scofield. I learned Bridge when I was younger, but I rarely play now, so I'm not very good and might bore you."

"Dad, I must get back to the hospital. I'm on tomorrow night, and I got very little sleep last night."

Andrea relaxed and breathed a sigh of relief. The thought of sitting at a Bridge table with Dr. Scofield scared her silly.

"Well, son, in my day we had to sleep every night in the hospital. We never had a night off for the entire year."

"You've told me." Tom's voice was harsh, and he turned away from his father. He kissed his mother's cheek. "Thank you, Mother, for a wonderful meal." Andrea watched his mother embrace and try to hold him tightly, but Tom moved away and shook his father's hand, then turned, took her elbow firmly, and steered her toward the front door. But Andrea stopped at the door and pivoted back to them with her hand outstretched to Mrs. Scofield.

"Everything was delicious--the fried chicken, gravy, potatoes, green beans, and what was that wonderful ice cream we had with that scrumptious Devil's food cake?"

"That's Breyer's burnt almond ice cream, Andrea," Mrs. Scofield said. "It *is* good, isn't it? Thank you for joining us for dinner."

"Thank you," Andrea smiled at her. "It was quite a contrast to our usual hospital cafeteria suppers, wasn't it, Tom?" She turned to Tom's father. "Good-bye, Dr. Scofield," and she shook his hand.

Tom gripped her elbow again, and pushed her out the apartment door.

"Tom, what is it? Are you angry?" she asked at the elevator.

"No, my parents just rattle me. Make me mad."

"But why? They're kind, especially your mother. Your father scares me. He is so stern and commanding, but I'm hoping that may be just a crusty exterior."

Tom held her hand as they walked down 66th Street. "Well, it's a long story, and though you don't realize it, you said all the right words, just because you are who you are, and that's why I love you." He stopped and turned to look at her. "Let's go to my room."

"But you just said you were tired and needed sleep."

"No. That was just to get out of there. It's only 9:30. I hate going to my parents' apartment, but I feel I have to go ever so often. After all, they support me. But I hate being dependent on them, or anybody."

Andrea stared at his taut, rigid face so like his father's. She saw a flutter wavering along his jaw.

Tom's voice was loud as they walked toward the entrance to the nurse's residence. "Please come to my room. You've said you would, but never have."

"How about going to the student lounge in the nurse's residence?"

Tom sighed. "That's what we did the few moments we got together last week, and we had to untangle twice when other couples walked in."

"But it's a week night," Andrea said. "One of the small date rooms across from the big lounge might be free."

Tom put his arm over her shoulders. "Come on, Andrea, just for a little while. "

"Will you behave?" she beamed up at him.

Chapter Seven

Andrea and Tom stood alone in the hospital elevator as it sped upward. It stopped and the door opened on the eleventh floor. Andrea immediately pulled her hand away from Tom's.

"Andrea, how nice to see you." Dr. Harris smiled and spoke in a loud voice as he stepped on the elevator. His deep brown eyes under bushy eyebrows glared intently at Tom. "And Dr. Scofield, how are you this evening?" Dr. Harris pushed the button for the fifteenth floor, then turned to her. "Have you been home recently, Andrea? How is your dear mother?"

"She's fine, thank you, Dr. Harris." Andrea looked at him and smiled weakly. She prayed she wouldn't blush.

"Good-bye now, you two," Dr. Harris said as he left the elevator. Then he turned to Tom, bent his head and looked at him over his eyeglasses. "Dr. Scofield, I expect you to take good care of this fine young woman."

"Yes, sir." Tom said as the elevator doors closed.

"Horrors! How could this happen, Tom?" Andrea put her hands up to her face. "He knows I'm going to your room. Dr. Harris was serious. I'd better go back to my dorm. I'm so embarrassed."

"No, Andrea. I'm sure he feels his warning will be well taken, and it will. I promise you." The elevator doors opened at the 23rd floor.

"Come on now." Tom took her hand, and led her down the corridor. He stopped and unlocked the final door on the left. White lab jackets hung on the corner of the open closet door immediately to the left as they entered his small narrow room. The white sink next to the closet was cluttered with shaving mugs, bars of soap, and toothpaste. The mirrored medicine cabinet door above the sink was open, and a toothbrush lay in the sink drain below. The gray linoleum floor was scattered with books, newspapers, trousers, and a pile of shirts was stacked in one corner.

There was a twin bed to the right, and across the little room, a dresser and desk. Andrea walked to one of the two windows and looked down at the tiny street lights and specks of people walking far below.

Tom looked around his room. "It's more of a mess than usual. During Neuro I haven't had time to bundle my clothes for the laundry."

"Don't you take them home?"

"Never. I don't depend on my parents one iota more than I have to. Come sit with me here on the bed."

Andrea sat down next to him, but she was uncomfortable. Seeing Dr. Harris made her feel guilty and Tom was acting so strange.

Tom kissed her and pulled her down with him on the bed. He held her tightly and then rolled over on top of her.

"Tom . . ." but he kissed her roughly again.

"Tom, I'm sorry." She wrenched herself free from his embrace. "I must go to the bathroom." She stood up. "Is there one for girls down the hall?"

"No," he rolled over. "This floor is just for interns. There's one on the floor below, just to the right of the stairs which are diagonally across from my door--at the exit sign."

"I'll be right back." Andrea sped from his room.

When she returned, Andrea stood by the window and looked at him. Tom sat at the side of the bed, his hands over his face. "I'm sorry I was a brute. That's why you left to go to the bathroom, isn't it?"

She didn't answer.

"I'm furious at my parents and myself for what happened at the apartment."

"But what happened?" She walked to the bed, and sat down next to him. She took his face in her hands. "Tell me."

He took her hands from his face, then cupped his own hands at the sides of his face and leaned his elbows on his knees. He looked down at the floor. She put her arm over his shoulders as far as she could reach.

Tom was quiet and Andrea gently patted his shoulder with her hand. She felt him take a big breath.

"After Billy died, my parents became *very* restrictive and possessive of both Sandra and me. They had not been this way prior to his death. It was awful, and went on for years. I became very independent, talked only a little to them, and finally only when I had to."

Andrea leaned over toward him trying to see his face, but Tom's expression remained hidden behind his hands. "How old were you?" She asked gently.

"Twelve." His voice was low.

"How about Sandra?"

"It was worse for her initially, but she's four years older than I am, so she escaped to Smith College two years after Billy died. Then, I was alone with them and it got worse. I felt I couldn't breathe without their permission."

Andrea thought of Muffy. "Did they pry into your mail and your friendships?"

Tom shook his head. "No. Their fear was I would die." He sighed deeply. "They controlled my sports and the car. Dad called my football coach at Scarsdale High and forbid my playing wide receiver. The coach told me a few months later. They forbid my getting a driver's permit, which all my friends had. I was humiliated, because they drove me and my dates to and from parties. These curtailments affected my dating, my social life and my already fragile ego. My friends laughed at me.

Tom shook his head. "I realize now, I was horrible to them, but I couldn't help it at the time. Finally, I started to act out, drink, sneak out with girls and do poorly in school. They insisted I see a psychiatrist." Tom raised his head, and looked across the room at the window. "I refused and ran away for days."

Andrea rubbed his shoulder softly. She said nothing, but watched the side of his face.

"When I returned, they lectured--said this was all due to my grief over Billy. I had heard that excuse so much and it hurt. I felt it had nothing to do with Billy. I screamed at them in anger, 'If Billy's name is *ever* brought up in front of the three of us again, I'll run away forever!' It was a horrible screaming scene. The very next afternoon, with my mother crying at the front door, my father put me in the car when I came home from school and drove me to Andover."

Andrea patted his back with her hand. She leaned her head against his shoulder. "How terrible," she whispered. "I always felt sorry for my friends who were sent away to boarding schools."

Tom looked down at the floor again. "I never let them come see me at parents' weekends or at any time at Andover--until I graduated. During those years, I went home to Scarsdale as little as possible. My parents knew very little of my whereabouts or my life. Every summer I worked at a Saint Simon's Island resort as a waiter or boat boy. My parents have owned a cottage there since the thirties. I stayed in the resort dorm for the help, and rarely saw them, even when they were there for the month of July."

"How long were you at Andover?" Andrea asked gently.

"Three years. I went at fifteen. My father was an alumnus and a big benefactor."

Tom sighed, and lowered his head again. "Things got better when I started medical school. I lived there with them, in that apartment. It's huge. It goes way back. I had my own bedroom and bath there, because it didn't make sense for my father to pay room and board for me to live a few blocks away. But even though we lived together, we communicated very superficially."

"Oh, Tom," she rested her head on his shoulder. He did not raise his head or look at her.

"Billy's never been mentioned by either one of us until tonight when your genuine response to his photo spontaneously elicited my words to you. That's why my parents were moved-- not because of their grief over Billy, but," he paused, " probably because of their grief over me." Tom shook his head back and forth.

"Sandra has told me they have regrets. They now realize how difficult they made our lives, but we still can't discuss it. It's how they acted out their grief and distress over losing Billy."

Andrea spoke softly. "But it's so long ago."

Tom turned to look at her. "You see, my father felt utterly and hopelessly inadequate and useless as a physician. He watched Billy die in his bedroom bed, a little bit each day. We all did. Now as a physician myself, I understand how he must have felt. I think of it when we lose a patient on the table after operating for nine, ten, or twelve hours.

"I've been involved with the families, more than most students or interns, and I know that's because of Billy. But for some horrible reason I can't share any of this with my parents, and my father is so eager to hear my experiences. You heard him tonight. I can barely choke out the words to him. I feel if I let down my guard, they'll move right in and take over. I'd be twelve all over again." He hesitated. "That's what I say, but down deep I know that's not true." He paused again. "I, I can't admit I was wrong, too."

Andrea tried to hug his big shoulders. He wouldn't move or open up so she could hold him. "Tom, look at me, please."

His taut face looked up at her in confusion.

She stood up then and opened his arms so she could snuggle into his lap and hold him. She held him for a long time, patting his back..

"Tom?" she said looking over his shoulder and out his window.

He didn't answer.

"Sometimes when hurtful words have been said, and time has passed, it's really difficult to bring up the subject and hash it out. It's easier to put one's regrets and apologies for the past into simple words and what you hope the future can be."

Andrea felt him let out a long slow breath. "You could do that now," she said, "now that there has finally been a breakthrough with your parents. Write a few words, explain how you felt as a teenager, and your hope for the future. That doesn't mean you have to give up one bit of your hard earned struggle for independence. It's words, but they would mean so much to your parents, and maybe even more to you, if you forgive yourself."

"I don't know," he said in a low voice.

"I never saw you like you were when you spoke with your father about the OR. You usually have everyone in stitches. You're a good person--full of life and love and incredible talents. Don't you think your parents deserve to see that? I bet they'd so appreciate the privilege to be in your life, they'd never interfere again. People react differently, and sometimes in strange ways to personal grief. Didn't I tell you about my mother?"

Tom shook his head back and forth. "I don't think I could."

Andrea leaned back and looked up at him. She kissed his cheek, then pushed his hair back from his forehead. "Tom, it's really late now. I'm going to my dorm. You don't have to take me. I can go down the elevator and go through the tunnel. Goodnight." She got up and gently pushed him back down on the bed, kissed his forehead, and left.

But when she got to the elevators, she looked at them and then walked quickly back to the stairway exit. She raced down 23 flights of stairs. She didn't want Dr. Harris or any other doctor from Pelham see her leave the interns' quarters at this hour.

Chapter Eight

The next morning Tom put on his green scrub suit. He checked his watch and started out his door, then quickly came back and stood by his window looking at the cars and people far below. He shook his head and walked to his desk and quickly scribbled some words on his note paper. He closed his fountain pen, lifted his writing paper, and re-read his letter.

December 19

Dear Mother and Dad,

Many years ago I told you if Billy's name were ever again mentioned in our presence, I would run away forever. Last night, unexpectedly, I broke that taboo myself, but I do not feel like running away. Instead, I want to ask you for your forgiveness. I have not been a good son.

Would you please call me after you return from your Christmas holidays at Sandra's. Perhaps we can have dinner then.

Love,
Tommy

Tom quickly stuffed the note in the envelope, licked the four cent stamp, and pasted it on the envelope. He walked from his room and dropped it in the hospital mail shoot between the elevators. He watched it sail down through the glass slot. *That's the best I can do.* He sighed, relaxed his shoulders and took the elevator to the OR.

#

"Mother," Andrea said in their small living room. She was unpacking familiar Christmas decorations from tattered old boxes.. "I'm so happy to have five days off. Isn't it wonderful?"

"Yes, dear, but your excitement wouldn't have anything to do with Tom Scofield's joining us for Christmas, would it?"

Andrea laughed, her hand in the air. She sensed her mother's eyes on her. She stretched up higher on tip-toe and placed the crooked gold star she'd made in grammar school on the Christmas tree, which they had bought on their way home from the Pelham station. Andrea pulled down the red knit top that had risen high on her waist line over her matching skirt. She turned to look at her mother, noting how tired and thin she looked in her straight dark brown dress.

"I've never seen you interested in any boy until Tom, and there've been a lot of boys around here over these last few years."

"Guess so," she giggled. "Do you like him?"

"Yes, I do. He's very bright, charming, and he captivated me with his mirth and hospital stories. It's his humor that's good for you, Andrea. Also, I think he's very much in love with you."

"I hope so."

"Did you like his parents when you met them last week?"

"They seem older than you, and Dr. Scofield is frighteningly stern--just the opposite of Mrs. Scofield." And then, she told her mother about the entire evening.

"Sounds like you were the catalyst to bring about a reunion of sorts, which by the way, doesn't surprise me." Her mother smiled at her. "And Andrea, you don't realize it, but you're pretty independent yourself. I guess you had to be." She sighed. "I always feel guilty that I worked evenings, but the day charge position was taken, and we needed the extra $20 dollars a month I earned for working evening charge duty."

"Mother, you're independent, not me. And I loved your working evenings. I got away with murder here alone with you in the hospital--could drink, smoke and sleep with boys and all those things," Andrea grinned as she selected a Santa decoration that her sister had made, and slipped it on a low Christmas tree bough.

"Now stop that," her mother said severely. Then she smiled, "Or I'll take you over my knee and spank you!" They laughed together at the old familiar bribe. "Are you ready to go to Muffy's?" her mother asked. "Did you pack my gifts for my sister and dear Orville."

"Mother, do you realize that since I was little you always change the subject when you don't want to discuss something with me? And yes, I did. I'll mind my table manners and say ma'am and sir with my Southern cousins, if I can remember, and all those other things. So spare me--don't go over it again . . . please."

Her mother laughed. "That's the independence I'm talking about." She handed Andrea some tinsel. "What time do you pick up Tom at the Pelham station?"

"He's taking the 6:25 train from Grand Central. I'll buy the groceries for our dinner after I drive you to the hospital. After our dinner, I want to drive Tom around Pelham to look at the pretty Christmas lights. We'll go to the midnight service at Huguenot Church, then pick you up at 1 a.m--at the usual place."

Her mother started to close the boxes and stack them together to take to the basement. "Fine. I made up Tom's bed with fresh linens in Roddy's old room. In the morning we'll have a light breakfast. Louise and her family will come about noon as well as Roddy and Bruce. After gifts and dinner they'll all go on to their in-laws, while I go to the hospital."

Andrea turned to look at her mother. She shook her head. "Mother, you've worked every Christmas since Daddy died."

"I think so. Since you're away at school I now work the weekends, and let the younger nurses off with their families. Remember, I always tried to be off on weekends when you were in high school so I could be here for your dates. That was the only time we had any real time together, without my rushing to the hospital or you to school."

"Do you think that's why we got along so well?" She grinned at her mother.

"Andrea, don't say such things," her mother admonished in a stern voice, but her face was smiling above the boxes she carried in her arms.

#

Tom jumped off the train step onto the platform. He wore a tan overcoat and the wind blew his dark hair forward over his forehead. He put down his suitcase, hugged Andrea and kissed her gently. Then he stared at her. "You're hair's different."

Andrea watched his cold white breath break out between his lips as he smiled with every muscle on his face.

"It's a pony tail."

"Oh."

"You don't like it."

"I didn't say that." But he kept staring at her. "Here," he said, and he handed her an envelope.

"What's this?"

"Open it."

"I will in the car. It's cold." They walked quickly to the old green Chrysler next to the lighted lamp post in the station parking lot. Andrea sat behind the wheel in the dimly lit car and opened the letter.

December 21

Dear Tommy,

We were overjoyed to receive your letter. Your mother and I deeply appreciate your words. We accept your apology, and we would ask that you forgive us for the error of our ways in raising you. We have wanted to ask your forgiveness for many years now.

We leave tomorrow for Sandra's, and will return the 27th. Could you come for dinner on Thursday the 28th?

We hope you have a meaningful and spiritual holiday.

Again we thank you for your fine thoughts. They are the most precious gift you could possibly give us this Christmas.

Lovingly,
Mother and Dad

"Oh Tom, how wonderful! You *did* write. Why didn't you tell me?"

"I don't know."

Andrea studied his face in the car. "I don't think it's your pride." She hesitated, then smiled. "I guess you'll protect your self-reliance for a long time."

Andrea turned the key in the ignition, and the radio blared. "U. S. television sets number an estimated forty one million, up from approximately eight million in 1950." She turned it off.

"Did you listen to the radio when you were little?" Tom asked.

"Yes. I loved *Portia Faces Life* and *Stella Dallas.* They were on late in the afternoons. And then another favorite was the mystery, *Mr. and Mrs. North.* That was later, after dinner. I had a flashlight hidden in my room so I could dial my programs after I was put to bed, and mother and daddy wouldn't know."

"You listened to all the sissy programs. I liked *Terry and the Pirates, Hop Harrigan, Ace of the Airways,* and *Jack Armstrong Jack Armstrong, the All American Boy."* Tom's voice sang out.

Andrea laughed. "On Saturday mornings I used to wait what seemed like forever for my older sisters to wake, so we could play Hearts on my sister's big double bed in her green, ivy wallpapered room. Then, almost at noon *Henry? Henry Aldrich?"*

"Coming Mother" Tom joined in.

"That's when we'd quit Hearts, and I'd watch my beautiful sister get out her red nail polish and paint her nails for her Saturday night date."

"Still the sissy programs," Tom said. "But, you must have listened to: *"The Lone Ranger rides again! Return with us now to those thrilling days of yesteryear when from out of the West came the thundering hoof beats of the Great Horse Silver! The Lone Ranger Rides again!"* Tom's voice rose in a high crescendo as Andrea drove to a stop in front of the house.

"And how about this!" She said. *"Who knows what evil lurks in the minds of men? The Shadow knows; Eh, Eh, Eh, Eh."*

Tom laughed out loud. *"The Inner Sanctum, eek, eek, eek."*

"But your creaking door voice needs some oil," Andrea said. See, I didn't watch only sissy shows. In fact, I ripped my slip listening to that one night when mother let me spend the night in Roddy's room."

"Spend the night?"

"It was a big treat to sleep in her pink and peach flowered room with her twin beds and matching maple furniture. I can't quite remember, but I think I 'spent the night' when my parents went out for a Saturday evening.

"Don't forget Sunday evenings," Andrea said, *"Jack Benny* and--"

"Jingle Bells," Tom said, "Are we going to sit in this cold dark car all evening or do your Christmas plans include dinner?"

"You're always hungry, and we're going to have dinner here," Andrea said getting out of the car." She told him her plans for the evening. "We only have one car so I drove mother to work."

In the tiny kitchen Andrea brought out all the makings for dinner from the cupboard and refrigerator. "Now I'm going to cook this steak and try to make dinner for you."

"Perfect, except I'll cook dinner."

"You?"

"Yes. I'm a very good cook. Two years after Billy died, I cooked for my parents and all their friends every night, and breakfasts, too. It was my paid summer job."

"Holy Cow!"

Tom came and kissed her for a long time.

"Tom," she gasped, "you always take me off guard."

"All your other boy friends never kissed you impulsively?" He laughed loudly.

"You sure like to laugh at your own jokes and you're a lot older than most of my boyfriends, except maybe this one obstetrician who always took me to the ballet or to the theater and later to Ruben's for cheese blintzes. Because he'd finished training, he was rich." She grinned up at him.

"You sure are a tease." Tom said, before leaning down to kiss her again.

Andrea breathlessly pushed him back gently. "And where did you cook for your parents?"

"On Saint Simons Island, Georgia. They vacationed there every summer. My parents employed me for six weeks as a way of keeping me at home under their supervision. That summer, it was the water they worried about.

Tom sighed. "I'd been on the water every summer since I was little. I fished, swam, sailed, water skied, and was handy with motor boats, and yet, that summer, at 14, it was like I knew nothing. We had enormous fights when I wanted to go out on the water with my friends. They stood on the dock one midnight as I drove up in the speed boat with all my friends. I was so embarrassed. I could have killed them at the time."

Andrea gently patted his cheek and rested her fingers on his lips. "It's over now, remember?"

"Right." He smiled, taking her fingers in his hand and kissing her fingertips. "I brought the ingredients for Whiskey sours. I'm going to get you drunk so you lose all your inhibitions."

"Tom!"

He brought in his suitcase from the small front hall and brought out the supplies. "Now, you sit here on this red kitchen stool and watch me make you marvelous drinks and a magnificent meal. Do you have a Waring Blender?"

"No, you'll have to 'make do' as my mother says. Here's an egg beater."

"All right. This'll be a first," Tom said, washing his hands at the sink.

"This is great," Andrea said. "I honestly don't know much about cooking. I ate mostly minute steaks, canned Spam, and corned beef hash with a poached egg on top when I was in high school--right here on this stool at this white enamel table, right next to the stove. I didn't even have to get up for second helpings because the stove was so close."

Tom raised his eyebrows. "Your mother didn't teach you?'

"A little, but there was never enough time."

"That summer I cooked for my parents, I did all the grocery shopping, too. My Dad took me and showed me. I remember I got an extensive lecture on the cuts of meat in the local Piggly Wiggly."

"Your Dad?"

"He was a powerful, energetic man and father. My conflict was mainly with him. That's why he wrote the letter. My mother tried to interfere with his dogmatic domination, but it was useless."

"It didn't mean he didn't love you."

"I know that, and knew it then, but still it was impossible for me."

"I think you're a little like your Dad."

"Oh God." Tom looked up at her while quickly turning the egg beater in the bowl. "How's that?"

She grinned up at him. "You wouldn't know anything about being dogmatic or stubborn yourself, would you?"

"You're taunting me again," and he pulled off the red ribbon from her hair. "It's like spun gold." He lifted up her hair with his hands over and over stroking her neck, and letting her hair fly down, like he so often did. She was excited immediately. He picked her up and carried her to the living room couch, leaving the dinner and drink ingredients strewn about the kitchen. He kissed her many times, and with such exquisite tenderness that waves of rapture carried Andrea away and she forgot where she was.

Finally she heard, "Andrea, open your eyes. Look at me."

"Oh, I'm always embarrassed when you catch me with my eyes closed. I feel exposed, but you have the most wonderful lips." And she reached up and outlined them slowly, over and over with her finger, and then reached up and kissed him.

"Andrea, you're tormenting me."

"It's mutual," she smiled, and then giggled.

Tom looked at her seriously. "Andrea, I know you'll only let me go so far."

"Yes . . . but it doesn't mean I don't care . . . It's just--it's just . . . I can't."

"Andrea, I'm trying to tell you something, but you keep interrupting."

"I do?"

"Yes. I want you to know I love you. I want to marry you, and soon, as soon as possible." He rushed on breathlessly. "I'll not tell you anything but the truth about this, and you probably have suspected. I've been lonely for many years, because of my problem and stubbornness with my parents. I've dated many, many girls, because I was so lonely, but I'm not lonely with you.

"What I'm saying is I've been with many girls since I was young because I hurt, felt homeless, but now, now I need you, Andrea. You light up the tiny, melancholy well hidden deep inside me. I'm obsessed by you. I thrive on you. I've become addicted to your sunniness, teasing, goodness, to say nothing of your sexuality. Please say yes.

"Why are you crying. Did I hurt you?" Tom frowned and took both her hands in his. "Is it about my being with the girls?"

"No," she smiled, tears rolling down her face, "I love you, Tom. I'm happy."

He sighed, then smiled. "You've a funny way of showing it. But you didn't answer me."

"It's so soon," her aquamarine eyes serious above her smile. "I hadn't planned to marry for years. There's so much I have to do, want to do, and then, I wanted to play and have some fun. I wanted some of that, too." She saw his jaw line flutter.

"Like what?"

Andrea looked at him earnestly. She reached up with her fingers, and stroked the light hairs on his temple. "I had planned to earn money and get my degree from Hunter. I had wanted to go to Europe and play for a summer, like my older sisters did before my Daddy died, and since high school I've visualized a glamorous single life in New York. Most of my friends wanted to marry early, but I wanted to work and date a different boy every night."

"I'll take you to Europe, just as soon as I finish my training." His voice was urgent, sincere. "That's another six years, and then I have to go into the Army for two years. I'm in the Berry Plan, which allows me a deferment until I finish my surgical training. We could apply for the Army hospital in Paris. We could marry while you're a nursing student, and you could still get your Hunter degree. My parents supplement my intern's salary a little, and I think we could live on that and if you work as--"

"If we marry, I'll work as a nurse," Andrea said right away. "We won't need support from your parents."

"Now, who's self-sufficient?" Tom smiled at her and patted her hair.

"It's funny--that's what Mother said this afternoon. I never thought of myself that way."

Tom took her chin in his hand and turned her face up to his. "Andrea, please answer me."

"I love you. I want to marry you. Do you think we could wait a little?" She smiled at him. She hesitated, and her bluish-green eyes glistened with moisture. "Could I say yes, but not exactly when?"

Tom took her face in both his hands, "Yes, you master of taunt. You'll always know how to get your way with me."

"I certainly hope so!" Andrea laughed up at him.

"But I want it soon. I need to speak to my parents, and of course I must ask your mother for your hand. Would you think about a date that's not too far off--that you feel would be possible for you?"

"Maybe, but--"

Chapter Nine

Tom had tried to kiss her objections away, Andrea remembered two days later. Her eyes were closed as the plane hovered over Hobby Airport in Houston. She had tingled most of the flight as she felt Tom's kisses and caresses over and over again. Andrea opened her eyes and smoothed down the skirt of her navy suit. She reached the back of her legs with her hand to feel if the seams in her stockings were straight.

"Ictaminigoalagosectobingolady, yoo hoo!" Andrea heard Muffy the minute she stepped from the airplane onto the air field.

She whirled around and saw Muffy running toward her, her long blonde hair blowing out behind her in the wind, her pink pocket book bouncing up and down at the side of her pink dress. "Oh, Muffy, it's so exciting to see you and be here."

"I thought you'd *never* get here," Muffy yelled breathlessly. They hugged each other tightly.

She's thinner, Andrea worried. But she said, "There's my suitcase." The stewardess placed it on the ground from the rear of the plane.

"Is that all you brought? Just one little suitcase? Wow, you should see how Momma and I pack. We take *loads* of suitcases."

"It's only three days," Andrea laughed.

"I know, and that's awful." Muffy frowned and squinted into the late afternoon sunlight. "Couldn't you please stay longer?"

"I can't, Muffy." Andrea took her hand. "I have to be back from Christmas break. My nursing school vacations are short, not like college, but I'm thrilled to be here for your engagement party."

Muffy picked up her suitcase and led her from the airfield. "It's tomorrow night, and Momma made our hair appointments for 1:00 in the afternoon so we can nap before the party starts at 5:00." They walked together toward the parking lot. "Many of my sorority sisters are coming from UT, but I asked them to stay with other friends in Houston, so I can see you all to myself at home. I'm not willing to share you.

"Here's my car." Muffy dropped Andrea's suitcase over the rear door and into the back seat. Then she whirled around. "It's my Christmas gift from Momma and Daddy." The top was down and they climbed into her red Chevy convertible with beige leather seats. "Are you weary from the trip?"

"Oh, no. It was fun, and I already wrote Tom a letter on the plane. I'll mail it on the way to your home." The car smelled new and Andrea patted the seat.

"A love letter, Andrea?" Muffy grinned impishly.

"Oh, yes," Andrea said. "He's so wonderful."

"Has he asked you to . . . you know what?" Muffy turned the ignition on. "Alaska has become the 49th state of the United States," the radio announced. Muffy quickly turned the dial to "Christmas Don't Be Late."

"What do you mean?"

"You know, *do it?*" She steered the car quickly around a curve to avoid another car coming toward them. Muffy's perfect thick pageboy stayed in place while Andrea's swirled about her head in the open car.

"I'm driving us straight to the club," Muffy breathlessly rushed on, "so we can talk privately before mother demands all your time to find out about Aunt Marie, your sisters, and 'new friend,' as she calls Tom."

"Jingle Bell Rock" blared out as Muffy raced her red Chevy up the circular driveway to the River Oaks Country Club. Andrea felt the valet attendants had their car doors opened before they even came to a stop.

"We'll have two Martini's, Charles," Muffy ordered in the cocktail lounge a few minutes later. She lit her Pall Mall, and held out her lighter for Andrea. Andrea studied Muffy's wrist and arm as she leaned over with her cigarette to get a light. "Andrea you'll simply love this cocktail. It's Bucky's favorite and now mine. They're *divine.*"

"Oh, Muffy, you're such fun! I've never had a martini. But tell me about the party, your Christmas, and the wedding. Is the date set?"

"It's June 24th, only two weeks after we graduate, but I can't wait any longer than that--neither can Bucky."

"You will be my maid of honor, won't you? You never answered in your last letter."

"Of course I will." Andrea took her hand. "I'd love to and I'm honored. I only hope I have enough money for the dress and the bus trip."

"Andrea, I'll talk to Momma and Daddy. They'll want to pay. You simply must, must, must be my maid of honor! You're the only one who really *knows* me."

Muffy leaned forward over their drinks on the table. "It'll be a candlelight wedding at St. John's Episcopal at 7:00, and the reception will be right here at the club. Momma's already made the reservations for everything--the club, flowers, caterers, photographers, and, best of all, we're going to New York in February to buy my dress! We must see you there, and Aunt Marie, and meet your Tom. Promise me you won't have to work."

"Oh, Muffy, there's no one like you--who loves life so! I promise to see you and have mother and Tom join us. And he did ask me to marry him on Christmas Eve!"

Muffy jumped up and hugged her. "Wow! When will you marry?"

"I don't know yet, but certainly not till after you, and you will be my matron of honor, won't you? You must keep this a secret, for Tom wanted to ask my mother, but there hasn't been time or an opportunity for him to do that. You're the only one who knows!"

"But your sisters?" Muffy asked.

"It's perfect, because I have two, so they'll both be the same--my married bridesmaids and you'll be the matron of honor!"

"It'll be wonderful to see you in New York. Momma has made the hotel reservations at the Waldorf, and we'll be there over Valentine's. Isn't that thrilling?" Muffy put her hand on Andrea's arm. "I hope we can go ice skating at Rockefeller Plaza. Have your ever done that?"

"Daddy took us there many times on Sunday afternoons when I was little." Andrea smiled at her. "It was especially beautiful during the Christmas season when the enormous tree was all lit and decorated."

"Charles, we'll have another round, please," Muffy said, and she lit another cigarette.

"I hope we don't meet Aunt Elizabeth when we first get home," Andrea giggled. "She'll see me punchy drunk, and my mother told me Aunt Elizabeth thought I was a *good influence* on you!" They both burst out laughing.

"Andrea, I've missed you so! Isn't this fun? I'll get Charles to get us some coffee before we go home. Muffy's brilliant blue eyes shone with excitement. We can *prepare* in my car before we get home, because I always carry a tube of toothpaste and perfume in my pocketbook in case Momma shows up unexpectedly. She still watches me like a hawk. She'd never, ever let me take a bus to the reunions like you did, even as a teen-ager, or fly here alone from New York."

"Tell me about the wedding," Andrea said as she lit another cigarette.

"It's going to be beautiful--spring colors with all the bridesmaids in light pink, carrying darker pink roses with baby's breath, except you. As the main attendant of honor, I want you to wear a soft pale yellow and carry deep yellow roses. Because since I was 5, you've been my sunny summer joy, my fun, and recently hope regarding this condition." Muffy frowned for a moment, but then smiled. "I've already seen in a magazine the dress I'd like you to wear. I'll show you later at home."

"How many bridesmaids will you have?"

"I'll have a total of fourteen."

"Fourteen?" Andrea gasped.

"Yes, and two little flower girls--my cousins who live here. Not Macphersons, but cousins on my father's side of the family. But I do hope all our reunion cousins and relatives will be here. It won't feel right if they aren't.

"But we'd better go now, because Momma will just kill me if we're late for dinner. She's having Bucky and his parents join us. His brother is away now, but you'll get to see Bucky again and meet his parents for the first time. I told you, didn't I, Ella Louise is Momma's best friend? I think Aunt Ella Louise and Momma cooked this up when Bucky and I were babies, and luckily it's worked out perfectly."

"Wait," Andrea said. "Before we go, tell me about your eating. I know you're going to lick this and get totally well soon, but how are you now, honestly? You look awfully thin to me, thinner than at the reunion. How much do you weigh?"

"I weigh about 115 pounds. It's always better when I'm at UT than when I'm here in Houston, but I know it'll be much better after I'm married and living with Bucky."

"Muffy, we're both five foot eight. I weigh 128 pounds, and I'm not fat as Marilyn Monroe! Does Bucky know about this?"

"Heaven's no! I'd never tell him. He'd think I were crazy or something. Only you and John Taylor know. He followed me and caught me at it again on Thanksgiving Day. Oh, it's so awful." Muffy lowered her head over the table. "But you've given me such hope. You said at the reunion you'd seen a patient like me, and the literature you sent said it was a disease, and that made me feel maybe I wasn't just crazy. I feel once I'm on my own with Bucky, I can conquer this. You haven't told anybody, have you?"

"No. I promised you. Remember? I know you can do it, but I think you'll need a doctor's help. Can't you do that now?"

"Never." Muffy looked at her intently. "Mother would find out. But the information you sent has a place I can call, and I know, now, if I can't do this on my own after I leave home next June, I can call and get help. It was a hospital in Atlanta."

"You must remember, you can always call me in New York. Tom would help us, too, if we needed him."

#

Every light in every room sparkled at the elegant engagement party. It's like something out of an Esther Williams movie, Andrea thought, looking at the hundreds of people mingling among the impressive rooms of the Davidson's River Oaks Boulevard home. She stood, enchanted, in the center of the grand foyer, next to the long mahogany table and inspected the twinkling red and green centerpiece of flowers so artfully arranged for the holiday season. She heard the piano and harpist's music waft over the crowd and at that moment it changed to "Silent Night." *How kind of Aunt Elizabeth and Uncle Orville to fly me to Houston for Muffy.*

The great hallway glowed in flickering incandescent light from the huge crystal and silver chandelier overhead. She looked up at the radiating teardrop crystals that shimmered and spun in iridescent burgundy-blue tints picked up from the immense Oriental rug beneath her feet. The Persian carpet spread from one set of twinkling, leaded glass entrance doors completely across the hallway to an exact replica at the other end. And outside those doors, at the foot of the curved circular steps, set a shining, lighted blue pool that always looked so tempting, even at Christmas.

Andrea looked at the archways of many rooms that fanned out from the massive foyer. Only the special music room located behind the grand staircase was hidden from her view. She glanced at Muffy surrounded by her friends coming from the living room--a formal room covered in a gold trimmed rug surrounding white and beige figures and patterns that swirled and turned like the gold filigreed rococo furniture legs that stood upon it. Gold tapestry draperies swooped about the many windows, and the gold piano in the corner rang out lilting Christmas carols. Rich walnut, glass, and gold tables were laden with porcelain china figurines and silver bowls of cut red and white roses. She could just see the edge of the hearth--the golden glow of the flickering fire made it warm and inviting.

Andrea turned to look at the dining room where the enormous table was bedecked with gleaming silver platters filled with sliced meats, tureens of soup, compotes of shrimp, clams and oysters with sauces, and rolls, then cakes and pies. Glimmering candlelight from tall silver candelabras on the English sideboard and dining table sumptuously bathed the gourmet repast.

Waiters wore black uniforms and white napkins graced their arms as they refilled guests' glasses. The maids in black uniforms with white aprons walked by and surrounded the brightly dressed guests. The maids passed silver trays filled with tall glasses bubbling with champagne, or took orders for drinks.

All of a sudden Andrea heard the music change to "Tender is the Night" and she yearned for Tom to be in her arms. She felt alone and remembered vividly her feeling in the Greyhound bus station when she looked at the Davidson's in all their finery. That was the first time she'd realized how worlds apart they were.

"Are you having a good time, Andrea?" John Taylor interrupted her thoughts as he approached her from behind. "Let's go sit in the library." He looked elegant in his tuxedo as he selected two tall glasses of champagne offered by the maid. He handed Andrea a glass as they walked under the large rectangular archway into the library. Uncle Orville's imposing writing desk sat at one end of the room in front of book-lined walls. They walked across another splendid red Oriental and sank low into the midnight-green velvet cushions of the Chippendale sofa in front of the lighted fireplace. It felt warm and cozy.

"You look beautiful tonight, you know." John Taylor smiled at her.

"No, I didn't. Thank you." She looked down at her simple black sheath dress that she'd bought last October. She looked up at John Taylor's serious pale face.

"I want to talk about Muffy, Andrea. I'm terribly worried about her and about her health. She told me you knew and had written her there was help and treatment for her condition."

"There is, but she must face her illness, see a psychiatrist and be in a totally different environment. Away from all this," Andrea said, sweeping her hand in front of them and toward the living room thronged with guests. "I'm worried too," she said. "Sometimes Muffy admits her problem and wants help, and then at other times she glosses over and denies it. I've promised her that I won't tell anyone, but I do think Aunt Elizabeth should know how sick she is. It's hard to imagine she can't see how Muffy looks--sallow coloring, big bags under her eyes, and the weight loss. There must be some times that she sees Muffy without her make-up. Couldn't you talk to Aunt Elizabeth about this, John Taylor?"

He sighed deeply. "I brought it up twice recently--at dinner since Muffy's been home this Christmas. Muffy glared at me, but Mother just said all brides lose weight or something like that. I got nowhere."

Andrea leaned forward toward John Taylor. "How about Uncle Orville?"

He sighed again. "Oh, I don't know. Though he dotes on Muffy, he primarily just thinks seriously about his oil business. And I don't think he'd interfere with Momma. It's mostly her doing."

"You have the most loving, wonderful, generous parents in the world." Andrea frowned. "I know they mean well and adore Muffy. Who couldn't? It's just they don't realize what they're doing to her."

John Taylor put his champagne glass on the table to his side. He lifted his hand in anguish, and rubbed his hand over his eyes. "Believe me, I know."

"Muffy's thinner than when we were at the reunion last summer. I think she believes she'll be all right as soon as she's married and out from here." Andrea looked around the room. "But I'm afraid Aunt Elizabeth will still be near by and remain in her life on a daily basis. If only Bucky worked in another city or state." Andrea stared into the fire. "Sometimes I think I hear fear in Muffy's voice. That's awful, but good, if it makes her face the truth."

"You know, don't you, that Momma and Daddy and Bucky's parents bought them a house over on Ella Lee, about three blocks away."

"Oh, no." Andrea wailed. "Muffy didn't tell me that."

"I'll try once again to talk about Muffy to Mother when she's alone, after the holidays are over."

"I feel better, knowing you're here and can watch her," Andrea said. "And how about you, John Taylor? Muffy told me it was hard for you--that you'd wanted to be a doctor, but ended up in Uncle Orville's office tending to his oil business."

"Right, but Andrea, I maintain a secret life that nobody, not even Muffy knows about. It sustains me. That's how I survive."

Andrea watched his sad dark eyes. "Oh, I can't imagine. I'm sorry," and she patted his hand. "It's tough to live a secret life. If you ever need a family friend or a cousin, I'm in New York. You know I know how to keep a secret."

But he looked toward the living room where they heard the beginning strains of "Oh Holy Night." It's hard to believe you've a steady boyfriend, too It seems like yesterday we were playing hide-and-seek when you came here in the summers. Tom's a surgical intern, I hear. What's that like? What's *he* like?"

"It means it's hard to get enough time to see each other," she laughed. "Between his every other night 'on' and my senior charge duty. He has six more years of training and then the Army, but he's a wonderful doctor--six years older, smart, handsome, fun, and serious."

"Serious?" He raised his eyebrows.

"It strikes you funny I'd mention that?"

"Yes, a little . . . but come to think of it, no, not really. You're more serious than you were or maybe I just see it now as I'm older and surrounded, as I am, by Muffy's fun-loving giddy friends. No, I'm not surprised. You've changed over the last years here and at the reunions. It was probably Uncle Paul's death, and the changes you and your family had to make."

"I guess, but I've had such fun--such a wonderful time since that happened. When so much comes your way, you can't help but be overwhelmed and genuinely appreciate it. That's what's made me serious.

"I'm lucky to live in Pelham, a town that has supported me in many ways. I'm lucky to be a Macpherson, that wonderful clan at the reunions and have your parents provide this fabulous trip and wonderful experience for me. But that's why Tom attracts me--underneath, he's serious too, but then," and she winked with a wicked grin," I guess there are a few other reasons why I like him, too."

John Taylor laughed out loud. "I'm happy for you, Andrea, and I'm also a little envious. It's something I'll never have."

"But why? Oh, please don't ever say *never* when it may be your life and happiness you're talking about. You're only three years older."

They stood up from the sofa, and he hugged her as she heard Aunt Elizabeth call him a second time from the grand foyer.

Andrea was distressed and saddened to see tears in his eyes as he broke their embrace and went to his mother.

Music trumpeted forth a call for all the guests to come to the formal living room for toasts. Andrea raised her glass as parents and older guests sang out their toasts and praises for the beautiful, beaming Muffy, shimmering in her sparkling red gown with tall fair Bucky at her side. He held his arm around her waist and leaned over and kissed her forehead. Andrea held her glass on high and waited for Muffy's eyes to find hers and when they did, Andrea winked and mouthed, ictaminigoalagosectobingolady, yoo hoo. Muffy smiled back a warm, sweet smile, hiding her secret angst behind shining sapphire eyes. Andrea sighed happily for her. They looked like the Prince and Princess of Fairyland.

Chapter Ten

"Merry Christmas, Mother, Dad," Tom said at the front door of their apartment and handed his father a large rectangular Christmas present.

His mother held him for a long time. They parted and looked at each other, tears in their eyes, "I'm sorry I hurt you, Mother. I didn't know how else to grow up."

"I hurt you also, Tom. For a long time." She smiled up at him. "But I rejoice you're here and it's over now."

Tom turned to his father. *This will be harder.* He took a deep breath. "I'm sorry, Dad," he held out his hand, but his chalk-haired father, still taller than Tom, but slightly slumped forward, walked to him and embraced his son. Tom cried as he felt his father's stiff lean frame hold him and shake with emotion. "It was mostly my fault," his father stammered. "The whole damn situation." He caught his breath. "I was too stubborn to ever acknowledge that to your Mother, who suffered terribly, or to you. I apologize now, son."

Tom patted his father's back as he held his trembling body. Then they turned and walked arm-in-arm into the living room. "I don't know how we start over again," Tom's father said, "but mother and I'll not intrude on your dignity or integrity ever again--at least we'll try hard as hell not to!" He grimaced tentatively.

"How about we communicate," Tom said looking at his dad, "in Billy's honor, instead of holding him between us."

"Amen," his mother said, and she laughed. "Pretty solemn for the fun and laughter I hope is ahead for us."

"I'm going to fix a Scotch for Mother and myself. How about you, Tom?"

"I'll help you," Tom said and followed his father to the kitchen.

As Dr. Scofield opened the freezer for ice, he looked at Tom. "Do you see the Breyer's Burnt Almond ice cream in there? I bought that for charming Andrea, in case you bring that beautiful girl around again."

Tom raised his eyebrows, his face wreathed in smiles. "We needed to be a threesome tonight, Dad, but anyway, Andrea's in Houston for a few days, visiting her cousin." They walked back to the living room, and Tom sat on the couch.

"Mother, I'd like you to sit here next to me and open your Christmas present. No, Dad, please sit here," Tom said as he saw his dad follow his mother to the side of the couch. "I want to be between you."

Tom watched his mother with pleasure as she opened the box filled with photographs of Tom at Andover.

"Oh, Tom, what a special present," and she leaned over and kissed his cheek. "We missed those years."

"It's catch-up-time, Mother. They're all here. My Andover roommate for three years is still an avid photographer. In fact, that's how he makes his living--mostly selling to the National Geographic. It may take more than one showing for me to explain all these, but I separated them into the three classes. Let's start with Lower Middler where I started."

"Let's go, son!"

Tom laughed at his father, who smiled across him at his mother. *Why had he never appreciated him before? The tight-lipped old goat.*

Mrs. Scofield looked at Tom. "I read in today's paper the 'Beatnik' movement originating in California has spread throughout America and Europe. Do you think that will affect Andover?"

"Steeped in tradition and discipline, I rather doubt it, Mother." And the three Scofield's sat with heads bent over the photographs for over an hour. Dr. Scofield reminisced about his years at Andover, sharing old stories with Tom and his wife.

After dinner and over dessert later in the dining room, Tom said, "Now I'd like to share with you about Andrea." Tom saw his parents look at each other across the table and he smiled to himself.

"I met her in August in the OR. I took down my mask after a difficult, but short, three hour case, and there she was--this beautiful green-eyed student scrub nurse looking up at me. I fell in love with her at that moment. We've dated all fall and I asked her to marry me on Christmas Eve."

"Oh, how wonderful," Mrs. Scofield exclaimed, looking at Tom with a big smile. "Your father was so taken with her, not only because she brought out your words by her genuine, empathetic reaction to Billy's photo, but also because she was so unassuming, warm, . . . just delightfully refresh--"

"That's not it, Mother," his father butted in. "She's beautiful and innocent."

"She's all of what you both say, and a hundred times more." Tom grinned at them. "I can't believe I found her, and she's agreed to marry me."

"Congratulations, Tom."

"I'm still a little numb about it all. She said yes, but she wouldn't commit to a date. I had asked her to marry right away. She said she'd let me know when she returns from Houston."

"Does she want to graduate from nursing school first?" Tom's mother asked.

"I'm afraid that's a given, which takes us till next August-- eight long months away. But then I'm afraid she may want to finish her degree at Hunter, too. That's at least another two years, because she'd go part time outside of working as a nurse. She'd need to work to earn the tuition money. Maybe you heard Andrea say that she promised her father she'd get her degree. Nothing will keep her from that."

"Oh, dear," his mother sighed.

"Having found Andrea, I realize now just how lonely I've been, and perhaps that's why I dated at such a hectic pace all through college and med school. That cognizance and Andrea, herself, made me realize how I'd probably made both of you feel the same way."

"Thank you, son," his father said, looking at him over his eyeglasses. "Mother and I have longed to know you, but we're happy you share with us now. If mother and I can help you in any way, financially or otherwise, you must let us know, because we don't want to infringe on your independence. We'll continue to mail you a monthly supplement as we planned to do for the final years of your surgical training."

"My salary won't always be fifty dollars a month." Tom laughed. "Each year it goes up some."

"Have you asked Andrea's mother for her hand?" his mother asked.

"I meet Mrs. Deck night after tomorrow, before Andrea returns."

"Will you need money for an engagement ring?" his mother asked.

"No, I have savings from my summers' work. Not much, but I think enough. Dad, you've always bought mother such beautiful antique jewelry. Would you help me with a ring? I don't know the first thing about this."

Dr. Scofield cleared his throat, and his eyes stared at Tom again. "I'll show you what I know and I can introduce you to the dealers I trust."

Tom looked at first his father and then his mother. "But it's late now, and I must head back to the hospital. Thank you for a wonderful dinner as always, Mother, and for the comfortable evening."

They walked together to the front door. "Here's your usual Christmas present, Tom." His father handed him an envelope. "Maybe next year we'll know you a little better, and Andrea, too, and can give you both a more personal gift."

"Thank you, Dad." They shook hands, hesitated, then embraced warmly. Tom shook his head in the elevator. *Why had he always felt his father was so cold and distant?*

#

"Mrs. Deck," Tom said two nights later. "I think you probably suspect why I'm here." They were sitting together at the small dining room table in the green painted dining room. The overhead light, as well as the light from the lamp on the grand piano at one side of the room, helped to illuminate their dinner. When he had telephoned about meeting her, Mrs. Deck had insisted he come for a roast beef dinner. She had been hungry for such a dinner for a long time, she had said.

"Perhaps, but I'll let you tell me," she smiled warmly at Tom.

"I proposed to Andrea on Christmas Eve. I don't know if she told you, but to my great relief, she agreed to marry me." Tom smiled happily and took in another breath. "I am truly the happiest man in the world. But, of course, I need your approbation and your blessing.

"I'm very much in love with Andrea," Tom said, not giving Mrs. Deck time to speak, but looking directly at her. "I want to marry soon. I spoke to my parents and they'll help us financially, because as you know, we can't live on an intern's salary.

"Andrea lights up my life, which sometimes, I've just come to realize, has been lonely. She's beautiful, tender, caring, funny, and I find her attractive in every way, and I speak of her sexuality as well.

"I guess I should stop." He grinned sheepishly.

"This is no surprise to me." Mrs. Deck smiled softly. "I knew you were in love with Andrea the first time I saw you with her. But I have seen that before, many times. Andrea has always had many boys hanging about her, but you are the very first one she's been interested in. When Andrea told me on the phone about your first date in the hospital cafeteria, I suspected she'd fallen in love."

"It happened in the OR, just like that." Tom clicked his fingers and laughed with happiness.

"Andrea told me," Mrs. Deck said. "I'm pleased for both of you, and I give you my blessing with eagerness and love." She patted his hand on the table.

"Thank you," he said, and he took the last bite of his meat. "This is such a good roast beef dinner, Mrs. Deck."

"I'll warm up the gravy and get you some more. But Andrea can hardly cook like this, I'm afraid." She said as she walked to the kitchen. "We've never had time to work much in the kitchen with my working evenings and her days filled with a busy school life. Through her high school years, I left out only the simplest of suppers for her to prepare for herself on school nights."

Mrs. Deck returned with a full plate of dinner and a refilled basket of warm rolls.

"I can cook, Mrs. Deck. I worked for my parents one summer as a cook, and I had to do all the grocery shopping as well."

"How unusual . . . and fortunate." She smiled as she sat down again at the dinner table. "But Andrea knows from her childhood that her responsibility as a wife is to have your dinner warm and ready when you come home from work.

"All the things you said about Andrea are true, Tom. She is an unusually caring person. Her father used to say that she was born with compassion, a sense of fairness and empathy to see both sides of any situation.

"Andrea lost her very protected, happy childhood abruptly, as her family of five decreased to just us, but she went out and made her school and everyone she met her family. She revels in people, and they fascinate her.

"That's why she was voted Miss Pelham High, Queen of her junior and senior proms, captain of her cheerleading squad and then her scholarships. She's out-going and happy, but she has another side--a secret seriousness combined with her personal commitment to do her best in everything. She hides that, but it's there. Then, our financial reversal brought out those secret goals even more."

"She helped me with Billy and my parents."

Mrs. Deck went to the kitchen. She returned and placed a plate of homemade apple pie covered with two slices of cheddar cheese in front of Tom. "That may be one of the reasons she fell madly in love with you. She sensed your inner unrest, something she could relate to. She's never found that seriousness or earnestness in the typically, happy-go-lucky, Joe College boys who've surrounded her."

Tom looked at Mrs. Deck seriously. "Maybe."

"And you may not know it yet, but Andrea has a temper that smolders and grows blindingly revengeful if she or anyone near her, is unfairly taken advantage of. It's a temper we both witnessed in her wonderful father."

Tom's eyes opened wide. "I'm surprised, Mrs. Deck."

"Sometime in the future, when you're comfortable with it, you might want to call me Marie, like my other two sons-in-law.

I think most young people are only comfortable calling their own mother, *Mother*."

"I guess so, and thank you for talking to me. I'm glad you approve."

"Oh, I do, Tom. I do."

#

After the Christmas holidays, Andrea received a call from Dean Lyman. It had been two and a half years since she'd been summoned to her office. When Andrea entered, she saw the Dean had what looked like her school file in front of her on her desk. Andrea shuddered and remembered how frightened she'd once been in this office.

"Miss Deck, I've noted that this January, for the first time since you commenced studies at New York University-Lexington Avenue School of Nursing, you have not attended Hunter College."

"Yes, Dean Lyman. I'm on senior charge rotation. It's demanding and my schedule rotates from evenings to days to nights, and that's not compatible with classes. It was all I could do to complete classics and get an A in the fall semester."

"I'm glad to hear you say that, Miss Deck. What do you plan to do when you graduate?"

Andrea smiled at the Dean, then knew she reddened. Tom had taken up residence in her mind.

"I'd like to work for the Visiting Nurse Service of New York. It pays $4200 a year. I'll earn enough to pay tuition for hopefully two courses a semester. I can go to Hunter in the evenings and on Saturdays and then study on the weekends."

"Did you like your student nurse VNS rotation better than hospital nursing?"

"No. I prefer the challenge and excitement of hospital nursing. The Recovery Room has been my favorite rotation up till now, but as I said, the money and hours as a VNS nurse will allow me to get my degree more quickly."

"You have a fine academic record, and as well, you've been class president, a basketball team player, and helped with the annual hospital benefit to raise money for the hospital and nursing school."

"This is a wonderful institution, and I hope the money we raise helps. It's my small way of paying back for the wonderful scholarship I've had here every year. It was fun to be involved, because so many of the doctors and their wives are from my hometown. I've known them since I was little. I especially loved helping with the spring Bridge party held in our enormous lounge. It was fun to see my mother and so many Pelham friends here."

"Miss Deck, would you like me to speak to my friend, the Dean at Hunter, about what they might be able to offer you in the way of a scholarship for your tuition?"

Andrea smiled broadly. "That would be wonderful, because you see . . . ah, I fell in love in the OR with a surgical intern. He wants to marry now, but I've told him I must graduate from nursing school and get my Hunter degree first. His salary is meager, so if we marry, my income would support us. Then I doubt there'd be enough for my tuition."

"I see. Well, I wanted to see if your plans were the same as two years ago. They are, except of course for one lucky young man." She smiled.

"It's just . . ." Andrea hesitated and looked down. "It would have been so much easier if I'd met Tom a few years later." She sensed Dean Lyman's eyes on her.

"I lost someone I loved, Miss Deck, when I went on to get my B. S., then a Master's, and then a Ph.D. Think carefully if you've found the right person."

Andrea looked up at her in surprise. "Oh, I'm sorry, Dean Lyman. Thank you for talking to me." Andrea hesitated and looked at the rug again. "Ah, Miss Lyman, could I ask you one more question, please?"

"What is it, Miss Deck?"

"It concerns my cousin, who's very ill. This must be confidential, because I promised not to tell anybody, but I need a reference for a doctor for her, just in case I can get her to a doctor when she visits New York next month." Andrea told the Dean the details of Muffy's health problem.

"In a few days I'll put some literature in your mailbox, as well as the name and number of Dr. Lillian Hillerman. She's the country's authority on eating pathology. I'll call her first and prepare her for your call. That is about all I think I can do. It would be best if your aunt would accompany your cousin to see Dr. Hillerman."

"I hope she will, but I'm not sure my cousin will want that. Thank you for contacting Dr. Hillerman and for the literature. I feel committed to help Muffy, and I can't tell you how badly I feel for her and worry about her. Her parents are wonderful and I just can't understand they're not seeing Muffy's illness."

Andrea stood up and shook hands with the Dean. "Thank you so much for talking to me . . . and, for everything. I really appreciate it."

#

"Mother, how do you do this, night after night, week after week, and year after year?" Andrea said loudly into the phone a few nights later.

"Andrea you always exaggerate so, and I'm not sure what you're talking about."

"Nursing!" she screamed. "I'm in charge on G-5 . . . a very busy medical ward, much like your *snake pit* at New Rochelle Hospital, I would imagine. It's impossible to do all the work and on time. I've got one patient on Levophed who has to have his blood pressure taken every fifteen minutes, two patients in oxygen tents who have to be checked frequently, and their families are about all the time. I finished my four o'clock meds after six, and then the six o'clock doctors' rounds added more treatments than I could possibly do. Mother, there are 22 patients on my ward," Andrea gasped. "Lord, Mother how many do you have?"

"Andrea! Do not take the Lord's name in vain. Is that clear?"

"Yes, Mother."

"I have 29, but you must train your aides to do as much as possible."

"Mother, they sit in the kitchen and eat, and they don't listen or take even the kindest requests from a *student* charge nurse."

"Andrea, there is always a supervisor to call for help."

"I had to last night. I even had the medical students helping me with blood cultures. It was so busy. I didn't start writing my chart notes until 1:00. I left my 3:00 to 11:00 shift at 1:45 in the morning, later even than you usually are."

"To be in charge of a busy floor demands the professional nurse be rigorous in detail, to meet the constantly changing challenges. You may need to tell your day charge nurse about it when you go on at 3:00 today."

"I did yesterday, Mother, and she said, Miss Deck, you're probably disorganized. But she did agreed to stay, give my 4:00 medications and observe until 7:00 tonight."

"I'm glad you asked for help, Andrea, because when you're rushed and more emergencies arise, one can make medication errors. It's crucial to check 3 times the med order, the patient, and the medicine before you give any medication to a patient."

"Mother, I'm not even finished. I had 2 admissions last night and 1 death and you know what that takes."

"You must be tired. Remember to eat well and sleep."

"I will," Andrea complained in a high voice. "But I have an exam in two days that I have to study for."

"How's Tom and your friend, Gerry?"

"Mother, you *always* change the subject if it's the least bit unpleasant, or when I get upset." Andrea hesitated. "They're fine, but we're all working all the time now. I hardly see Gerry anymore or any of my other friends because we're on different shifts, and I couldn't go out with Tom on two different occasions while I've been on this horrible rotation, but only another five days. Then I start charge duty again, but nights on urology, which I think will be easier."

"You'll do fine, Andrea. You always do. Try to stay calm, and sleep as much as you can. Good-bye now, dear."

"Now I know why you always sleep late in the mornings."

Her mother laughed. "One afternoon at 3:00, Dr. Rezen brought in a pedometer to my floor. He told me to attach it to my shoe. He wanted to know how many miles I walked on my shift."

"How much was it?"

Her mother paused. "It was 20 that evening."

#

"Mother," Tom said on the phone from his intern's room. "This coming Saturday Andrea and I both have off for a change. We'd like to come for dinner. Are you and Dad free? Would it be okay?"

"Oh how wonderful. Your father, dear, bought a piece of jewelry for Andrea last month. This will be a good time to give it to her. And we'll expect you anytime late Saturday afternoon, or certainly by 6:00."

"Dad bought Andrea jewelry? He didn't tell me that when he helped me with her ring two weeks ago."

"I told you he was taken with Andrea that first evening you brought her home. Like father, like son, I guess. He fell for her right away, before she even saw Billy's photo." Tom heard her sigh into the phone. "Of course, he wouldn't tell you. You know his quiet ways. I have to drag most information out of him, that is, except talk about medicine."

"Guess Dad and I love the same women to death."

"Thank you, son. We'll see you Saturday."

"Mother, would you have *ever* thought that Dad and I had anything in common?" Tom heard her laugh as they hung up.

Chapter Eleven

Andrea and Tom burst into the Scofield's apartment the following Saturday. Andrea stopped at the powder room in the hallway before she joined them in the living room.

"Did Tom already tell you what we did today?" Andrea exclaimed with a big smile as she walked into the living room. Andrea wore a light blue sweater over her plaid pleated skirt. She had worn stockings and comfortable ballet shoes as she walked about New York City all afternoon with Tom.

"Tom hasn't told us what he's done, any day, since he was twelve," Dr. Scofield barked.

"Oh," she was so taken aback by this exacting man that she hesitated for a moment, then nervously spoke quickly. "We went to the top of the Statue of Liberty and took a Staten Island ferry, just like when I was young with my father. Then," she rushed on, "we ate lunch at the Metropolitan Art Museum and Tom suggested we stroll in the Cloisters, which is where, on a little stone bench, he gave me this precious ring. Isn't it beautiful?" She stuck out her hand and then lowered it to her lap as she sat in her favorite chair in the room, a maple rocking chair with a wicker back. She wondered if Tom's mother had nursed her babies here.

She looked out the window across from her as the darkening sky began to show off twinkling city lights. Then she looked down again, and touched her gold ring with its tiny diamond shining in the antique marquis setting. His father had helped Tom look at rings, but she was glad Tom had paid for it himself, from his own summer earnings. He had worked as a drug representative the last free summer he had at medical school. It was quiet in the room, and Andrea looked up to see them all studying her.

'This is exciting for us to share your joy tonight," Mrs. Scofield said. "Isn't it Harold? Would you please bring out the champagne, dear?"

"Mrs. Scofield, I love this comfortable rocking chair. Is it old?"

"It is." She smiled at Andrea. "Do you like antiques?"

"I do, but I don't know too much about them."

"They have a wonderful antique show at the Armory every spring. I particularly like to look for pattern glass--the ribbed ivy pattern in goblets, wine glasses, compotes. Just anything I can find in ivy, "she laughed. "Maybe you'd like to join me one day."

"I would. Thank you."

At dinner, Dr. Scofield kept asking her about nursing. She told them her recent harried stories on G-5.

"And when the day charge nurse stayed on to give my 4 o'clock meds, she called the supervisor, insisted we be sent another aide as well as a practical nurse who could give meds and do treatments. We had only one death and one admission that night. When that charge nurse left at 9, not 7, and told me I *was* organized," Andrea laughed. "I felt vindicated!"

"I'm so glad my senior charge rotation on medicine is over. And this sounds silly. Now that it's over, I think I liked it better than Recovery Room, which had been my favorite rotation."

"Some people thrive on a challenge," Dr. Scofield said, keeping his small beady eyes locked onto hers. "And the demands of a busy ward can challenge one in many ways. The rewards of being helpful, useful, and needed can be heady."

She smiled at him, and to her delight, she saw a smile flicker cross his face for the first time that evening. *What a crusty old badger, but he smiled, so he must like me a smidgen.*

But the exacting man kept his piercing eyes on her. "What was your worst experience at nursing school?"

"The very first morning--being told by Dr. Fawlett to pick up my scalpel and cut down the chest of the black cadaver on the table in front of me. A formidable formaldehyde stench pervaded our lab filled with groups of four around each cadaver, but the professor stood by our table and pointed at me first."

"Did you do it?"

"I *had* to!" She stared at him. "Since then, I've heard hundreds of times in all different classes and services about preparing the patient and anticipating his fears, needs, etc. It seems to me they could have anticipated *our* needs and told us the night before that our first class was anatomy with a cadaver."

Dr. Scofield's severe countenance broke into laughter, and Andrea was relieved when Tom took over and transported them to his anatomy lab days with the same professor. She was happy to see Tom more like his usual self, and she watched the three of them interact with pleasure.

Andrea helped Mrs. Scofield clear the table and bring in the dessert. Like Evelyn, their maid didn't seem to work on Saturdays. "Harold bought more of this burnt almond ice cream the day after you were last here. It's been sitting in the freezer since then," Mrs. Scofield told Andrea in the kitchen.

Andrea stepped back and looked at Mrs. Scofield with raised eyebrows. "He did?"

"Harold has a funny way of showing people he likes them," Mrs. Scofield laughed.

After dinner in the living room, Andrea looked at a photo of a large stone residence in a gold frame on the antique mahogany desk. She bent to look at it. "What a beautiful English looking estate," she said.

"It was our home in Scarsdale," Mrs. Scofield said.

"Oh, it's lovely." Andrea was embarrassed she'd noticed the photo, but was horrified when she thought of Tom in her tiny triplex home. He'd never said a word about living on such a grand scale.

Dr. Scofield came back into the living room from the hall and placed a little wrapped gift in her lap. "This is from Mother and me, to welcome you into our family, Andrea," he said gruffly. He looked away as she looked up at him from her rocking chair.

"Oh my, what a surprise. Thank you," she said, and she sat there in the rocking chair looking at the silver wrapped gift in her lap.

"Please open it," Dr. Scofield said. It sounded like a command. Andrea stole a terrified look at Tom, and he laughed at her from the couch. She bent her head over her gift and her blonde hair fell forward by her cheeks. She did as she was told, oblivious as three people watched in fascination as she hesitantly, tenderly unwrapped the gift as if it were magic from heaven. For Andrea, it *was*.

She was speechless when she first glimpsed the gold bracelet in the white tissue. She drew in her breath, her mouth open. She carefully, gently picked it out from the tissue and turned it over in her hands. "Oh, it's lovely . . ." she said quietly, "so sweet," and she threaded the gold band around in her fingers. "Why it has three lovely little stones embedded in the delicate filigree."

"They're little emeralds, Andrea. The color of your eyes," she heard Dr. Scofield announce.

She didn't look up, but continued the examination of her gift. "How utterly exquisite." She held it in one hand and circled the band with the index finger of her other hand. She unclasped it and put it on. She looked up in the silent room and again saw all their eyes on her.

Andrea got up and walked to Dr. Scofield across the room in his chair. She put her hand on his shoulder and bent over and kissed his cheek. "Thank you," and she did the same to Mrs. Scofield. "Thank you both very much. I'm happy to be a part of your family," and she sat down on the sofa next to Tom, who further embarrassed her by kissing her on her lips right in front of his parents. She pulled back gently, knowing her face was red.

Tom broke into laughter. "You're one red tomato," he said. She saw Dr. Scofield smiling a little as he cleared his throat in embarrassment.

I hope this gets easier. She sighed.

"Have you lovebirds thought about a date for the wedding?" Mrs. Scofield asked.

Andrea quickly answered as she felt Tom's discomfort. "No, Mrs. Scofield I must graduate first and that's not until next August. And then, well, we're just not sure."

"Mother, we must go," Tom said. "I have to be on duty at five in the morning, and Andrea has exams next week."

"Thank you both for the wonderful dinner and special gift," Andrea said. "I've never had two such meaningful and lovely pieces of jewelry my whole life. I'll always remember this day."

"Andrea, Andrea we're here!" she heard Muffy shouting into her phone in her room. "You have the time and place, so don't be late!"

"I'll be there, but you're sure it's Rockefeller Center? First you wrote the Stork Club, then Pen and Pencil, and now you tell me Rockefeller Center."

"That's it, Andrea, and after an enormous family battle!"

"Could Bucky come?"

"No, he had to go with his parents to see his sick grandmother. See you in a little while."

Andrea, her mother, and Tom walked into the restaurant overlooking the ice skating rink. One look at Muffy from a distance and Andrea knew she was worse. Her embrace confirmed her worst fears as she felt Muffy's skinny body through her sophisticated black silk dress and mink stole. Andrea looked down at her light blue Sunday School dress in comparison, but nothing could daunt the joy of seeing her childhood cousin and friend.

Between Billy and John Taylor's talk, Tom entertained them all with stories. Her mother radiated happiness as she sat and talked with her sister and big Uncle Orville, who seemed ruddy faced and in good humor as always. Andrea studied him for a moment. Maybe she should ask Muffy if she could tell him.

As soon as dinner was over, Muffy insisted she and Andrea skate, and off they went in high enthusiasm. Donning their skates, Andrea said, "Muffy, I made you an appointment for tomorrow at 2:00 to see Dr. Hillerman, the specialist in eating ailments. I set it for the time you're to visit me at school. Your mother will never know."

"All right, Andrea," Muffy said slowly. "I think it'll be all right, but the very next morning you must come with us to look at wedding dresses.

"I will. I promise."

"Don't you like my little green dorm room?" Andrea asked Muffy the next afternoon. The last refrain of "He's Got the Whole World in His Hands" ended and the next record flopped into place. "Everything's Coming Up Roses" sang out.

"You've an exciting view of Lexington Avenue right from your bed." Muffy leaned over the bed and looked out the window and then around the room. "I love this picture of Tom and you on your dresser. And it's great you can have your Victrola on at just any time. With a roommate, I can't do that."

"Muffy, I want you to get on this scale next to my sink." She pushed her on quickly before she could say no.

"Oh, God, Muffy, it's 98 pounds! You must see the doctor."

Muffy grabbed her hand. "I want to. I'm scared." Her voice was high. "I have diarrhea of the mouth. Should we go now?"

"Yes. I'll show you around the hospital afterward, and then John Taylor called this morning. After you go back to the Waldorf, he wants to stop by and tell me something."

"What, I wonder?"

"I don't know. Maybe it's some surprise for your wedding."

"Oh. He's so special, but he's secretive now, about a lot of things--especially his whereabouts, when I'm home."

Andrea took hold of Muffy's hand and walked her out her dorm room and to the elevators. A little later Andrea sat skimming magazines in the waiting room while Muffy had her appointment. Finally, Dr. Hillerman stood in her white lab coat at her door and asked Andrea to join them. Dr. Hillerman was only about 5 feet in height and her fine white hair seemed to go in all directions about her heavily lined face.

She smiled warmly at Andrea. "You did a good thing to make this appointment, Miss Deck. Muffy has promised to go to this hospital just as soon as possible. It's written here, on the back of my card.

Dr. Hillerman sat down at her desk and turned to Muffy. She spoke softly and with a gentle smile. "Please remember to call me when you're ready to go, Muffy. I'll call the hospital and set it up for you. Do you understand?"

"Yes ma'am," Muffy said with a weak smile. "Thank you very much. I'm relieved to talk to you about this awful condition and learn there's a hospital full of people like me."

Dr. Hillerman leaned forward over her desk toward Muffy. "Are you sure your mother won't come to see me today or tomorrow while you're here in New York? I'll make room in my schedule."

Muffy shook her head. "No, that's not possible."

Andrea turned to Muffy. "How about Uncle Orville?"

"No," Muffy said slowly, shaking her head. "I think I have to do this on my own."

Andrea studied her anguished, woeful face. "Muffy, I'll come and help you."

"You will?"

Andrea saw relief wash over Muffy's face.

"Can you get off from school?" Muffy asked.

"I will somehow. I'll help get you admitted."

"I want to reiterate, Muffy, that it's very important for you to go just as soon as possible, "Dr. Hillerman said. "In fact, you could be admitted here temporarily--today. I really feel I must contact your mother." Dr. Hillerman persisted. Andrea heard the concern in her voice.

Muffy jumped up from her chair, her face in terror. "No. Never! You mustn't! She'd find a way to prevent it. I have to get there first. Then call her. It's the only way. Believe me, I know." Muffy took out her checkbook. "Dr. Hillerman, how do I make this out?"

Dr. Hillerman came from behind her desk and put her arm around Muffy's waist. "We'll keep with our original plan," Dr. Hillerman reassured Muffy. "If you would talk to my secretary outside in the office, she will advise you. Thank you, and good luck." They shook hands.

Andrea held Muffy's hand as they walked toward the elevators. "Before you go back to your hotel, Muffy, I want to show you a little of this famous hospital and especially the chapel that I love so much. It's small and beautiful, and I like to sit there sometimes."

#

Later in one of the small date rooms off the large student lounge, John Taylor said to Andrea, "Any luck with Muffy?"

"Yes." Andrea hesitated. "But she's the one who must tell you about it. I can only tell you that she agreed to get help, and that must remain between us."

John Taylor smiled at her. "Gee, I'm glad to hear that. You sound hopeful."

Andrea looked directly at John Taylor. "I am."

"You know how to keep a secret, and I need a listener."

Andrea smiled tentatively. "I'm here."

"I'm in love with Helen Saros, the most beautiful, talented, loving girl in the world. I see her all the time, but secretly, because her father is the High Holy Priest of the Greek Orthodox church in Houston. You know how Momma hates Catholics. She doesn't exactly keep it a secret, so you can imagine how she'd feel about Helen as a Greek Orthodox. My entire time at UT she continuously sent me newspaper articles about the Catholics--all about their horrors and dangers."

Andrea frowned. "Oh, I'm sorry."

"But I'm not like Muffy." His face was grim. "I'll defy mother. It's just Helen's parents will totally disown her. More than that," he sighed. "They will consider her dead and never recognize her or her future family in any way. She will be cut off from her family permanently and forever. She's prepared to do this, and I pray it won't turn out to be too big a price to pay in years to come. We plan to elope soon after Muffy's married in June." John Taylor spoke quickly. "I needed to tell you, and I may never get an opportunity at Muffy's wedding. It will be crazy at that time."

"Wow, I admire your courage, and know Helen must be special. How can Aunt Elizabeth be so rigid and not see the anguish she causes Muffy and you?"

"Momma loves us, but she *really* cares what her friends, her church, her relatives think about her and her family, and how we look to all those people. That overriding pride prevents her from really feeling about any of us, including Daddy, who's starting to drink too much. And so is she, for that matter."

"Oh, no." Andrea shook her head.

His face was grim. "The calamity of the Davidson family. But I'm not going to collapse with it. If Helen can be courageous, I can be defiant."

"How will you support yourself?"

"Helen has an excellent job now. She has a B. A. from Boston University and a M. S. in Library Science from Simmons. She's applied for three Boston jobs starting next September and I've applied to six medical schools in Boston. I'll be three years older than most students, but I hope they'll take me anyway. I'm prepared to take my family trust funds with me and leave Texas. If Momma and Dad block me or the funds in some way, and they may, I'll manage somehow--borrow, work, whatever, but I'm going to do it."

"You make my life look easy," Andrea said, taking his hand. "I admire your strength and wish you luck. Remember I'm here. And if I can help you in any way, will you let me know?"

"I will. I like your Tom Scofield. He really knows where he's going."

#

In the bridal salon at Sak's Fifth Avenue the next day Andrea looked at the two wedding dresses under consideration. Muffy watched Andrea. "Of course I prefer this one—"

"I do too, Muffy. It's exquisite. The pearl beading is so delicate."

"And mother prefers this one, so I'm sure you know which one I'll get."

"Can't you fight for it, Muffy?"

"No. Let's go to the Biltmore and have a martini."

"Yes," Andrea agreed quickly. After lots of giggles and two martinis, they headed from the Biltmore to the top of the Empire

State building. They held hands and skipped and danced around the top, their hair blowing in the wind like carefree children they knew they weren't anymore.

Andrea yelled to her above the howling wind. "We make a pact here and now, Muffy! Within four weeks, you call me and I'll meet you at the hospital in Atlanta. You'll have to give me as much notice as possible so I can play sick or somehow get out of school. It won't be easy for either of us, but we must do it. Promise?"

"I do, I do, I do," Muffy sang out loud. And they headed back to the Biltmore to seal their bargain with one more drink under the clock. As they strolled over the lobby to the bar, they heard the wolf whistles, "cute 'n oh those legs," and "blonde bombshell" and finally, "come dance with me, my twinkle toes."

"Muffy, I've got to run to the head."

"You go," Muffy smiled. "I'll order our drinks."

When Andrea returned to their table, she saw Muffy out on the dance floor, bitten by the jitterbug. "Come baby blue-green eyes, come dance with me," a crew cut boy with an enormous smile grabbed Andrea's hand and danced her to the floor where she spun around Muffy, "Oh my gosh, I got nabbed just like you!"

Many boys cut in and for two hours they whirled round and round to happy tunes tickled on the ivories by a wonderful Negro who bellowed out their favorite fast songs. The music got louder, and Muffy and Andrea's hilarious high laughter filled the air till Muffy led Andrea and many dancers in a Congo Line that snaked through the lobby. Muffy and Andrea turned their faces to the skylight above and screeched out, "Ictaminigoalagosectobingolady, yoo hoo!" The uniformed manager came running to them and ended it all.

"It's so glamorous. Don't you just love living in New York?" Muffy asked breathless with laughter and excitement.

"I never want to live anywhere else," Andrea said seriously. "It's the most exciting city in the whole world, but it's even better with you here with me." She took Muffy's hand and they walked slowly back to her hotel.

At 10:00 in the hospital cafeteria the next night, before Andrea had to go on duty, Tom said, "Muffy surprised me. She's not like you, your sisters, Gerry or any of your friends in nursing school."

"Don't you just love her? She's always been my best friend."

"She seems so giddy and light-headed, not like you at all."

"But that's how I was when we were little and best friends at the reunions, and every August we were together until I was thirteen. I love her to death. She's peppy, full of love and life and an energy all unto it's own, even though she's sic. . ."

"She's sick?"

Andrea coughed. "No, I said 'she's scintillating.' I was more like her before Daddy died. I was so carefully protected by my wonderful parents that I was really more like ten, not thirteen, when he left us."

"You're more down to earth."

"Yeah, because I lost my childhood overnight, but she brings it back to me--the times before I had to worry about mother's health, baby-sitting money, when the $18 Aid to Dependent Children government check was coming, and the importance of high grades on my report cards and many activities for scholarships. Then the summer jobs--selling dresses at Lorelie Dress Shop in New Rochelle, working in the factory at Sanborn Map Company in North Pelham, waitressing on Cape Cod, and eating dinner and breakfast alone in an empty house, and always another achievement to be accomplished, another challenge to be faced.

"That's why I didn't want to marry right away, but wanted to be free to work during the day and play on a different date every night. I've been weighed down with responsibilities for . . . it seems forever."

Tom stared at her. "I didn't really know all this."

"Muffy brings me happy pre-thirteen times to relish and rejoice. I have other friends, but I speak of this 'something' only my cousin, Muffy, can give me.

"She's always carried me along with her for the ride wherever we were. I guess I can't really describe how I adore her or what she means to me. Only recently I realized how different our lives are--hers elegant, rich and glamorous in a unique way, far away from mine in a nurse's uniform, burdened with the responsibilities on G5."

Tom stared at Andrea and shook his head. "You're complex, Andrea. There are so many facets to you. I'm not sure I understand them all."

"Me? You're silly. It's time now," she said looking at her nurse's watch, "for me to get to my charge duty on F17 and face today's challenges of post-op urological men." She patted his hand, stood up, and was gone.

#

The next week, on Sunday night, Muffy telephoned Andrea from UT. "Do you think you can meet me next Thursday afternoon?" She spoke breathlessly. "Bucky leaves Wednesday night to go on a four day deer hunting trip with his father. I plan to catch a jumper flight from Austin to Dallas and from there to Atlanta. I get in at 2:00 in the afternoon. I've called Dr. Hillerman. She said they will expect me at the hospital sometime late that afternoon, and to ask for a Dr. Ashworth.

"Can you be there, Andrea? Do you have the name? The Atlanta Institute, 1919 Atlantic Boulevard at the corner of Emory Road."

"I'll be there. Give me your phone number now and I'll call you late Wednesday night to confirm." Andrea tried to sound confident, but she felt frightened. "Okay? Good, Muffy. I'm proud of you. Keep strong."

"I have to," she whispered. "I'm weak and I'm scared. I weighed 92 pounds this morning."

"Oh, no!" Andrea screamed.

Chapter Twelve

Andrea walked in her dorm room from evening duty. It was after midnight. She took off her uniform and sat on her bed, Indian style, in her slip and underwear. She dialed her mother's number. When the ringing stopped, she heard her mother's voice. "Darling, is that you?"

"Mother?" Andrea was confused. *How did mother know this was me calling?* "Is that you?"

"Why, Andrea, what a surprise." Andrea heard her breathless voice. "You never call when I get home from work. I just walked in the house. It's 12:20. Are you all right?"

"Don't change the subject. Whom did you think you were talking to?" There was a long silence. Andrea heard her mother's soft breathing. "Oh . . . I know," Andrea said slowly. "You thought I was Bill Graham, your bridge partner. Well, well, w*eeell.* That's wonderful! What a surprise. Why didn't you tell me?"

There was again silence on the phone. Finally, her mother spoke in a calm gentle voice, "I thought it might upset you."

"It doesn't. It makes me happy. Mother . . . do you hear me? *Very* happy."

"Why did you call at this hour?" Andrea knew her mother would change the subject, but it *was* an unusual time for her to call.

"I need to borrow some money," Andrea said.

"Well, I'm not surprised. I don't know what you live on sometimes, except maybe air. How much do you need?"

"Three hundred. To be on the safe side."

"Three hundred?" Her mother's voice rose higher. "Are you in trouble?"

"No, but could you meet me at 10:00 at the Pelham Railroad station tomorrow morning, and could you bring your checkbook with you? I can only stay for an hour, because I need to study for an exam and be back on duty at 3:00 in the afternoon. Maybe we could have a cup of coffee at the Fifth Avenue Drug Store across from the station."

"That'll be fine if you assure me you're all right," her mother said.

"Yes, I'm fine. You'll see tomorrow."

#

"But why can't you tell me?" her mother said handing Andrea the check, as they sat over their second cup of coffee at one of the few tables in the Fifth Avenue Drug Store.

"I made a promise to help someone--someone you know well. It's something very important I feel I have to do. I know you'd agree with me. It's just I gave my word not to tell anyone." Andrea felt her mother studying her face.

"I've had to trust you from a very early age, and I will now. You've always been a responsible girl, and I'm proud of you. I want you to know, however, I don't like this. It just doesn't *feel* right."

"I promise you, Mother, that I'll tell you as soon as this person says I can. Okay? Now smile a little. Did I drink and smoke and sleep with boys all those years of evenings alone at home while you were working at the hospital?"

"Oh, Andrea, shuush," her mother said, looking around. "Someone may hear you."

An older woman ambled to their table. She peered down at her mother. "I think you were my nurse. You wore that special white, cupcake cap on your head when you dressed my burns. I never screamed when you dressed them. Why was that?"

Mother stared at her for a long moment. "Why, yes, you were in room 321. You'd been severely burned--an accident. Your kitchen stove blew up. I remember now, Mrs. Picarelli."

"You were so gentle and talked to me when you changed the bandages. I screamed horribly the other two times that they were treated everyday. You were my wonderful nurse. And you warmed the bedpan. No other nurse did that. I'm so glad to see you. Thank you for being so kind to me."

"I gave you all the pain medicine ordered for you, then did all my other eight o'clock treatments before I returned to do your dressings last. I always hoped the pain medications would have taken effect by the time I returned and I guess they had."

"I told my neighbor about you," Mrs. Picarelli said, "and you took care of him, too. He said when he got well enough, he met you every day, and walked you to the nurse's station. He said you were always spotlessly white--shoes totally white, even when it rained or snowed."

"That was Mr. Phillips. He met me at the elevator every afternoon I came on duty, once he was well and I took him out of the oxygen tent. Please do give him my kind regards. But we must go now, Mrs. Picarelli." Her mother sat up straighter in her chair and smiled at Mrs. Picarelli. "My daughter must catch the train to go back on duty at the well known Lexington Avenue Hospital in New York. She's a senior student."

"Mother, it never stops, does it? You've an incredible reputation. I hear it from the Pelham doctors at my hospital, too." Andrea walked to the car with her mother, her arm in hers.

"Andrea, I want you to get some rest and let me know as soon as you can what this is all about. It makes me uneasy. Also, now that you're engaged, I want you to read this important newspaper clipping that I saved for you." She slipped an envelope in Andrea's coat pocket, and stopped the car at the station as the train approached the platform.

"Say 'hi' to darling," Andrea teased her mother, but she hugged her fiercely. "Thank you, Mother, for the trust and the money. I'll pay you back as soon as I can." She opened her car door and raced to the train step.

Andrea sat at a window seat on the New Haven. She looked out her window and sighed with relief. Then she quickly looked again in her pocket book to make sure her mother's check was safely in place in her wallet. Before opening her text to study, Andrea read her mother's article, "The Etiquette of Being a Good Housewife," March 7, 1959 *New Rochelle Standard Star*. This is a review by Abigail Flanigan of the New Rochelle Women Club's seminar held March 1.

It is important to give our husbands our utmost care and respect considering their hard work supporting the family. They need a haven in which to rest and replenish their strength and spirit at the end of each day.

With this in mind it is essential to prepare for our husbands' home-coming each evening by having a tasty and well prepared meal ready and by looking chic and appealing, perhaps by donning a fresh housedress and adding a touch of make-up to one's face.

Preparing a cool cocktail and providing soft background music is soothing for our husbands returning work-weary after eight hours in the city. Sitting together for some time can allow him to unwind while he tells you about his day. Serving a warm appetizer with his drink might just hit the spot, and it might be best to keep your own little trifling troubles to yourself and let him ventilate his concerns about his harried day.

Should you have children you might want to bathe the little darlings and have them in their nighties and ready to welcome their father as he walks in the door before they play quietly, *seen but not heard,* during this quiet hour that you share with your husband.

At the end of your welcome home visit, you might want to have each child tell his daddy what he did during the day--maybe even show him some art work or project that you organized and supervised. For example, this might be a good time to model for him mother-daughter dress alike outfits that you've sewed throughout the day.

At the conclusion of the seminar it was reiterated that the purpose of a good wife is to be always ready to anticipate the needs and wishes of her husband. Andrea read over her mother's article twice. She sighed and wished she had learned how to cook and she felt fortunate that Tom liked to shop and cook. She had no idea how to shop for different cuts of meat. But she had to study, so she'd worry about being a good wife some other day.

The very next morning, Andrea made an appointment to see Dean Lyman, and was delighted that she could see her right away.

"Dean Lyman, I came to talk to you because you helped me with information about eating ailments early in January. My cousin, Muffy, had an appointment with Dr. Hillerman when she was in New York over Valentine's. Dr. Hillerman has arranged for my cousin to be admitted to The Atlanta Institute Thursday afternoon this week. I need to go and help admit her and be there when she calls her parents. I promised her."

Dean Lyman's eyebrows shot up. "Miss Deck, how did you plan to miss school?"

"I didn't, Dean Lyman but Muffy weighs 92 pounds. She's my height, and I weigh 128. This is very serious. As I say this, I wonder why I didn't force her to go earlier.

"*Please*, Dean Lyman." Andrea burst out crying. "I love her so much, and I'm *scared* for her. I could lie and say I was sick. I've never missed a day of school since I started. I've got to help her or she won't go to the hospital. Dr. Hillerman said I did the right thing. She knows all about this!"

"All right, Miss Deck, don't cry. You did the right thing to come here." Dean Lyman said picking up the phone. She talked with Dr. Hillerman for a long time. Then she turned to Andrea. "Dr. Hillerman has explained to me that your cousin may have bulimarexia, a combination of anorexia and bulimia, and that she is dangerously ill. She agrees that it would be beneficial if you were with your cousin. However, have you told your mother about this, Miss Deck?"

"My mother gave me $300 dollars yesterday morning. She knows only that I need to help someone, someone whom she knows. Mother does not know the details, but I'll call her every other day so she doesn't worry about me. Mother's had to trust me for a long time and I promised Muffy I'd tell no one. I broke that promise when I told you, but I needed a doctor for her."

"What are your plans, Miss Deck?"

"I need to leave first thing Thursday morning. I will fly to Atlanta. I will meet Muffy and help her get admitted Thursday afternoon and evening. I plan to spend the night in the hospital. They have guest quarters where I've made a reservation. I'll stay with Muffy Friday morning, if they'll let me, but then head back home in the afternoon, by plane if I have enough money, or by bus.

"I've traveled alone several times to a family reunion in North Carolina by Greyhound bus. If all goes well I hope to be back in school late Friday evening or very early Saturday morning."

Dean Lyman shook her head. "I will excuse you, but I want you to call me the moment you return. Is that clear?"

"Yes, Dean Lyman. Thank you."

"Good luck, Miss Deck." Andrea stood, shook her hand, and left quickly.

#

That evening at 10 Andrea went to the hospital cafeteria. She was packed and ready to leave. She'd told none of her friends-- not even Gerry. She would leave as soon as she changed her uniform when she got off duty at 7:00 the next morning.

"Andrea why can't you tell me where the hell you're going?" Tom slapped his hand down on the table and frowned at her. She saw a flutter along his jaw.

"Please, Tom. I promised this person I'd help with this situation long before I'd even had a date with you." She gritted her teeth, "Tom, I'm going on duty now. Do you want to meet Saturday night? I should be home."

"Not till then?" He stared at her and saw her eyes narrow.

"Yes. That's right." She turned abruptly and was gone.

#

In the Atlanta Institute, Muffy and Andrea found Dr. Ashworth as nice a woman physician as Dr. Hillerman. Andrea breathed a sigh of relief. Dr. Ashworth wasn't as old as Dr. Hillerman, and she spoke in a similarly kind manner. Her dark hair was pulled back in a clip and she wore a stylish black suit under her lab coat. Muffy explained again that money was not a problem. She brought out her check book, made out a check, and showed the balance to the doctor and admissions administrator. Andrea was shocked Muffy had so much money in her checking account.

They started Muffy on I.V.'s as Dr. Hillerman had explained. Muffy looked so tiny in the white bed sheets that it frightened Andrea even more. Andrea stayed and talked of old childhood games they'd played together in the summers. Muffy closed her eyes and screamed when Andrea suggested they call Aunt Elizabeth.

Muffy spoke firmly. "No. Not until tomorrow just before you have to leave."

But it still wasn't easy to think about and Dr. Ashworth agreed to be there at nine the next morning.

#

Muffy looked better in the morning. Dr. Ashworth had talked with her for two hours that first evening, after Andrea had left exhausted for the hospital guest quarters.

Lying in bed, Muffy dialed her home. Andrea stood at the edge of her bed, her arm around her and Dr. Ashworth sat in a straight chair across the room.

"Momma, this is Muffy. I have some important and sad, but also good news for you. I have been very sick, Momma. I have an eating condition and weighed only 89 pounds yesterday. I have signed myself into The Atlanta Institute, because if I don't, I will die. They have a good program here, and I know they will have me well soon."

Muffy's face twisted in anguish. "Momma, I'm not exaggerating. Please don't say that. I must stay here to get well. Is Daddy there? May I speak to him, please? Momma, please. Momma, please be reasonable. Momma, I don't care what you say to your friends," her voice rising.

Andrea leaned over and crawled onto the bed next to Muffy. Muffy took a big breath and Andrea lay down next to her and put her arm around her.

"I can't come home," Muffy insisted. "I don't give a hoot what your friends think. That's your problem," she screamed. "In fact my illness is in part your problem, so tell them whatever you want. Tell them I'm pregnant and having a baby. I don't care. I'm sorry you're embarrassed. Momma," she cried. "Why do you care so much what people think? Are they more important than me?" She screamed red-faced into the phone. "I can't go home.

Did you hear me?" Muffy sobbed. "Here, here is my doctor. Talk to her."

Dr. Ashworth took the phone and clearly, slowly explained the situation and then hung up.

"Muffy," Dr. Ashworth said at her bedside. "I will speak to your father as soon as he calls me, perhaps in an hour, as your mother suggested. She's trying to reach him on his hunting trip. I'm going to send the nurse out for your next dietary supplement. After you eat, we'll start another I.V., and after you talk with your cousin, I want to talk with you again, like last night.

Dr. Ashworth turned to Andrea. "Maybe it's time now for you to return to school. Muffy and I have work to do." She smiled down at them lying together on the bed.

"You girls did the right thing to come to us. We can cure you, Muffy. It will take a little time, but you are strong, motivated and will be successful. I'll be back in about two hours."

"Muffy, I need to run to the bathroom. I'll be back in a few minutes," Andrea said immediately and climbed down from her bed. She walked quickly down the hall to the nurse's desk, where she heard Dr. Ashworth say, "Mrs. Davidson is not to be connected by phone to Muffy Davidson's room, 422, until I authorize differently. Is that verbal order written?" she asked.

"Yes, Dr. Ashworth," the nurse said, writing in the order book.

"Dr. Ashworth," Andrea said behind her. "May I please speak with you for just a moment. I need to know how it's best for me to reach Muffy--that is, when she's not working with you or having some treatment."

Dr. Ashworth's serious face broke into a smile. "I can tell you're a nursing student, Andrea. Those are good questions. I should have reviewed this with you. I'm used to dealing with parents. Muffy's fortunate to have such a fine friend."

"I'm the fortunate one," Andrea answered.

"It would be good if you didn't call her." Dr. Ashworth brushed back some loose strands of hair that had escaped from the bun at the nape of her neck. "Our session went very well last night. Muffy is an excellent candidate for our treatment program.

It would be better for you to write your cousin frequent, short letters. Show your love and support, but also write about funny incidents, your work or things you've shared in the past, not about the grave concern you have, and which I share with you. But as I said, I'm extremely hopeful about Muffy's prognosis, even as seriously ill as she is today."

#

"Oh, Andrea, I'm so relieved to be here," Muffy said as Andrea returned to her bedside. "Thank you for helping me. I like Dr. Ashworth and I know I can get well. You need to know that Bucky and I discussed this. He knows everything, and that I'm here, but could you call him Sunday night after he returns, or maybe Monday? He'd never tell my mother or Aunt Marie about your helping me. He's very much aware of both my mother and his mother trying to run our lives. It's a problem for him as well. That's why I'm so glad you could help me here--not Bucky."

"I will, and I'll write you daily little notes, so I don't disturb you when you're working with Dr. Ashworth," Andrea said. "I'm so happy you're here, and I know you'll get well, but I need to leave now, as Dr. Ashworth said. She kissed Muffy on her forehead, then whispered, "Ictaminigoalagosectobingolady, yoo hoo!" Muffy said it with her, and Andrea raced from the room so Muffy wouldn't see her tears.

Andrea boarded the Greyhound bus at noon and walked into her dorm at 2:00 a.m. Saturday morning. At the front desk she asked the receptionist to telephone Dean Lyman at her home and tell her she had signed in.

"Now?" the receptionist asked her.

"Yes, please. That's what the Dean requested."

#

Andrea slept late the next morning, but she called her mother as soon as she awoke. "Hi, darling!" she said as soon as her mother answered.

"Andrea, you'll be the death of me," her mother said.

"I hope not. I want you know that I'm here in my dorm and I can return $25 if you want me to bring it out or mail it to you."

"Andrea I'm fine this month, so you keep it. You probably deserve it for some good deed you've done. I've started to save a little each month for your wedding."

"I'd like to start baby-sitting more so I can too, but my schedule changes every week so it's difficult."

That evening Tom had $2.00, standing-room-only tickets and they saw Sidney Poitier in <u>Raisin In The Sun</u>. Back in the private date lounge later, Tom said, "Why won't you tell me where you were? You weren't in the dorm or hospital. I thought you'd always tell me everything and the truth. You, who are so genuine and truthful."

"I'll tell you, I promise, at a later date. Have you told me every truth about your life?"

"Since we met, yes. And I'd like to tell you something we briefly talked about earlier. When I told you how desperately lonely I'd been and dated, you know, many girls. I wanted to tell you the worst. I was with three in one night."

"What?" Andrea looked at him aghast. "Are you telling me you did 'it' with three girls in one night?"

"Yes."

Andrea stared at him, her mouth ajar. Tom watched her eyes narrow. She stood up with her hands on her hips, stamped her foot, "How could you tell me that? I didn't know that was possible. You braggart!" She leaned over, her slit eyed face almost touching his. "You're proud of your conquests, your sex drive and lust, aren't you? Aren't you?" She screamed. Her spit hit his cheek. "I think it's cruel and disgusting of you to tell me that." She turned on her heel, ran to the elevator, and was gone.

Tom stood in the foyer looking at the closed elevator doors. He went to the phones around from the elevator that connected to her room and called her.

"Miss Deck." He heard her taut, strained voice.

"Andrea, I'm sorry. Please come down. Let's discuss this like adults."

"Now you insinuate I'm a child. You're very good. You know how to add insult to injury." Tom envisioned her slanted, slitty eyes.

"Andrea, you've never been sarcastic like this. Please, I love you. I want to marry you today, yesterday, last week. I can hardly work, I'm so distracted by love for you."

"It's just your lust!" Her biting sarcasm lashed his ear.

"Please, don't cut me out of your life even for a minute. It hurts me, so now I hurt as much as you. There's no point to this. I made a mistake, but let me explain, please."

"I'll be down when I'm good and ready." *Click.*

Andrea lit a cigarette. She left it hanging between her lips as she opened her closet door and kicked off her pumps into the closet. She watched herself in her full-length mirror and lowered her nylon stockings being careful not to get a run. She unclasped her garter belt at the back of her waist and threw it into her chair. She unclasped her brassiere in the back.

She looked at herself nude. She took a deep drag and put her cigarette in the ashtray on her dresser. She cupped her small breasts in her hands and held them up and out as she exhaled her smoke through her nose and watched it trail and circle over the front of her body. Then she straightened up and put her shoulders back. "Chin up, shoulders back, sugar titties out, Muffy says."

A slow curve on her lips spread into a sly smile. She turned to her side and looked at her behind and legs. "Stick up the hiney, Muffy says." Andrea followed her own command, inspecting herself from different angles and positions. She slipped on her bathrobe and headed to the shower room. No waiting line at midnight Saturday.

She returned to her closet searching for her tight navy skirt. She tried it on without her panty girdle or garter belt, and only her nylon panties--not her cotton ones. She posed in her hiney out position before the mirror. She studied herself sideways, then reached in her dresser drawer for her bra with falsies. She tried it on, then took it off and selected her bra with only the lower half a falsie. She adjusted the straps to make them shorter, tighter. She put on the bra and leaned over, cupped her breasts and raised them into her bra. She smiled, at first her side, and then her frontal view.

She put her robe on again and banged on Gerry's brown metal door next to hers. "Gerry, are you there?"

"Yes, I'm coming, I'm coming. What is it? I'm asleep." Gerry opened her door. Her eyes were half closed, her short hair a mass of light brown ringlets.

"Could I borrow your red sweater? You know, the tight one."

"You? Do you think you can get in it?" Gerry laughed, rubbing her eyes.

"Yes. Come with me." They went into Andrea's room. They lit up their cigarettes.

"Sexy, sexy," Gerry sang as Andrea paraded in front of Gerry and the mirror, smoke curling about her. "What *are* you up to?"

"I'm mad at Tom."

"Yeah, I can tell." Gerry smiled, her brown eyes teasing.

"I've kept him waiting long enough for now. Thanks for the loan. I'll return it tomorrow." She chuckled at Gerry, "If I don't wear it out."

She doused herself with Chanel No.5, brushed her teeth and tongue, and put a swipe of toothpaste on her tongue before she locked her door.

"Let's plan breakfast for tomorrow morning, if you're off," Gerry said. "Right here on the hall. But Andrea, don't get pregnant tonight." She winked.

As Andrea stepped out of the elevator, Tom took her off guard and kissed her gently, tenderly in front of all the people coming in from Saturday night dates.

"Tom, stop this." And she unexpectedly burst out laughing. "How can you do this to me in front of all these people I know? I'm embarrassed, but it's so funny typical of you. Do you always get your way?"

"No. But Andrea, I need to explain."

"All right, but in the date room, not here."

"Andrea, what I spoke to you about has bothered me since I fell in love with you in the OR, because you're so good, pure, and innocent. That's why I wanted to tell you my most worse sin, so I could start out with you on a clean sheet. Can you understand?

"Your secret vanishing act made me angry and jealous," he rushed on, "And I think quite honestly, I'm jealous of your close friendship with your Cousin Muffy. I don't know what's happened to me except I want you and need you. You don't need me as much as I need you. I think I love you more than you love me."

"You made me furious as well as hurt," Andrea said. "If I'd gone all the way with someone, which I haven't, I'd never have told you. I don't go around hurting people's feelings intentionally. How can I ever trust you again? Are you going to do that after we marry? Cause if you do, I don't want to marry you."

"I swear I haven't even looked at another girl since I took my mask down and saw you looking up at me. That's why I told you the truth. I promise you, I won't. That's all in the past."

Andrea stood up very straight, remembered Muffy's words and, put her hands on her hips.

He saw her eyes were slits again. He smiled at her.

She saw the exposed emotion on his face. But she said, "Let me tell you, if you ever date another girl or have an affair during the course of our marriage, I will pull a disappearance act so fast you won't believe it!" With hiney out, she turned to her side, "Even if we have children--one or six. It doesn't matter. I'll be out of your bed and house so fast it'll shock you, and you'll never find me or the children."

She swung around to face him directly, her hands still on her hips. "Don't you think for one minute I'm exaggerating. I will not tolerate it. I saw my suddenly widowed mother get up, and go to work to support three teenagers, a formerly wealthy child and later wife, and I can do that, too!"

Andrea looked at his face and saw what was there. She knew that he loved her so much at that moment that he couldn't speak. She watched him lean back into the couch and stretch out his arms wide. She smiled and climbed into his arms for a long time.

But later she whispered, "Now, I have to worry about how I compare to all your other girls."

"No, you don't. I've never kissed anyone who responds like you do."

"Mother talked of 'chemistry.' Do you think this is it?"

Tom laughed. "You're so naive it startles me and makes me love you all the more. Andrea, you climaxed just petting on your living room couch."

"Isn't that normal?"

"I guess I honestly don't know, but I think it usually takes more stimulation."

"It's not bad then?" she said, shaking her head.

"Just the opposite. It means we'll have a lot of fun making love."

"Good. Let's kiss some more."

Chapter Thirteen

Sunday evening Andrea telephoned from her student nurse's dorm room. It was very unusual for her to make a long distance call and she realized that she was holding her breath when she heard Bucky's voice. She sighed with relief, stretched out in her chair, and took a big drag from her cigarette. "Bucky, it's Andrea."

"Thanks for calling," he said in a loud voice. "I'm relieved she's there. Muffy told me everything about her health four weeks ago. I've known for a long time she was terribly upset, and I begged her to tell me. She's believed all along that she could conquer this with her indomitable spirit, but she really liked Dr. Hillerman. That's when she told me she'd go to the hospital, but she didn't know exactly when. She made her plans when I told her about my hunting trip with Dad."

Andrea told Bucky every detail of the weekend, and the doctor's suggestions.

"This is unfortunate, because at the last moment Uncle Orville joined us hunting, then he decided to stay on with my Dad until next Friday. Dr. Ashworth won't be able to reach him for a week. They're way out at a hunting lodge where there's not even a phone, but I'll call Muffy tonight so she can tell Dr. Ashworth." Andrea heard him take a drag on his cigarette. "But you know Andrea, this may be good," Bucky continued, "because I don't think Muffy's mother will do anything until she can talk with Uncle Orville.

"I hope you're right," Andrea said, watching her cigarette burning in the ashtray. "I'm about to write Muffy now."

"I mailed two letters to the hospital before I went hunting," Bucky said. I miss her like hell. She's been part of my soul forever."

"Mine, too," Andrea said as her voice broke. *I can't cry now.* "Bye Bucky. Good luck." Andrea put down the phone, put her head in her hands, and cried silently.

Student nurses were not allowed to take calls when on duty, but the next day at noon the charge nurse on orthopedics called Andrea to the phone.

Andrea picked up the receiver. "Miss Deck speaking."

"Miss Deck, today you are to come directly to my office from your shift," Dean Lyman said. She sounded severe. Andrea shivered and worried. She finished her work wondering all the time what would happen in the Dean's office.

At 3:00 that afternoon, Andrea went directly to her office. Dean Lyman sat erect at her desk. "I called you in about this, Miss Deck, because your aunt was hostile this morning on the phone. She wanted you called from duty. I explained to her about our policy and told her I'd have you call her from my office when your hospital duty was over. You can use the phone in the outer office, or right here, as you choose."

Andrea gripped her hands together sitting in the chair across from the Dean's desk. "I'd prefer to call from here, please."

"Aunt Elizabeth, this is Andrea." Andrea said after she dialed the number.

Her aunt spoke very slowly and enunciated every word with emphasis.

"Andrea, I am very . . . *very* . . . disappointed in you. After trying all weekend, I was not able to talk to Dr. Ashworth until this morning. She told me you were with Muffy when she admitted herself . . . to that crazy . . . hospital in Atlanta."

Andrea heard her aunt draw in a big breath. "Aunt Eli--"

"I was *shocked* to learn of your involvement into our family's affairs. I've not decided . . . *what* to do about this. I'll make that *determination* when Orville returns from his trip. I'll not bother my dear sister, Marie at this time, but I do not want something like *this* . . . *ever* repeated again. Do you hear me, Andrea? *Is that clear?*"

"Yes, Aunt Elizabeth, but Muffy has an excellent doctor who is very optimi--"

"*Stop that!*" Her aunt hissed. "My sister may allow you to talk back to her, but you are *not* to be rude to me. Do you understand? There is absolutely *nothing* wrong with Muffy--

every bride loses weight. I'll not discuss this with you--*you nosy little up-start!"*

Andrea covered the mouthpiece quickly with her hand, as if to stop the spit from hitting her ear. *Click.* Andrea looked at the receiver, then slowly reached over and hung up the phone on the Dean's desk.

Dean Lyman could hear the caustic tone of some of the outraged words.

Andrea looked down at the rug. "I guess I should have expected th--"

"Miss Deck, I will not interfere into your family business, but I do have some news for you," Dean Lyman smiled. "Dean Matthews at Hunter College reviewed all your school records and feels you can win a Jessie Smith Albright Foundation scholarship, which is an assistance program for anyone trying to earn a medical or nursing degree in New York City. Here is the application, but you must return it to me by this Friday in order to meet their March first deadline."

"Thank you very much." Andrea stood and shook the Dean's hand. "I'll have it back in your office before then. Well, maybe not until Friday." Andrea gave her a weak smile as she looked at the large application booklet the Dean had handed her.

"It's a lot of work, but you must put down all your expenses--tuition, books, transportation, food, rent for housing, phone, utilities, everything. Good luck."

#

Lost in concentration filling out her scholarship application the next day, Andrea jumped when her buzzer jangled.

"Miss Deck speaking," she said after she picked up the receiver.

"Andrea, this is Esther Scofield. Would you like to join me for lunch on Saturday, and then accompany me to the New York Armory Antique Show?"

"I'd love to, Mrs. Scofield, but we work a 44 hour week and I don't finish until one. It's an unusual school day this Saturday, because we take practice New York State license exams."

"Come at one thirty then, and we'll have a quick bowl of soup before we go."

#

Andrea felt more relaxed at the dining room table without Dr. Scofield present on Saturday afternoon. She looked at Mrs. Scofield at the head of the table. Her thick silver hair shone in the overhead light. She wore a beautifully tailored red suit with a bright print blouse. Andrea looked down at her worn navy suit which she had worn with her low heeled black pumps as she knew they would be walking a lot. She wished she'd blue pumps to match her suit, but she didn't.

Mrs. Scofield smiled at her. "You know Andrea, I trained at your hospital too, many years ago, but as a nutritionist. At my last reunion we had a tour and I saw they hadn't upgraded the nutrition labs much since my day."

"Did you work after you graduated, Mrs. Scofield?"

"Yes, right in your hospital. That is, until I met Dr. Scofield and we married. I didn't work after I was married. You see, Dr. Scofield was finished with his training when we met, but then students, interns, and residents rarely married in our day. Tommy's had quite a few medical student friends marry already."

"We have a wonderful and well known professor of nutrition at the nursing school. She's quite elderly. Her name is Miss Rynhampton. She's very strict, but she has an energetic and colorful personality."

"That's a very apt description of her, but I'd say crusty, not colorful. I felt she was old-fashioned even in my day, but I agree she was an effective teacher. I can still hear her instructions when I work in my kitchen today."

"A nutritionist." Andrea smiled at her hostess. "No wonder Tom cooks better than I do and I've enjoyed such good meals here. Is this homemade soup, Mrs. Scofield?"

"It is, but you'll have to start calling me something other than Mrs. Scofield, now that you're engaged, Andrea."

"What would you suggest?" Andrea said, looking at her.

"When our daughter, Sandra, had her first baby she asked me what I wanted to be called. I said, 'Honey,' because no one had ever called me that. That's what our dear three-year-old grandson, Michael, calls me."

"How lovely. I'd like to call you Honey, too." Andrea hesitated a moment. "Mrs. Scofield, would you mind if I smoked?"

"Why no, I might join you."

"I didn't know you smoked," Andrea said smiling. "I was afraid to light up the two times I've been here for dinner, thinking none of the Scofields smoked."

Mrs. Scofield got up from the table. "I'm going to get our cigarettes from the refrigerator."

"The refrigerator?"

"Yes. I keep them in a glass jar and I like to fill my little cigarette boxes when guests are coming. They'll get stale if I leave them out." She chuckled. "And if I don't see cigarettes all the time, it's less temptation for me to smoke. I generally have one after lunch everyday. I try not to have any more than that, though occasionally I have one later in the afternoon."

"That's good," Andrea said. "Only two a day."

"Harold doesn't know I smoke. I believe you don't have to tell your husband everything, because if he gets upset about things that he doesn't want to hear, then he needlessly upsets his wife."

"Oh." Andrea stared at her as she lit her cigarette.

"Andrea, Tom told us that you might marry in two years after you earned your degree from Hunter. Perhaps Dr. Scofield and I, maybe, could assist you with your tuition. We would be happy to do that, especially if you and Tom wanted to marry earlier."

Andrea stopped in the middle of flicking the ashes from her cigarette in the ash tray. She looked up directly at Mrs. Scofield and smiled. "Thank you for your generous, kind offer, but I couldn't possibly accept it. I was raised since thirteen never to discuss money or accept it unless I earned it. Mother even made me keep it a secret that we received Aid to Dependent Children checks till my sister and I were eighteen."

"Would a loan appeal to you more?"

"Oh no . . . thank you. I don't think so." Andrea hesitated. "You see, Mother never once complained or talked about being poor, and she was once the daughter of the richest man in her little town of Neenah, Wisconsin and she'd been a wealthy wife before the depression." Andrea put her hand on top of her future mother-in-law's. "I thank you and Dr. Scofield, but I could not accept a loan." She laughed softly. "Some of my mother must have rubbed off on me."

"I thought you ladies would be long gone by now," Dr. Scofield's voice bellowed to them from the front door.

"We're just leaving," Mrs. Scofield said, getting up from her seat and hiding the ashtray under the dining room table before joining him in the hall. Andrea quickly followed.

"I'll drive you," he said as they approached him at the front door. "Then I'll get to look at my lovely, new, future daughter-in-law to be." His oval eyes twinkled above his tentative smile.

Andrea kissed his cheek and began to wonder why she'd been so intimidated by him.

As they walked to the elevator, he turned to her. "Andrea, are you seeing Tom tonight?"

"I don't know. Our schedules didn't gibe yesterday so we haven't talked."

"How about I call him," Dr. Scofield said, "and we all meet at Longchamps for dinner tonight. It's right at the corner of our building."

"I'd love to," Andrea said as she got into the car. "I've never been there, and I've heard it's elegant."

"Esther, shall I pick you and Andrea up here at six?" Dr. Scofield asked as he stopped the car in front of the Armory. "If Tom agrees, we can go to the restaurant, or home for a drink depending on his time."

Mrs. Scofield put her hand on her husband's arm. "Remember to suggest, not tell Tom about dinner."

"I haven't forgotten. I will. I promise you." Andrea chuckled as he smiled in his sheepish unsure way at her, as if he'd been found with his finger in the sugar pot.

#

Sunday morning the phone awakened Andrea at 9:00 in her dorm room. She picked up the receiver.

"Andrea?"

"Muffy! Hi! Dr. Ashworth let you call? How are you? It's so good to hear your voice. How do you feel?"

"Andrea," Muffy giggled and giggled. "Let me get a word in! I'm here at school, but in Bucky's bedroom."

"What?" Andrea screamed. "You're not in the hospital?"

"No. I'm in Bucky's new apartment at UT. What happened is that Momma and Daddy drove to The Atlanta Institute as soon as Daddy returned from his hunting trip. Momma insisted I leave, and she signed me out of the hospital. You should have seen her. She created an uproar. They had to call in Dr. Ashworth and the head administrator Saturday morning at 9:00. Fortunately I had paid my first week in advance when you were there, because Momma refused. It's a *wonderful* place."

"Oh, Muffy, how awful. You were only there about ten days."

"Yes," Muffy rushed on, "and then because Daddy insisted on paying the additional costs despite Momma's refusal, they learned I'd paid and so Momma took my check book from me, and then she cut my allowance. What Momma forgot is, Bucky has his own trust fund."

"But Muffy, your health," Andrea cried out. "Can you get well?"

"I refused to go home. Dr. Ashworth stood next to me. But I agreed to return to UT. I called Bucky, and when I arrived Saturday at the airport, Bucky brought me here. In one day Bucky rented this darling furnished apartment, just off campus. I'm not going to live in the sorority house. Bucky's going to help me do exactly what Dr. Ashworth instructed all week. I'm going to call her tomorrow for a referral of a therapist here in Austin. She was *so* helpful."

"Do you think you can get well by yourself?"

"I'm going to try. If I can't, Bucky wants me to return and he'll pay. And Andrea I'm going to tell you a huge secret. This morning after church, the minister, whom we've known since we started UT, is going to marry us."

"Oh, Muffy!" Andrea cried. "How brave! I want to be there."

"I know. I want you with me--like we planned when we were little. That's why I'm calling. I want you to go to your hospital chapel and say 'ictaminigoalagosectobingolady, yoo hoo!' exactly at 1:00 p.m. I'll say it with you just before our service starts."

Andrea shook her head in amazement. "Muffy, what are you going to wear?" She yelled and laughed into the phone. "I can't sit there and think of you at the altar *nude*."

"That's later." Muffy giggled.

"Tell me," Andrea commanded.

"My Chanel winter white suit with navy trim down the front by the buttons and around the collar and cuffs. I plan to be nude otherwise," she shrieked back excitedly. "Oh, I wish you could be here!"

"I do, too! We planned our weddings with our dolls, remember? But I'll be in the chapel."

"I'm so glad you took me on a hospital tour, and we were in the chapel together. I can think of you there! Andrea, you always think of the right things to do--like go to Dr. Hillerman and the Institute. Bucky did all this yesterday before I arrived home--rented the apartment, planned the wedding, met the minister. Isn't he wonderful?"

"He is." Andrea sighed. "He loves you, and so do I."

"Bucky even asked the minister's wife to be our witness. He knew if I couldn't have you, I wouldn't want anyone. No one must know, or Momma will have the wedding annulled, though I may call John Taylor and ask him to drive up some time this week."

"John Taylor would love that, Muffy. He won't tell anyone. Do call him. He was so worried about you when I saw him here in February."

"Momma will proceed with our wedding plans in Houston for June 24th. We'll go along with that so still plan on coming to be my maid-of-honor. Hopefully this will keep Momma busy and away from UT until graduation in three months."

"Please follow the instructions and get well."

"I will, you old spinster, you," Muffy laughed. Thanks again for helping me in Atlanta. You saved my life."

Andrea smiled. "Till 1:00 tomorrow. Give Bucky some of my love that's left over from you."

"I will. Remember, get to that chapel in time. I'll call you in a week."

Andrea stamped her foot as she hung up the phone. All their hospital plans smashed by that woman. *Darn. Aunt Elizabeth.* She wrote Muffy a letter, and dropped it into the mail on the way to the chapel. She went in uniform, because she was on duty later. She wished she'd thought to get Muffy's telephone number, though she knew she wouldn't spend the money on a long distance phone call. She wrote again on Wednesday. She could hardly wait for Muffy to call her on Sunday.

But on Sunday morning Andrea's phone rang and waked her. She heard her mother say, "I know it's early, dear, but do you think you could come out and go to church with me this morning? And do you think Tom could join us?"

"I can, Mother. I'm off the whole day. Celebration. I don't have to work until evening duty on Monday, when I start the Tuberculosis ward for one month, which I dread. And Mother, I have good news."

"What, dear?"

"Dean Lyman spoke to Dean Matthews at Hunter, and then Dean Lyman gave me a scholarship application which I completed and turned back into her office. They think I might get it, and it's very generous assistance. Isn't that wonderful?"

"It is."

"I'll call Tom now and see what he says."

"Tell him I'll have a roast lamb dinner for him."

"Oh, mother, you'll spoil him."

"I hope so."

Andrea heard her mother chuckle as she hung up.

Tom groaned when she called him about her plans for the day. "I need more sleep."

"Please come," Andrea begged. "It's unusual for Mother to call and ask me to come out. Something's up. She must be lonely or something. Maybe that Bill Graham, remember her widower friend whom I told you about--maybe he got sick or is giving her a go-round. She said she'd have a roast lamb dinner for you."

"I just woke up. Let's go," Tom said. "But what time is it?"

"It's 9:00 a.m. We could catch the 10:25, and she'll take us right to church from the station. Thanks. I'll let her know."

"I'll be in your lobby. Can you be ready in 45 minutes?"

Chapter Fourteen

In the living room after church, and then dinner, Andrea sat on the couch next to Tom. His arm was around her shoulders. Her mother came and sat on the other side of her, but at the edge of her seat. Her mother looked at her, tears welled in her eyes and slipped slowly down her face.

"Andrea, I have some great sadness to tell you."

"Me?"

"Yes," her mother said, taking her hand. "It concerns Muffy."

Her mother patted her hand with her other hand. She hesitated. "Andrea, this is very sad. I must tell you, dear, that Muffy and Bucky were killed last night."

"No! No!" she shrieked. Her head dropped low into her hands, her hair flying around over her head. She covered her eyes with her hands, and cried in great, noisy, heaving sobs. Tom, his arm about her shaking shoulders, drew her to his shoulder, and her mother patted her back. Tom looked at Mrs. Deck's distraught face over Andrea's back.

After a long time Andrea suddenly stopped. The room was quiet except for the hum of the noisy old furnace in the basement. Sun filtered through the glass curtain on the porch door across from where they sat. Andrea looked up and stared stupefied across at the windows in the porch door.

"I saw them. I just saw them, in Muffy's red convertible-- Muffy sitting up in the middle, high on the back of the front beige leather seat, her feet resting on the seat, her hand on Bucky's shoulder. They hit a tree. The car split in half, right down the middle, but they didn't. They were together on one side of the car, and their heads hit the tree together."

Andrea turned to her mother's shocked face, her mouth open.

"Yes, Andrea," her mother said. "That's *exactly* what Orville told me late last night. They'd had dinner in Austin, before they returned to campus."

Andrea, hypnotic in her staring across the room, said nothing. Tom patted her shoulder and kissed her temple.

Andrea's mother held her hand. "You see, Tom, when Muffy and Andrea met at a family reunion in North Carolina, they clung together from that moment on, often in the corn garden where no one could find them"

"You knew we were there?" Motionless, Andrea's monotone voice spoke as she continued to stare across the room.

"Yes I did."

"Did Aunt Elizabeth know?" Andrea asked.

"No. I didn't tell her. I didn't think you Bobbsey Twins could get into too much trouble there." She smiled at Andrea and again Tom saw her mother's pained face as she struggled and continued, for her daughter, to talk slowly and quietly.

"Then, Tom, they begged every reunion not to be separated, so for the next three weeks of most Augusts throughout their childhood they were together in Houston or here in Pelham.

"When Muffy came, I hardly knew they were about, except for their continuous giggling, which could be heard everywhere. It turned up in unusual times and places inside or outside. They played quietly and almost secretly."

Mrs. Deck patted her daughter's arm, but Andrea continued to stare across the room. "First, and for many years, with dolls," her mother continued. "They told stories to each other about their dolls and put them into fantasy families. They'd sit on Andrea's bedroom floor with the dolls all about, but sometimes they'd take all 30 of them into wagons, carriages, and strollers and explore the neighborhood, and then other lands and countries as they learned about such places over their grammar school years.

"Later, they moved to Andrea's stuffed animal collection, and the animals, like the dolls, went around the world with their twin mothers, and one time, the dolls, and then the animals, even came in the back seat of my car and into the A & P on Fifth Avenue in Pelham--all 30 of them.

"In between the Augusts, they wrote monthly--long letters, about what I'm not sure. But I believe it probably changed from dolls and animals to secret girlfriends and boyfriends.

"Muffy's family took Andrea on some beautiful August trips from Houston to the cool mountains of Winter Park, and another time to Grand Canyon. When Muffy came to us, we drove to Niagara Falls one year, and Paul took Muffy, Andrea, and her sister, Roddy, to Old Orchard Beach in Maine."

"To have a frappe," Andrea's heavy voice interrupted, as she sat mesmerized by the dwindling light filtering through the glass curtains on the porch window. "Like he had there as a child. And Roddy, Muffy and I got the giggles in a fancy restaurant where we used finger bowls for the first time." Andrea stopped, but remained transfixed.

"Paul took them to New York--his office, museums, theater, Radio City, Empire State, and all the things the great city has to offer. When teen-agers they went to the city, and did it all over again by themselves. We didn't tell Aunt Elizabeth everything, and Muffy sifted through what to share with her mother, that is, after my sister complained to me the first time."

"Muffy loved the Botanical Gardens the best," Andrea said in a low voice. "She always wanted to go back there. She loved coming here the best. Mother never bothered us," Andrea continued in her monotonous voice.

"That's because you behaved better with Muffy in residence to entertain you. They loved coloring books and games--Sorry, Monopoly, Carrom. Then, playing cards--first War, Go Fish, then on to Canasta, Hearts and then Bridge with Paul and me. They were a delight to have around and I looked away from their antics a few times."

"Like what, mother?" Andrea continued to stare straight ahead.

"Well, dear, when you two ran into the school and turned on all the wall vacuum hoses that made such a ghastly noise and scared that dear old janitor, Walter. And then you played some pranks with Taffy"

Andrea drew in her breath, "You knew about that?"

"Yes, dear, I thought it would pass. I guess it did. Taffy died."

"That embarrasses me."

"It's the normal exploration children go through. I don't believe it held any lasting damage for either of you."

"Oh, Mother, why were you so good to us when Aunt Elizabeth never seemed to understand. We had to look and act as if we were on stage--smiling, clean, and pretty with hats, gloves, and pocketbooks all matching, the seams in our stockings perfectly straight, our hems exactly the right length, and our noses powdered so there was no shine, and it went on and on and on, and always well behaved.

"How will I live without her?" she continued trance-like and stared at the darkening window.

"Like I've lived without Billy and you've lived all these years without your father," she heard Tom's voice.

"It's hard for me to watch you have so much tragedy in your young life," her mother said. "First, your father, then Granny dying six months later, and now your beloved, precious Muffy. It's these bumps in the road that God has chosen to throw your way--they'll enable you to catch life's daily events and appreciate them. They'll make you strong." She patted her hand. "I was so much older than you when I had to face this."

"But I already learned that, Mother. I appreciate each day and the good things, because I learned when Daddy died, they can be fleeting, gone in a flash like he was, and now, Muffy. Now I'm afraid for *all* my good things." She took their hands and squeezed fiercely as she stared in front of her.

"Bucky said she was a part of his soul."

"You were soul-sisters, Andrea," she heard her mother's words. "That's what you were, and will always be. In a way, you were closer to Muffy than your own older sisters."

"Yes, we were." Andrea thought of sitting in the chapel during Muffy's wedding, and then realized how little her mother and Tom knew of her recent life with Muffy.

Her mother walked across the room to turn on the standing lamp by her father's old reading chair.

Andrea watched her mother. "Mother," she exclaimed. "Your work! You need to go to the hospital."

"No, it's all right. I called in sick today." Her mother paused. "I am. For you."

"Oh. I've never known you to do that."

"No. But Andrea," she returned to the couch and sat next to Andrea. "Orville said Muffy's funeral would be next Saturday. He said Elizabeth was very upset, of course, and could not face anybody before then. They were notified at 2:00 a.m. last night and their doctor had to come to sedate my poor dear sister.

"We must go to the funeral next Saturday. I'll call your Dean and have you excused from school. We must be there for Elizabeth, Orville, John Taylor, and Billy. The Macphersons will all assemble in Houston for this family tragedy."

"No!" Andrea howled, and stood up. "*No!*" She turned, looked down at her mother, "*I won't go!*"

"Andrea, I know how hard funerals and other deaths are, once you've faced it yourself for the first time. But we must."

Andrea fell into her father's chair across from them. She splayed her legs out in front of her, looked down at the green wavy patterns in the rug, and held her face in her hands. "Does a promise end when a person dies?"

Tom put his arm over her mother's shoulder as they sat on the couch and watched Andrea, who remained frighteningly hypnotic. "I'm going to tell you about a promise I had with Muffy. It concerns my whereabouts two weeks ago."

Tom patted Marie's shoulder as he saw her tortured face watch her daughter's exposed pain.

Andrea's monotone took them in minute detail to the bathroom at the Macpherson reunion, Dean Lyman's referral, their visit to Dr. Hillerman's in New York, to Dr. Ashworth in Atlanta, and Muffy's phone call from her hospital bed to her mother, and ended with Aunt Elizabeth's phone call earlier in the week. She said no more. But Andrea closed her eyes and saw beautiful Muffy in her white suit saying her vows to golden handsome Bucky in front of the minister.

Tom handed Marie his handkerchief, and let his tears roll down his face.

"You do not have to go to the funeral," her mother said. "Louise, Roddy and I will go. It's no less than I have learned to expect of you, but it always overwhelms me with surprise and pride when I see how you help others and weather the storms in your young life."

Andrea stared straight ahead.

"You see, Andrea, my dear sister, Elizabeth, at 52 faces her first obstacle, at least to my knowledge. Perhaps she's never grown to her potential as a person. You learned long ago 'death bumps' can be the greatest, hardest of challenges to make you appreciate *everything, every tiny fleeting facet* that appears along the road in life's adventure.

"It's late now, Tom and Andrea. I'm going to drive you into the---"

"Stop!" Andrea stood up tall and straight in front of her chair. She gritted her teeth, and looked down at them on the couch. Her eyes squinted at her mother. "Don't you ever say 'my dear, sister Elizabeth' to me. *She killed her! She killed one of the best things in my life!"*

"And why?" Andrea put her hands on her hips and snarled at her mother.. "Because, and I quote, 'I'm embarrassed to tell my friends.' Those are the *very words* I heard go into Muffy's ear as she lay in my arms on her hospital bed!

"I saw Dr. Ashworth wince, as I cringed." Andrea's voice grew louder. "That shallow, hypocritical aunt of mine cared more about appearances and what her Houston friends thought than her own daughter. Muffy died knowing her mother didn't care two hoots for her. If she'd just left her very sick daughter in the hospital, Muffy'd be alive today. And I hope she remembers that for the rest of her life." Andrea screamed. "She killed her! I never want to see or hear from Aunt Elizabeth again."

"Now Andrea, don't make such rash statements."

"Don't you 'now Andrea' me!" she screeched, her eyes in slits. "You care one hell of a lot about appearances, manners, hemlines, too, but fortunately you love me more than let that *totally* rule us. That's why I won't go to the funeral," she taunted her mother with biting sarcasm. "It has *nothing* to do with my tears at funerals, but *everything* to do with my pain and eternal love for Muffy, and *everything* to do with how *I hate that woman and always will!*

"I'm going to take a bath!" Andrea said emphatically.

"What?" Tom and her mother said.

"To wash off the stench and *stink, stink, stink* of Aunt Elizabeth!" She marched out of the room and up the stairs.

Mrs. Deck sighed deeply. "Tom, I'm going to give you a big lamb sandwich and a glass of milk while we wait for Andrea. I'll wrap one for her. I hope she'll eat it in the car, or later," she said with a weak smile. "Then I'll drive you to the hospital, because it's already 9:00 o'clock."

Marie sat next to Tom as he ate his sandwich at the small dining room table. "You may remember I told you about Andrea's temper."

"Yes, I've learned about it since we spoke." Tom smiled tentatively.

"I'm sorry." Marie smiled weakly in return. "I think Andrea may be in shock now, but she uses the word 'stink,' because I forbade the use of that word as well as 'shut-up' when she was little." Marie put her elbows on the table and rested her head in her hands.

"This will be an enormous adjustment for Andrea, Tom. I can't tell you how close those precious children were. I'm glad Andrea has you in her life."

Tom leaned over and patted her shoulder.

#

The car wove through the night lights of other cars along Bruckner Boulevard, then down the East River Drive to the towering hospital on Lexington Avenue. Only Andrea's intermittent crying broke into the silence of the dark car.

Andrea clung to Tom at the doorstep as they said good-night.

"I know you don't like to come up to my room at night, but I think you should tonight."

She nodded, and they went into the dorm and down the stairs to the hospital tunnel. Andrea smiled. "Last time I ran down 23 flights from your room."

Tom's laughter ran out. Andrea took his hand. "I didn't want anyone, especially Pelham doctors, to see me coming from the intern's floor."

"Will you do that tomorrow as well?"

"Yes. We must set the alarm for 5:00 You can sleep while I sneak home to my dorm," she smiled.

"Just a little," Tom said. "In the morning I have to be on H8 at 6:00. I start Ear Nose and Throat."

"I'm not on till evenings. I start T. B. It's for 4 weeks."

"Why not meet me at the G cafeteria at midnight after you finish tomorrow night."

"All right, but don't call me on the ward. I got in trouble the last time you called me on G5."

"Oops, sorry." He smiled down at her, happy to see her smile, and he led her out of the elevator and down to his room. He closed the door, turned and kissed her. "And now, how do you want to do this, Miss Deck?"

"You get in your pajamas, into bed, turn out the light, and shut your eyes."

Tom laughed out loud and changed his clothes by his closet. Andrea looked out his window at the city lights. Tom turned out the overhead light and got into the unmade bed. "I need a light. I forgot to set the alarm."

Andrea crossed the room and waited by the light switch until Tom had put the little clock back on his table. Andrea stayed over by the door behind the bed, so Tom couldn't see her. She took off her skirt and sweater, folded them, and hung them over the towel rack by the sink. She left her slip and underwear on. She slipped in the other side of the bed and lay down next to Tom. He turned toward her and stroked back her hair. As his eyes adjusted to the dark with the city lights only dimly lighting his room, he saw her eyes close. She was asleep the next moment.

But later, she screamed in the middle of the night and sat upright. "I saw them."

Tom sat up next to her and put his arm over her shoulder.

"They were dressed as they were at their engagement party, standing in front of the gold piano in the living room," Andrea said. "They looked like a royal couple in fairyland. They were happy and smiling at me. I'm happy. It was real. I was with them. That never happened after Daddy died."

"I saw Billy a few times--always the same. He was playing Sorry on his bed with me. He smiled because he had won. Sometimes when he was sick, I had let him win. Other times he really won, but he got such joy winning."

Andrea shivered. "I'm cold."

"I'll get a blanket in the closet." Tom laid it out over the bed and got back in. He took Andrea in his arms again and kissed her and rubbed her back to warm her. Andrea couldn't stop her shaking for awhile. She felt Tom stroking her head until her breathing became regular, and she slipped back to sleep.

They slept until the alarm at 5:00 awakened Andrea. She washed her face at Tom's sink, put on her skirt and sweater, and quietly, quickly closed the door and ran down the 23 flights of stairs. She walked quickly through the hospital tunnel, and then up the stairs to her dorm lobby where she signed in. She took the elevator up to her floor. She banged on Gerry's door, but she wasn't back from night duty on orthopedics. Andrea took a quick shower, went back to her bed, and slept.

She screamed out loud as she saw Muffy's red car crashing into a tree. She heard Gerry pounding on her door.

"Andrea, Andrea let me in!"

Chapter Fifteen

Andrea opened her dorm room door, and stared into Gerry's brown eyes in a daze.

"Come on, it's cold," Gerry said. "Let's get back into your bed, and you tell me about your nightmare. I'm surprised you didn't set off the fire alarm."

They giggled down into bed and Andrea burst into tears. She told Gerry everything about Muffy.

"Oh, Andrea. It's such a sad story. I'm so sorry." Gerry gently patted her shoulder for long moments. "But you know what?" she said after a while. "We both need food." Gerry got up out of bed. "I'll run to the kitchen, and be back in a jiffy."

Gerry returned and they sat together on Andrea's bed and ate cinnamon toast and milk. The phone rang and Andrea answered. She looked at Gerry, frowning, then said into the phone. "Yes, Dean Lyman. I'll be there at noon," and she hung up.

"Gerry, I didn't sign in till 5:10 this morning." Andrea frowned. "Do you think that's why she wants to see me? I always get so nervous when she calls me in . . . though, she's been good to me."

"Where were you?"

"With Tom. I didn't want to be alone."

"Oh," Gerry said smiling. Then she winked at Andrea." You didn't tell me that part."

#

"Miss Deck, I'm sorry about your cousin, Muffy," Dean Lyman said to her later as she sat in the chair across from the Dean's desk.

"Thank you." Andrea burst into tears. "How did you know?"

"Your mother called. She was worried about you, and wanted me to know of your cousin's death."

"Oh," said Andrea, wadding her Kleenex in her hands.

"Do you feel well enough to go on duty at 3:00 this afternoon? If not, I'll write you an excuse."

"Yes. I want to keep my mind on other things and if I help T.B. patients, I'll be happier than I am now." She started to cry again.

"Maybe you'd like to talk to Dr. Hillerman."

"That I know is from you, and not my mother. She'd be horrified if I ever went to a psychiatrist. I was going to write to Dr. Hillerman and Dr. Ashworth to thank them for helping us. Also, I wondered how they would find out if I didn't tell them."

"I called Dr. Hillerman this morning. She was most distressed and wanted to see you. Let's call her now," Dean Lyman suggested.

Andrea felt the Dean watching her. "All right," she said slowly. "I've never been to a psychiatrist. It's scary, but if Muffy could do it, I can. You know, Muffy had more spirit and courage, except regarding her horrible mother." Andrea stared out the window. "Muffy . . . she loved life, and gave some of it to me,

"You know what we did in February when she was here?" Andrea, trance-like, continued to stare out the Dean's window. "We went to the Biltmore and had a drink or two under the clock. We danced like hell all over that place. I danced by her, 'Muffy, we're engaged, I said,' and she said 'and we'll still be engaged after we cut up this rug.' We jitter-bugged, did the Charlestown, the rag, and then she led the snake all over the dance floor and into the Biltmore lobby, and you know, Dean Lyman," Andrea turned to look at her. "Muffy was right. We had a ball, and I'm still engaged. I'd never have done that without her."

"*Joie de Vivre*," Dean Lyman said, looking at Andrea's sad face. "That's what she had."

"Yes, she was the *piece de resistance*, and everything else fun, exciting, and thrilling in life."

"She lifted you up and out of yourself, didn't she?"

"I guess so."

"Does your fiance have some of that spirit?"

"Yes, but in a different way. He's captured me into the center of his life. Of course, as a surgical intern, there's not a whole lot of life outside of the OR."

Andrea turned to the window again. "Tom has humor. Mother said that was good for me, too." She talked as if to herself, and then was silent for a few moments.

"Dean Lyman, if I can possibly win that scholarship, does it apply if I'm married and a student at Hunter? I filled out the needs column as a single person's living expenses, and wrote that I anticipated a VNS salary."

"I don't think it would change. Certainly a resident's salary can't pay your tuition or living expenses."

"Even if it goes from $50 to $75 a month?"

#

Later that afternoon Andrea was nervous, as she always was, on the first day of every new service. She just got comfortable trying to be a good nurse in surgery, then she was sent to medicine, then pediatrics, and then obstetrics, and then all the sub specialties, ENT, where Tom was now, thoracic, vascular, urology--each time a new and different environment. It never stopped--always adjusting to a new ward, a new set of patients, treatments, procedures, and always dozens of instructors, charge nurses, doctors, checking, correcting, criticizing.

On her way to the hospital, she stopped and reached into her mailbox. She pulled out a letter with Muffy's writing. She kissed the letter and cried.

She checked her watch, ran through the tunnel, and up to the chapel. "I'll read it here." But she looked at the letter in her lap and could not open it. She stroked it, knowing Muffy had touched it not long ago. She kissed it, and rubbed it over her face. She stood up, pulled her white apron forward, and put it in the pocket of her light blue uniform. She patted it as she rode the elevator to J12, Public Health and Preventive Medicine, Tuberculosis Quarantine Unit.

After her quick supper in the cafeteria where she didn't see anyone she knew, she returned to the chapel, just off the main lobby of the hospital. A few people were there this time. She sat in her usual spot in the first empty pew and looked again at her letter. She turned it over to open the seal, but didn't. "I have a little more of Muffy here. I don't want to use it up."

She put the letter in her pocket, and returned to her floor. As she walked to the nurse's station, Dr. McGiff walked toward her. "Andrea," he barked out with a broad grin. "How's my favorite student nurse from Pelham?"

Andrea burst out crying. Dr. McGiff stepped back. "I've never seen you without a smile on your pretty face. Let's go down here, Andrea, to my office."

"Oh, I can't. I'm on duty and need to give the 7:00 p.m. meds, Dr. McGiff. It's nothing. I don't know what made me cry. Honestly, I'm fine."

"Andrea, I'm going to be seeing patients for at least an hour. Then I'm going to tell Miss Scarlotti, that battle ax of a charge nurse, that I need to explain something to you in my office. I want you to come there at 8:00 p.m."

"Yes, Dr. McGiff."

"Now Andrea," Dr. McGiff said later, sitting at his desk in his office. "Dr. Harris and I were on the Pelham committee that made sure you received enough support for three years of nursing school. I want to make sure you're all right. Your father would expect no less of me and he'd do the same for me. Come on now, out with it."

Andrea took the letter from her pocket, put it on his desk. "This letter," she said crying, "is from my best friend and cousin, who was killed Saturday night."

Finally she composed herself. "If you just hadn't been kind to me, I could have gotten through my shift without crying. It was the same when Daddy died--all those days the next week in school. If people said nothing, I was all right, but if the teachers hugged me and said they were sorry, I'd have to run to the bathroom cubicle to cry. Mother had told me that if I cried, to go there."

"Nothing can bring your cousin back, Andrea, but good healthy cries help. You've been handed one of life's double whammies."

Andrea looked up at him from her chair in front of his desk. She smiled through her tears. "A double whammy? What a funny expression."

Dr. McGiff leaned back in his chair, shook his head, and rubbed his hand over his whispy gray hair. "I don't know why you got hit with this. Nobody does, but I want you to come in here any time, day or evening, and cry all you want. You can use the phone and call home, too. Here's an extra key to my office." Dr. McGiff passed it across his desk to her. "I don't know anything else I can do to help you, except I know you bravely handled this once. You'll do it again."

'Thank you, Dr. McGiff." Andrea smiled weakly.

"Have you been able to get off, and see your wonderful mother about this?"

"Yes. I was with her yesterday."

"I see her at New Rochelle Hospital all the time. I bet someday you're going to be just as fine a professional nurse as she is, and they don't come any better than Marie Deck."

"I hope so."

"Now you better get back out there on the floor, or that ornery charge nurse will have my head."

Andrea laughed. She stood up and shook his hand. "I sure am glad I grew up in Pelham."

"We are, too, Andrea."

After the 11:00 p.m. change of shift report, Andrea patted her pocket, and walked to the elevator to meet Tom. They went down to the first floor cafeteria.

#

"How are you feeling?" Tom asked as they put their trays down on one of the rectangular tables near the entrance.

"Nervous."

"First day bad on T.B.?"

"Yes, we had to learn the quarantine procedures, and it's hard and scary. And the charge nurse is awful. And . . . and, also this." She put Muffy's letter on the table, and Tom read the return address, Mr. and Mrs. Ward Buck Hamilton.

"Oh, my God. You haven't opened it?"

"No," she sighed. "I want to save it, savor it, enjoy it for as long as I can."

"But I hear you, and see how nervous you are. Once you open it, you can do all those things better," he said, smiling at her.

"You're laughing at me." She looked away, and her voice was low.

"No, but you've had an enormous shock and you're acting a little crazy."

"I know. I'm going to see Dr. Hillerman tomorrow. Do you know who she is?"

"Of course. She's famous, like most every other professor around this place."

"Have you ever been to a psychiatrist, Tom?"

"No, but my parents wanted me to, and that's why I wouldn't go. It may have helped me deal with the anger I felt."

"Anger?"

"Yes, and you're angry, too."

"Me? No I'm not." Andrea said emphatically.

"Well, what were the histrionics at your home yesterday where you ended taking a bath to rid yourself of your aunt's stench? That was quite a performance You could be an actress."

"I'm furious at Aunt Elizabeth. She killed Muffy!"

"Right, but your real anger is because Muffy's been taken from you. Your aunt didn't cause the automobile accident."

"She did, too!" Andrea's eyes narrowed. "If she'd left Muffy in the hospital she'd be alive today!"

Tom's brow wrinkled. "When do you see Dr. Hillerman?" he asked.

"Tomorrow. Muffy liked her psychiatrists. I'm going to see what it's all about. Do you think I'll have to lie on a couch? I'm so tired, I might sleep, and then she'd have to wake me up."

Tom broke out into loud laughter just as Dr. Harris and Dr. McGiff came into the cafeteria and stopped at their table."

"Is he entertaining, Andrea?" Dr. Harris said.

"Yes, Dr. Harris." She stood up, as did Tom, as the two Pelham doctors stopped at their table.

"What's this?" Dr. Harris boomed, taking Andrea's left hand. His shaggy eyebrows raised high on his forehead above teasing bright brown eyes. "You're engaged! Well, isn't that nice. Congratulations. Marie Deck's getting a third good son-in-law. When do you come to Thoracics, Dr. Scofield?" Dr. Harris asked.

"It's my next rotation."

"I'm going to give you hell if you don't take care of our shining light from Pelham."

"Yes, sir," Tom said.

But Dr. McGiff put his hand on Andrea's shoulder as Dr. Harris walked away laughing toward the cafeteria line. "I see that letter again," Dr. McGiff said looking at the table. "I think you need to open it, and get it over with, Andrea. You can use my office. I'm through for the night."

"I will." She hesitated. "I'll open it tonight--with Tom, but I'll go to the chapel. Thank you, Dr. McGiff." She looked up at him, tears spilling from her eyes.

"Come on, then, if that's what we're doing," Tom said, taking her hand.

It was quiet in the chapel. No one was there. It smelled of musty, old wood. It was darker, as no light sifted through the stained glass windows. The little lights on the altar were soft and Andrea sat in the first pew where she sat for Muffy's wedding. Tom sat next to her.

Andrea rubbed her fingers over Mr. and Mrs. Ward Buck Hamilton in the top left corner. She slowly broke open the envelope, and looked at Muffy's familiar monogrammed stationary. EDA -- Elizabeth Ann Davidson, *her initials* read. Elizabeth Ann for her mother and grandmother, but always Muffy for Uncle Orville, and for everyone else who knew her. Her personality demanded that nick-name. Tears filled Andrea's eyes. "I can't see. Would you please read it to me . . . slowly."

Tom put his arm around her shoulders, took her letter, and read to her quietly.

Wednesday, three days, two hours,
forty minutes after my wedding.

My dear Andrea,

You cannot begin to know the joy Bucky and I have shared these days since our wedding when I thought of you sitting in your beautiful hospital chapel saying ictaminigoalagosectobingolady, yoo hoo! with me. But I want you to know, should I never live another day, these last few will suffice. I've had to attend all my classes having missed last week, but Bucky has missed all of his to shop and cook my meals, according to the directions Dr. Ashworth surreptitiously slipped into my suitcase.

On Saturday, we'll celebrate our almost first week of wedded bliss. We're going to Austin for dinner and dancing. I'm not allowed to have any alcohol, and so Bucky does the same. It's not important, because we're drunk with happiness. We'll dance away the night to "Tender is the Night" and all our favorites. Wasn't our Biltmore dancing fun?

Keep our June wedding date on your calendar. Bucky and I will have our second wedding in Houston, as Momma, Daddy, and Bucky's dear parents' have planned. We wouldn't want to disappoint them. I'd never hurt Momma. I love her so. She's been good to me in many ways.

John Taylor's driving up later today--all the way up and back in one day. I can't wait to show him our new home, where I'll get well.

I've been in Heaven these days and I hope you and Tom will soon enjoy this marriage bliss. This is very naughty and secret, but I laugh and think of us when we were little, on your bed with Taffy. Naughty, naughty, but you'll understand someday after your future wedding.

I think of you often and all you did for me in Atlanta. With Bucky helping me in our own new love-nest, I'm confident I'll have a successful win over this eating disorder.

Though far away, I am with you in spirit. My love to Tom and to you always,

Your Muffy

Andrea took the letter and held it to her chest. "I feel a little better," she sobbed, tears slipping down her face.

Tom gave her his handkerchief. "I don't understand most of it. What is ictamini, etc.?"

Andrea wiped her face and blew her nose. She spoke softly. "That's our secret call from childhood. We made it up when we were little to call each other at the reunion. It seemed like a very big place at first. We used it later to avoid other cousins and Aunt Elizabeth. It's wonderful to have a secret call." Andrea took Tom's hand in hers. "Would you learn it with me? Now?"

Andrea practiced and rehearsed Tom and they laughed and laughed until Tom had it perfectly--even with a high pitched 'yoo hoo' at the end. Andrea leaned over and kissed him on his temple, where his white hairs shone in the dark. "I love you. You're so much fun. How would I have survived this without you?" Andrea hesitated. "The night you told me about Billy up in your bed, you said I didn't need you. That was right at the time, but now . . . now I do."

Tom, with his arm around her, kissed her gently on her forehead. "I had wanted to be more important in your life, but not for this reason. I'm sorry Muffy's death caused it. I grieve for her, too." He took Andrea's hand, then looked again at the letter.

"Does Muffy mean your skating in Rockefeller Center in February? You didn't go dancing."

"But we did--at the Biltmore."

"You didn't tell me."

"I know. Your mother told me I didn't have to tell you everything."

"What? My mother said that?"

"Yes. The day we had lunch. She said she didn't tell your father everything, because he would just get upset, and then upset her. So some things she said you don't have to tell your husband."

"Well, I'll be." Tom gasped. "All this time I thought Mother was such a sweet, docile wife under my father's domination."

"But dancing with Muffy at the Biltmore, until the management put an end to it, was hilarious. "She told him what they did." But when I told Dean Lyman, I didn't tell her the manager hauled us out of the lobby when we were screaming our secret call at the top of our lungs. Dean Lyman would have been upset and said 'that wasn't fitting of a Lexington Hospital student nurse.' "

"Muffy was spunky," Tom said.

"Yes, she was."

"And what I really want to know is what you two did with Taffy on your bed."

"I wish you hadn't seen that."

Tom's laughter filled the church and echoed off the high ceiling. "If it's what I think, I think it's so absurd. I'm trying to visualize this procedure."

Andrea laughed. "I don't know how it started."

"So, it went on for awhile."

"Well, I guess. It was so long ago that I can't remember all the details."

"You're pulling my mother's act again."

"No, I'm not. I just can't remember how it started. I guess we were on the bed and Taffy must have jumped up with us. And somehow he was licking our panties, and it felt good so we took them off. Then it felt even better. Taffy loved it, too."

Tom's laughter reverberated again and he could hardly breathe.

"Shuuush," Andrea said, looking around the pews. It's probably sacrilegious to talk about this here. We'd better whisper."

"How were you lying on the bed?"

"You sure are curious about this escapade of ours," she hissed. "We were next to each other on our backs, with our legs, you know, curled up. That is, our knees flexed and over our chests."

"Did it feel good?"

"Yes. That's why we did it." Andrea hesitated. "And Mother even knew. That's what she said on Sunday. I can't believe she didn't say something."

"Oh, Andrea, Andrea," Tom said, putting his arms around her. "You are so unbelievable, and innocent, and I love you. I'll ask you for the hundredth time since Christmas Eve, can't we marry before you get your Hunter degree?"

"I haven't decided."

"That's what you always say, but it's better than a 'no.' It's getting late. Will you please, please come to my room again tonight? I asked Gordon to cover for me. He's owed me a pay back call night for a long time."

"I was hoping you'd ask, because I had bad dreams in my dorm this morning. I screamed so loud that Gerry banged on my door."

Andrea carefully folded Muffy's letter, and kissed it before she put it in the envelope. She carried it in her hand as they headed toward the elevators.

Chapter Sixteen

"Because of You," Tony Bennett sang as Tom unlocked his bedroom door.

Andrea followed Tom in. "Don't you ever turn off your radio? You leave your lights on all the time, too. It's expensive to do that."

"I think the hospital has enough money to pay, because they pay me nothing. We're both cheap labor, you know. In fact, slave labor for this hospital."

"Tom, you can't do that when we're married, or our electric bill will be enormous."

"I promise I won't if you marry me tomorrow."

"Oh, Tom," she laughed. "You never stop. And this room looks worse than last night. Why don't you put your clothes in your dresser drawers, and then shut them? Look, they're all open."

"I'm normally very organized and somewhat neat, but I work about 1000 hours a week. I don't have time. Is this what you're going to do when we're married? Nag at me all the time?" And he lifted her up across his chest.

"What are you doing?"

"Taking you to my bed to enrapture you, my dear."

"Oh, Tom, you sound like the wolf in Little Red Riding Hood," she laughed.

"I'm starved for you like that wolf." He lowered himself next to her and kissed her for a long time. He unpinned her student's white starched cap and lowered it to the floor. He stroked her hair, and then moved down her throat.

"I have my uniform on," she whispered. "And I have to wear it out of here in the morning, so I can't get it wrinkled more than it is."

"Good, I'll take it off."

"You take every inch you can."

"I want you, Andrea."

She heard the emotion in his voice. "I can't go all the way. I just can't. I know some of my friends do, and you think I'm young and silly but it's against--"

"I told you I don't. I respect you and your wishes." Tom spoke slowly and seriously. "I have no intention of violating them. That's one reason I want you to marry me now and I told you I need you." He looked at her intently. "Now that I've found you, I'm terribly lonely in the few wakeful moments I'm here, and you're not with me. I want to come home to you, all the time, not just to this little room, now and then."

Andrea stood up and walked across the room to the chair. She unclipped the starched white collar from the top of her uniform. She reached around her waist and unbuttoned the two buttons of her white apron and the bib that was also buttoned to her waist band. She carefully slipped them off, and lay them on the chair. She looked over at Tom who was watching her as he lay in his green scrub suit on his back in the bed, his hands under his head. She unbuttoned the light blue cotton plaid uniform down the front, stepped out of it, and placed it carefully on top of her apron.

"Okay," Tom said. "Are the rules the same as last night?"

"We've already broken those. The light's on." Andrea walked toward him in her slip and underwear. She lay down next to him, rolled onto her stomach, reached up, and kissed him. She ran her fingers through his thick black hair, and felt him groan as he pulled her over on top of him. She felt the length of him, and shivered as he rubbed up and down her back and over her buttocks again and again. "I think you'd better get your pajamas on, turn off the light, and please, remember the alarm," she said.

Tom went to the sink by his door. She heard him brush his teeth and wash his hands and face. He flicked the light switch by the door and came back to bed. He lay on his back. She lay on her side and put her hand under his pajama top and caressed his chest. "I like the feel of your hair--next time I want to see your chest."

"I'll get up and turn on the light now," he chuckled and peered down at her.

"No, next time." And she was asleep.

But in the middle of the night, Andrea nudged Tom." I have to go to the bathroom. Why isn't there a girl's room on this floor?" she asked with her eyes closed.

"The floor's just for interns."

"No girl interns?"

"No. Come to think of it, there are five. I guess they use the floor below."

"Oh, Tom, that's not fair. I'm so sleepy." Andrea dragged herself from his bed. She walked by the sink and to the door. Then she stepped back to the sink. "I want to use the sink."

"The sink?"

"Yes. I can't go down like this in my underwear and slip and I don't want to put my uniform on. I don't dare be seen either."

"You see why we should get married."

"Tom, I want you to roll over and put your back to me. Close your eyes too. I'm going to sit up here and use your sink."

Tom burst out laughing and Andrea knew he was now wide awake.

"And I want you to close your ears so you don't hear me."

"How do I do that?"

"I don't know, but I'm sitting up here already and I don't want you to hear me."

"I'm a doctor, for Pete's sake. What does it matter?"

It's embarrassing. I know! Let me hear you do our secret call. I can't wait any longer. Go!" She heard his deep laugh and "ictaminigoalagosectobingolady, yoo hoo!"

"I'm not quite through." Andrea heard the sound of her tinkle hitting the porcelain. "So we'll do it together, one more time," she said loudly, then repeated the call with Tom. "This makes me think of Muffy. She'd do something like this. I wish I could tell her. Gee, Tom, you're so smart. That was good."

"Saying ictaminigoalagosectobingolady, yoo hoo! or urinating in my sink?"

"Toom, honestly, do you have to use medical terms?"

"It's what I know."

"I'm going to wash your sink or rather rinse it in the dark." She jumped down from her perch. "I'm going to brush my teeth, with your toothbrush, too. And I'm going to use a corner of this old towel here on this rack. You're right-handed aren't you?"

"Yes. Why are you asking me in the middle of the night?"

"I thought I would have noticed if you weren't. I'm trying to find the soap on the right side of the sink and I can't see."

"It's there. I wash my hands at least a hundred times a day. They sit in pools of infection most of the day. Rubber gloves could have holes. I always wash here when I first come in. Look in the sink."

"It's there. Oh, dear, I must have tinkled on part of it."

"Urine's sterile. Rinse it. Soap will take care of everything."

"I have to wash my bottom so I won't be smelly when I get back to bed."

"You see how more comfortable you'd be if we were married and we had a bathroom?"

"Where would we live?"

"Good question. Ma Freeman's is real cheap. Remember the party we went to at Hank and Lee's?"

"You mean the five flight walk-up with the tub in the kitchen with a board over it, and the 'john' with a pull chain in the closet?"

"Yes, we could live there in eternal bliss.

"Welcome home," he said as she lay down next to him on the bed. "Feel better? Empty bladder and squeaky clean?"

"Oh, Tom--"

He kissed her. Awake now, Andrea tingled with response. She edged up and lay to one side of him and took his face in her hands. She kissed his lips as she had learned from him. Slowly, gently, she traveled to his cheeks and nose and eyes. She smoothed his eyebrows with her fingers and outlined his ears and bent over him, her hair falling to the sides of their faces blocking out all the dim, night lights flickering in the windows from the city. She felt goose bumps on his skin as she stroked his throat and neck, as he had hers, so many times. She heard him groan.

"Andrea, I love you, and want to give you pleasure," he whispered. "And I promise I will not break your rules. I promise."

Tom caressed her, and gently pushed her bra and slip straps down over her shoulders to her waist. Andrea turned on her side trying to make her small breasts larger. She pushed them forward, embarrassed at first, and then caught up in her awakening of real passion, she forgot Muffy, who she was, where she was. She was only aware of Tom's hands as she waited, tensed for their next titillating touch.

His hands reached her waist. He raised her slip and gently rubbed over the outside of her panties. She'd never felt such intense pleasure, and arched her pubis higher, forward, to better feel his taunting, tantalizing tapping on her panties, and she thrust herself still higher, shivered violently and squealed out. "Tom, oh Tom, Tom." She turned, closed her legs to stop the piercing pleasure and buried her head into his shoulder and gasped.

It was dark in the room, but small patches of light came in the windows. Accustomed to the light, Andrea peeped open one eye and felt for his pajama shirt and slowly unbuttoned each button, exposing his chest She pushed herself up on her elbows and slowly kissed every inch of his chest, and buried her head and lips and hands in his hair that wound down his middle to his waist.

She felt him sticking out, and she tentatively, slowly touched him and then she encircled her hand about the pajamas and his penis, and he gasped, shook, and moaned all at one time. He encircled her with his arms. "Andrea," and, they slept.

Later she awakened--crying, trembling by his side.

"What is it?" he asked.

"A dream, but I can't remember it--only the fear and loss in it."

Tom stroked her hair, her face, throat, and then her breasts one at a time in the silent dark of the room. Andrea became alert, hypnotized again by his magnetic moving hands and knew she never wanted him to stop. She felt him stroking over her pants with the palm of his whole hand this time, and she felt them wet, and she sighed out loud as she moved up to meet his touch.

He whispered into her ear, "I want to give you more pleasure than before, but I will not violate your rules," and he deftly pulled her pants down over her knees. He moved down on the bed and she felt his fingers rub through her pubic hair, tickle her gently, and she cried out when she felt his soft, wetness.

She closed her legs together, "Tom," she hissed, "is this perverse? I'm embarrassed. Do you *like* that?"

He stroked the tops and sides of her closed thighs with his fingers and she heard him say, "This's normal lovemaking, Andrea, and I love making love to you and will forever." She felt her legs moving apart as if they weren't a part of her. She whispered to herself, *take me, take me,* as he brushed up and down the insides of her thighs, then fingering lightly over her pubic hair. He kept coming and going with his hands and fingers. She lay tensed, waiting, yearning for his touch again. She cried out when she felt his warm moisture on her labia. Then, in wanton abandonment, she spread her legs wide. "I love it, I love it. Take me. Don't stop. Don't ever stop." She raised up. She screamed out and shook violently. She felt the pounding of her heart in her chest.

He came back up to lie next to her. She ached to return ecstasy to him. She tentatively reached for his pajamas, slipped her hand in the open slit and felt him warm and stiff. She lightly rubbed him up, down, and over the soft top. He hollered out and exploded.

"Oh, dear, your pajamas are wringing wet," Andrea said. "What a soppy mess!"

Tom laughed out loud. "It is, my Andrea. It's wet, and warm, and gooey, and good."

"Oh, dear," she said, "when I think what I've done. Are you sure it's normal?"

"Yes," he grinned with pleasure. "And you're still a virgin. It's making love and it's wonderful and meant to be this way. That's what Muffy was referring to in her letter about Taffy and being naughty."

Andrea sucked in her breath. "Do you think Bucky did this with Muffy?"

"Read her letter again. Anyway, I hope so."

"So do I," she grinned. She turned over to cuddle him. "You're sure it's not perverse. Is it legal?"

"Yes, especially if we marry soon. We'll want to do this all the time now and we can't do it here. Do you want to void in the sink nightly?"

"Oh, Tom. Honestly."

"I start my first year of residency on July 1st. I think I get one week off. We could marry, and have a short honeymoon the last week of June."

"June? I won't even have graduated from nursing school," she wailed. "I wanted to wait until *after* I had my degree from Hunter."

"There's no way we can wait that long. What's your last rotation?"

"It's senior elective for six weeks. I'll do Visiting Nurse Service, because I want to work for them after I graduate, while I'm at Hunter. It's more money than hospital staff and I'll have weekends and evenings to study."

"And make love."

She snuggled up to him, and kissed his neck. "I love you."

Tom was still talking about their wedding date, but Andrea fell asleep.

Chapter Seventeen

"Want to play Taffy games?" Andrea heard when she answered her phone the next day in her dorm room.

"Oh, Tom, I'm so mortified when I think of last night." She heard him laugh out loud.

"It never fails to amaze me how innocent you are. How ever did you fend off all those medical students that I heard you dated over the last two years?"

Andrea shook her head. "I don't know."

"I'm on tonight, but let's meet in the cafeteria at your supper break."

"All right," Andrea agreed. "Try for six in the G cafeteria."

"If I don't show up, you'll know I'm back in surgery. Will you come up to my room when you're off? I'll leave the door open, because I don't know when I'll finish."

"No. I think I'll be all right tonight, and besides, you must be exhausted."

"Yes, but happy exhausted over you. It was great. I was surprised you even knew what to do with me--what to look for," he said laughing.

"I didn't until a few weeks ago on urology."

"What?"

"I never had brothers and I tried to peep in the little front slit of my Daddy's underpants when he lowered his trousers every night at six, and gave himself his insulin shot in his right thigh, but I never was able to get a good view. I figured time was running out so two weeks ago--remember, I was on urology nights?" Well, I took lots of peeks when the patients were sleeping."

"And what did you learn, Miss Deck, you ole peeping Tomasina?"

"They come in all sizes, shapes, and colors."

"That's the first time you ever saw a man's penis?"

"Oh, Tom, you embarrass me. How else was I to see it before now?"

"Didn't your mother ever tell you anything about this?"

"Heavens no! When I was about five, a new neighborhood kid, Alice Hoffberg, told me the facts of life, and you know what? I wondered for years if the boy went to the bathroom in the girl."

"When did you discover the answer?"

"Freshman year at this grand old venerable institution."

"Oh, how I love you. We're going to have so much fun playing school in bed. You'll be a brilliant student, and I, the ardent instructor."

"But tonight, are you sure you won't have bad dreams again?"

Andrea giggled. "You waked me now. My dream just came back to me. It wasn't scary," she tittered again," just sexy."

"Gee, Andrea, you said the big 'S' word. I hope you turn into a sex temptress next."

"*Toom!*"

"Are you still thinking about the last week of June? Why don't you ask your Dean, who's been so decent, if you can take a week off then, and pay it back a week after your graduation in August? But, I've got to run. I hear my name paged over the intercom. Bye."

The telephone rang again. Andrea rubbed her eyes, picked up the telephone, and listened to her mother's voice.

"Did you sleep all right last night? And did you get *enough* sleep?"

"No, Mother. I slept all night with my eyes open." She waited for her mother to change the subject.

"Andrea I've telephoned Houston and ordered flowers for Muffy's funeral. I've talked to Elizabeth. She cried and was terribly upset, but she says she's a little better everyday. I'm leaving tomorrow, and will return on Monday. Why don't you come home, and get a little rest if you can."

"Maybe. Will you give a special hug to John Taylor for me. Tell him I *hate* not being there with him and I want him to come see me whenever he can. He could stay with you, couldn't he mother?"

"Please don't use that word, dear, and why yes, of course. Do you think he's coming for a visit soon?" Andrea heard the surprise in her voice.

"Oh, I don't know," she said casually. Andrea had written J.T. to flee his home immediately. She dreaded to think of what her aunt would do if she discovered his plans. It's not safe there, she wrote. *That witch would probably kill John Taylor and Helen, too.*

"Andrea you must write Uncle Orville and Aunt Elizabeth a condolence letter."

"I have Mother, but I wrote one letter to all of them, including John Taylor and Billy. It was the only way I could do it. Then, I wrote a separate letter to John Taylor."

"Well I guess that's all right. I'm proud of you, dear." Her mother paused. "Andrea?"

She knew something was coming by the tone of her mother's voice.

"We've discussed this several times before, but it's been two months since you've been engaged. I've wanted to have a little family engagement party at home with your sisters, Aunt Anna, and the Scofields, whom I've yet to meet. We can use your high school picture, and announce it in the Pelham Sun and the New York Times, if we can get it in. Don't you think it's time?"

"But, Mother," Andrea said emphatically. "You had agreed to postpone that because I didn't want to marry for two years."

"The Macphersons at the funeral will all be asking about you and your wedding date? I'm embarrassed because I don't even have one photo newspaper clipping to show them."

"It's just Aunt Elizabeth you're worried about." Andrea's voice was loud.

"Don't be sarcastic with me, Andrea, or I'll wash your mouth out with soap and water."

"I won't have that woman at my wedding, whenever it is and I think I may move the wedding up."

"You do? To when?" Her mother's voice rose an octave. "I think that's good. I don't like long engagements, as I've told you."

"At least one hundred times, Mother." Andrea laughed. "I'm not sure. I'm only thinking about it. I'm waiting to hear about the scholarship for my Hunter degree. I thought I'd have heard by now."

"I'll call you when I return." her mother said. Get some rest now, Andrea."

"Mother, if I got all the rest you keep telling me to get, I'd sleep all day and night."

Andrea closed the door to Dr. Hillerman's office two hours later. She looked around the corner, and scooted to the elevator before any one could spot her. She'd been relieved not to recognize any other students from the medical or nursing school in her waiting room.

She did feel better. She wasn't crazy. No wonder Muffy had liked talking to her. She had taken the sample pills that Dr. Hillerman had offered her for sleeping, though she didn't think she'd need them. Certainly not if she were in Tom's bed every night. I wonder if she knows what I did there last night. *Do I look differently today, because I did those things?*

Andrea took out her compact from her shoulder bag, and looked at her face as the empty elevator descended. It looked the same. *I can't imagine the renowned Dr. Hillerman ever doing anything like that. Maybe I need to read a book about 'it.'*

But, Andrea thought to herself. One thing Dr. Hillerman was *absolutely* wrong about. It was *not* displaced anger toward her aunt over Muffy's loss. It was real, unadulterated *hate*--no displacement. *Why couldn't Dr. Hillerman understand? I could call Muffy at the hospital today, if proud, pushy Aunt Elizabeth hadn't butted in. How could Aunt Elizabeth cry over Muffy's death when obviously she'd rather have Muffy dead, than alive with an eating disorder?*

Andrea hurried back to her room, changed into her uniform, and started back to the hospital for her 3 to 11 p.m. shift. She stopped in the lobby for her mail and was overjoyed to see John Taylor's letter and one from the Jessie Smith Albright Foundation. She quickly stuffed them in her uniform pocket and hurried to the tunnel underpass.

As soon as Andrea had a free moment, she walked to Miss Scarlotti's desk to ask permission to go to the girl's room. Miss Scarlotti looked askance, as if students should never need to go to the bathroom. Her eyebrows jumped high on her forehead and her firm bright red lips opened. "Miss Deck, you have only been on duty for one and one half hours. Is this absolutely necessary?"

"Yes, Miss Scarlotti. It is."

"All right, then. But don't tary."

Andrea walked quickly down the hall and turned right. She passed the ladies room door and quickly turned to Dr. McGiff's office. She unlocked, then locked his door from the inside of his office. She turned on the light, and looked at the two letters. John Taylor's felt heavier. She put it back in her pocket, and opened the scholarship letter.

She read only "we are pleased to inform you," and hugged the letter to her chest. "Oh, thank you, God." She read it quickly. The living stipend was more than she had even hoped for. The food allowance was seventeen dollars. She'd written down thirteen dollars and sixty-five cents, like the food allowance check she cashed each week in the basement of the hospital. *Maybe they think I'll eat more next year.* She giggled with joy. *Maybe this will feed Tom's gigantic appetite. Wait till I tell him. We're rich!*

She read it over carefully a second time. She noted the Board of Directors listed on the left side of the first page. She recognized two Pelham names--Dr. Harris first and then Dr. Rezen. She thought of Dr. Rezen examining her father on the stretcher in their front hall long ago. "I can get that degree now, Daddy," she said out loud. "I got the scholarship. I'm so lucky. Everything's come to me."

She looked up and saw Dr. McGiff's calendar. She turned to June. The 24th was the last Saturday. Wow, the day she was to be Muffy's maid of honor. She looked up at the ceiling in Dr. McGiff's office. "Ictaminigoalagosectobingolady, yoo hoo! Get ready to say it with me, Muffy. I'm going to marry Tom on your wedding day!" She stared at the ceiling and waited. *Why doesn't Muffy come to me again? Like in my dream?* Suddenly conquered by the weight of her crushing loss, she broke down and wept, inconsolably, her head on her arms over the desk.

Tom didn't come to her table later in the cafeteria that evening. She ate, and then smoothed out John Taylor's letter next to her plate.

Tuesday

My dearest Andrea,

Now we're closer than ever, aren't we? Closer, but never to be the same without Muffy between us, in us, around us, and all over us. For that was her enchantment, her very essence as a person, wasn't it? She was all encompassing. But, because of her force of spirit and zest for life, she's left enough for us to treasure for the rest of our lives.

I feel now, I will cry and long for her always, but we know that's not how she'd want us to be. Not our Muffy. So we must sing, Andrea, dance, and shout out our joy to the skies for her and with her. Knowing she had six days of married bliss with Bucky and knowing she felt she was recovering, makes this possible.

The Wednesday after Muffy was married, Helen and I drove to Austin to see them. Muffy radiated with happiness and I think, from the health of her new life. Bucky told me she was remarkably disciplined and motivated to get well. Bucky looked far more mature, and seemed to thrive on his new role of leader, provider, nurturer. Our strong effervescent Muffy needed him and it brought out his very best.

We four sealed a life time bond that night when I announced Helen's and my imminent secret marriage and plans to move to Boston. Muffy, as only she could do, became a sister to Helen in three hours, grasping immediately Helen's future of total estrangement from her parents and family.

I have been accepted at Harvard Medical School. It seems unbelievable to me, but they receive few applicants from Texas. Helen has been accepted as a librarian where she attended college at Boston University.

Our plans are not made as of yet. I remain unsure whether to, or when, to share our plans with Momma and Dad at this time.

Helen and I marvel at Muffy's courage to defy Momma, and Muffy's death demands the consummation of our plans. We will, of course, see you en route to our new home whether it be late spring or in the summer.

Dad and I, along with Ella Louise and Ward painfully closed Bucky's and Muffy's apartment. Momma was too distraught to go to Austin with us, though she knows now about their wedding and apartment. I return to you your two letters, which I found opened and well worn on Muffy's bedside table.

With love to you and regards to Tom, I remain,

Your devoted John Taylor

Andrea smiled a sad smile and put the letter carefully away. She looked around the cafeteria for Tom and saw Dr. Harris coming toward her, on his way out of the dining room.

"Lose your boyfriend tonight?" Dr. Harris said, smiling at her.

"Guess he had to go back to surgery like he thought."

'That's the life of a lonely surgeon's wife. Ask my wife." He sighed, rubbed his hand over his eyes, then looked at his watch. "It's seven--time to be home for a family dinner. And, here I am, as usual."

"Dr. Harris." She took out the letter from the Jessie Smith Albright Foundation. "I noticed your name on the letterhead of this--"

"Oh, you got it, did you." He beamed, and sat down next to her. "You were our only nursing applicant this year, but Andrea you would have won if one hundred had applied. You've had a fine record both at nursing school and already at Hunter.

Congratulations! You should be proud of yourself. Your dad sure would."

"Dr. Harris, I have a question to ask you about this." She hesitated.

"Go on, Andrea."

"When I filled out the application, I fully intended to have a two year engagement and marry after I got my Hunter degree, but if I were to marry this spring, would I still be entitled to all this money?"

"You could support your fine fiance' in grand style, couldn't you," he winked. "Yes, it would apply," Dr. Harris said. "You have my word as a board member. Tom's little house officer check wouldn't influence our decision, and Andrea, you earned this scholarship, only you. The money is yours. Your stipend starts August first."

"I'm so lucky that I grew up in Pelham, where everything came to me in high school and in the community--years of ice skating at Playland, Miss Covington's dancing classes and the Westchester County Assembly dances. Did you know after Daddy died, there was always a little white card in those invitations which read, 'you will be our guest?' If I'm ever able to make a lot of money some day, I'm going to give back to your foundation, and the Pelham Manor and Pelham Men's Clubs, who gave me scholarships to get to this great hospital."

"Have you enjoyed nursing?"

"Yes, it's the best education. Especially at this school where we have the same great professors and Nobel Prize winners who teach us as well as the medical students. It's great preparation for being a wife and mother as well as a nurse. And you know, Dr. Harris, I'm not positive I'd've chosen nursing if Daddy had lived."

"Your father was a fine, generous man and he'd have liked Tom Scofield, too."

"Do you really think so Dr. Harris? I've often wondered about that."

"Andrea, I don't suppose you would know, though I told your mother when I last saw her at New Rochelle Hospital. Tom Scofield is one of the finest young interns we have here. Not only is he bright and technically going to be a very facile surgeon, but also he has the rare ability to handle patients who have to deal with death. Several of us old geezers have talked about it. We don't often see that in a first year intern."

"Did you know his younger brother died after a long illness at home?"

"No. I didn't."

Dr. Harris stood up to go and Andrea stood with him. "Thank you for talking to me, Dr. Harris." She shook his hand. "It's nice for me to run into you, Dr. McGiff, Dr. Rezen and Dr. Rice in the hospital halls, elevators and dining rooms. You're always so nice, and it makes me feel at home in a way."

"We like to watch over our Pelham medical and nursing students here. Congratulations, Andrea."

Andrea walked out the cafeteria with Dr. Harris, and returned to her Tuberculosis Ward.

"Miss Deck, You're five minutes late back from dinner. Start the seven o'clock medicines immediately."

"Yes, Miss Scarlotti."

After she'd finished the med rounds and eight o'clock treatments, Andrea went to talk with Mrs. Meyer, her favorite patient. It would be so hard to stay in bed all the time. All the patients could do was take Isoniazid pills and rest. Then, they waited interminably for their next scheduled X-ray appointment. Many of the men and women read, wrote long letters, and saw the occupation therapist frequently.

Mrs. Meyer was knitting a long aqua scarf for her daughter, Amy. Andrea listened as Mrs. Meyer told her about her sons, Michael and David, and their family life on the farm where they lived near Troy in upstate New York.

Miss Scarlotti appeared at the door, "Miss Deck, come here now."

"Yes, Miss Scarlotti."

"I want you to go to the pharmacy and ask them to fill this requisition. When you return, you busy yourself rather than talking to the patients."

"It was unusually quiet tonight. That's why I started to go around and talk to the patients. They seem so bored and lonely."

"I think you're projecting, Miss Deck. When you return, if you find it quiet, I want you to clean the treatment room."

"Yes, Miss Scarlotti," Andrea said before heading toward the elevator.

Andrea stepped out of the elevator and turned around the corner to the pharmacy door.

"Ictaminigoalagosectobingolady, yoo hoo!"

She whirled around, but he wasn't there. She smiled and went down the hall, poking her head into the spaces where the pharmacy office doors were located, back from the corridor. When she sneaked a look in the third space Tom pulled her to him, put his arms around her, and kissed her for what seemed like forever.

"Where did you come from?" she gasped. "How did you know I was here?"

"I didn't. I just came out from surgery and headed toward the elevator to go down to dinner when I saw your sassy hips swinging down the hall."

"I almost jumped out of my skin when I heard our call. Isn't it handy?"

"I'll say," and he kissed her for a long time again.

"Tom, I've got to go. The charge nurse will kill me if I'm late."

"Come to my room tonight. I think I'll finish about eleven."

Andrea shook her head. "No. I told you. Someone might come to your door. If you're there, you can answer it, but if you get called out and I'm there alone, I'll be uncomfortable."

"Just don't answer."

"Tom, no, and I've got to turn in this requisition." Andrea handed the slip to the pharmacist at the window. "Tom," she turned to him, "did you see that big woman in the gray aide's uniform walk by?"

"Yes."

"Do you think she did?"

"Did what?"

"You know, played Taffy last night?"

Tom burst out laughing, "Probably. Why?"

"Really? I've looked at everybody I've seen today and wondered--Dr. Hillerman, Dr. Harris, and Miss Scarlotti, the charge nurse."

"What conclusions did you draw?"

"A definite no for Miss Scarlotti and for Dr. Hillerman, but a yes for Dr. Harris."

"Do you think they know you were evaluating them?"

"I hope not," she said, her eyes wide. "Do you think they can tell I did . . .ah, you know, the Taffy thing?" She blushed. "Does it show?" The pharmacist gave Andrea the medicines through the slot at the bottom of the glass topped counter.

"I'll take the elevator up with you," Tom said.

"Okay, but don't come near my floor. I'm already in trouble."

"Miss Scarlotti probably needs to play Taffy."

Andrea burst out laughing with Tom.

He pulled her to him. "I love these empty elevators in the evenings. We can neck."

"Tom you mustn't mess my hair or knock my cap askew." Miss Scarlotti will notice. "She doesn't like me." Andrea put her cap in place. "You didn't answer my question. Does it show, anywhere?"

"Well now, maybe it does, hot pants. You do look sexier tonight, sashaying those cute buttocks down the hall." He grinned at her blushing face.

"*Toom!* Don't laugh. It's a big thing to me." In the empty elevator speeding up quickly to J12, Andrea tiptoed, whispering in his ear, "The ecstasy of coming is almost violent, isn't it?" The elevator stopped, the door opened, and there stood Miss Scarlotti.

"I was just coming for you, Miss Deck. Go to the nurse's station."

"And you, young man. You wicked interns are told repeatedly to keep your hands off our students. I'll have no more of it. Leave this floor."

"Yes, Miss Scarlotti." Tom said, and pushed the elevator button.

Chapter Eighteen

The next night after finishing their dinner, Andrea lit up another Camel as she sat across the booth from Tom at Charlie's--the local hamburger hang-out around the corner from the hospital. She put away the second letter.

"Do you have to do that? You just finished one?" Tom said.

Andrea looked up at Tom. "I like to smoke. It makes me look less of a Sunday school goody-goody-two-shoes person. It's fun to be glamorous and blow the smoke out my nose, or curl it like Gerry and I practice for hours. Besides, I'm used to it now. It would be hard to quit."

Tom looked at her directly. "But I want you to."

"Why?" She looked back at him.

He frowned. "I hate it."

"Oh, hell." Her elbows on the table, Andrea put her head down in her hands.

"My parents both chain-smoked when I was young," Tom said. "It was awful. They smelled horrible, both of them. There were full, stinking ashtrays all over the house." Tom sighed. "Every room in our house reeked of their nicotine habit."

"They didn't smoke when I was there for dinner."

"They stopped a few years ago when it was discovered that cigarettes cause cancer. They both quit cold turkey. And you should, too. It's lousy for your health. I don't want you to die young and leave me with lots of children to take care of."

"Children? How do you know we'll have any?"

"I sure hope we will. I want a baby, Billy, and you want a baby, Muffy. A couple more might fill the bill."

"I could never call a child Muffy. There was only . . . one Muffy. She looked away and was quiet. She squished her cigarette butt in the ashtray. "But a Deborah, I'd like that. It's so unusual to hear you talk about wanting babies."

"It's Billy, I guess," Tom said. "And then, I worked at a crippled children's camp in Vermont for two summers. That's when I decided I'd be an orthopedic surgeon, although I changed to general surgery after the first two months of my internship.

Those camp kids were so fabulous and brave that I thought I'd like to work with them. There was one boy in particular who reminded me of Billy. He came both summers when I was there, and he still sends me a Christmas card every year."

"Why did you change to general surgery?"

"Ah, some of the cases are so tough and the patients really sick. I think I could be more useful than in orthopedics. The families need more help. And then the variety of surgery is fascinating and perhaps more of a challenge."

"You'll be a great surgeon," Andrea said, thinking of Dr. Harris. "Do you send that little boy a Christmas card?"

"Yes." Tom hesitated. "Would you please think about giving up smoking?"

Andrea sighed deeply. She felt sad and annoyed. "Is it that important to you?"

"Yes. I'll play lots of Taffy, and other games, too, if you will." Tom grinned and raised her hand from the table and held it to his lips, kissing it.

"If I know you, you will anyway. I'm not saying yes, but I'll think about it. How's that?"

"A deal." He rubbed his finger over her thumb. "How did you get this big scar here?"

"Oh, dear, do you really want to know?"

"Yes."

"One afternoon I got mad when Mother wasn't home like she usually was. I think I was in first or second grade. I remember that I turned the kitchen door knob, but it didn't open. I dropped my school books on the aluminum milk box at the corner of the concrete back stoop, cupped my hands around the sides of my eyes and peered into one of the small rectangular window panes in the top part of the door. The long string hung down from the big globe light in the center of the kitchen ceiling. It was off, but I could see the box over by the sink marked *World War II Effort*, filled with crushed aluminum cans, a big shiny tin foil ball, Taffy's half eaten red rubber ball, and rubberbands all rubberbanded together. I saw the calendar, June, 1944, to the right of the door and heard the whirl of the motor on top of the old icebox to the left."

Andrea picked up her cigarettes, then put them down. "The white enamel-topped table, edged in black, stood in the middle of the kitchen, and the green and chrome orange juice squeezer was out on the counter, in its usual place, under the many red-trimmed cabinets and cupboards that surrounded the kitchen walls. Test tubes were sticking up from the bottom of the old double boiler on top of the stove across the room, so I knew Mother'd been putting Daddy's urine in those tubes."

"Your mother tested your father's urine for sugar?"

"Yes. All the time. It was always brick red, because he cheated and ate sweets constantly. Anyway, I ran down the steps, and concrete path, then crossed the front yard under the giant maple tree and raced up the steps to the front door. I hit the door with one fist and punched the door bell with my other hand at the same time. I turned and quickly found a stone in the big red geranium-filled urn on the front landing. I hit the door with the stone. No one came."

Tom laughed out loud. "I imagine your eyes turned to slits about now, like they do when you get mad."

"Tom, I don't get mad very often."

"I see," he said smiling. "I'm glad about that."

"I turned and ran back to the kitchen door. I screamed, pounded on the kitchen door, stamped my foot, then took my stone and banged it into the glass pane."

The glass spun out and into my thumb. Blood gushed out in spurts. I gulped and pulled my white blouse out from the waist band of my blue dirndl skirt and covered it.

"I cried, raced across the side yard, and raced up the street."

"Where were you running?" Tom asked.

"All I could think of was Miss Kornay, the school nurse. I was hoping that she wouldn't have left school. I raced around the corner on the sidewalk and ran past two big St. Bernard dogs on the Boulevard, who picked up my pace and followed me behind their black wrought iron fence. They were slobbering as usual.

"Mother had just read me a story about how these dogs with kegs of brandy attached to their red collars saved people in the snow-covered mountains in Switzerland. I'd wished they'd save me with a bleeding thumb.

"My blouse was bright red with blood, and it ran down one leg and seeped into my white sock. I'd hoped it would ruin my brown oxfords, which I hated. I thought mother would never let me wear brown-and-white saddle shoes or loafers, like the bigger kids."

Andrea fingered her matches on the table, then looked back at Tom. "I saw the grammar school playground with relief. All I had to do was run through the playground to the back door of the school, then up two flights of stairs to the nurse's office.

"A car horn honked as I dashed across the black-topped road to the anchor-fenced playground gate. I looked up to see mother at the wheel of our bright green 1942 Chrysler. I started to sob in big heaving gasps. Mother got out of the car at the side of the road. She helped me in and shut her door. I remember Mother slowly opened the blood-saturated blouse. Blood gurgled up and into her palm. "It will be all right. We'll fix it at home," she said. She took a neatly folded white handkerchief from her pocket book, flicked it open and wrapped it tightly around my thumb. I can still smell the Chanel No. 5 that filled our car from her handkerchief. She made me hold my thumb up high and tight with my other hand to stop the bleeding.

"That's my story."

"No wonder it's a big scar. You needed stitches." Tom kissed the scar again. "How did your mother dress it?"

"She talked about butterflies while she showed me how she put the skin surfaces tight together like butterfly wings."

Tom kept holding her hand in his, rubbing over the scar with his index finger.

"You mentioned your World War II Effort Box. Ours was filled with old rags, papers, and old scrap metals. My job was to crush the aluminum cans and put the scraps of tin foil into a big ball. We also saved string. My father was called up as a doctor into the Air Force. He had orders for North Africa, but he never left the air base in Maryland, where we lived for two years. I loved being the privileged son of an officer."

Tom smiled and went on. "I used to read the *New York Herald Tribune* everyday about the battles, especially the air battles, first in Europe and then in Japan. Each week I studied the gory details, graphically photographed in *LIFE* magazine."

"Every week I looked at *LIFE*, too!"

"I'm surprised you remember."

"But I do, and when the air raid sirens started blaring, often in the early evenings, I'd run to Daddy, who might be listening to Lowell Thomas's war news."

Tom leaned forward. "Andrea, do you remember 'Good evening Mr. and Mrs. United States and all the ships at sea?' "

Andrea answered quickly, "That was Walter Winchell! And Daddy listened to Gabriel Heater, and then the FBI in Peace and War."

"Did you have a victory garden?" Tom asked.

"Yes, did you?"

"It was my job to tend to it every day--my contribution to the war effort, Mother said, and she'd asked me to mix the orange coloring into the margarine to make it look like butter. She said she needed my strong muscles. Of course," Tom smiled, "another contribution to the war effort."

"Me, too," Andrea said. "But it was hard. I could hardly mix it."

"We had a maid, but I had to entertain Billy when Mother drove for the Drivers Corp. She paid me for that, but I had to buy war stamps with most of it. I remember she read to Sandra and me from a little red pamphlet, *The Citizen's Handbook For War,* about what boys and girls should do at home, in school and in town. She made us walk everywhere. Of course gasoline and sugar were rationed, but she always talked about saving the rubber tires."

"In the Air Raids," Andrea said, "Mother would run upstairs to her hall closet, and put on her uniform. The sirens would blast every minute as she kissed us all and whispered something I couldn't hear in Daddy's ear. She walked out the front door, across the street to the high school, where, as a former nurse, she prepared with the Pelham doctors a make-shift hospital for people who might come in wounded and in need of medical care in the event of enemy attack.

"You know," Andrea went on, "Mother even helped the war effort by selling war bonds, and years later, she received a plaque from the government for her patriotic contribution. She was so sad when Peter Cornwell died, the first serviceman to die in our town of Pelham. Mother later was on a committee to help make a Memorial for the Pelham servicemen who were lost or killed."

"You mean Dr. Cornwell from this hospital?"

"Yes, and she worked with Dr. Harris, Dr. McGiff, and Dr. Rezen in the air raid drills, too. Daddy and I would lower the downstairs blackout curtains, my sisters did the upstairs. I'd peek out and watch the air-raid wardens and doctors drive to the school with the top half of their car headlights taped with black adhesive.

"Daddy always sat with us on the living room floor in front of the couch during the air raids and read a story from the *Saturday Evening Post*. Occasionally he'd talk with us about the pictures in the current week's *LIFE*. I could never believe the Kamikazie pilots." Andrea rubbed her hand over her eyes and smiled," I guess I liked the *All Clear* whistle peals the best of those air raids.

"But V.J Day on August 8th was really fun. There was so much noise and celebration. We all walked in a parade down Fifth Avenue and Wolf's Lane in Pelham. Mother gave me an aluminum pot from the kitchen cabinet and a spoon to bang. I walked a long time. This was more fun than walking as a Brownie on Memorial Day, because everyone marched and wore different things and carried American flags and yelled and screamed."

Andrea smiled at Tom. "What did you do?"

"Our whole family went into Times Square with lots of other people."

"After the town parade, Mother and my sisters did, too--in the evening. I wasn't allowed to go. Daddy stayed home with me."

Andrea took a cigarette from her package on the table and lit it quickly. She blew the smoke away from Tom, but she saw him sigh deeply. "Daddy talked a lot about General McArthur in

Japan and General Eisenhower in Europe. Twice at 6 a.m. he drove us down to the city and we sat for hours on the lions in front of the New York Public Library waiting for their ticker tape parades to begin on Fifth Avenue. My sisters and I were so happy to miss school." Andrea put her cigarette out in the ashtray.

Tom took her hand and smiled. "Did you vote for Eisenhower?"

"Are you kidding?" Andrea laughed. "I can't vote till the next election. Did you?"

"Forgot I'm robbing the cradle." Tom chuckled. "But I did vote straight Republican."

"That will sure please my Macpherson relatives. They are *very* Republican. In the final prayer of the reunion they bless a Republican President, but never a Democrat. Muffy told me once her parents would probably *die* if she didn't vote Republican."

"My darling child bride, would you have voted for Eisenhower?"

"Definitely, but my father talked about politics a lot, especially when my older sister went to college. He thought she 'turned a little pink.' Both my parents voted Republican, but Daddy always said look at the issues, especially the candidates, then make up your mind.

"He probably didn't say that out loud in front of mother's Macpherson clan--nobody would. But his philosophy makes better sense to me. I'm glad one way of thinking wasn't forced down my throat when I was little, so I can be open to think and make my own decisions."

"You told me you had three pieces of good news," Tom said. "The two letters and what else? It's tough to top the good news of the stipend, which even includes a food allowance. We'll be totally independent of my parents."

"The Dean called me to her office about Miss Scarlotti's report. I had to go immediately, and I finished just in time to see Dr. Hillerman."

"How'd it go with Dr. Hillerman?"

"A lot of talk about my anger at my aunt, about getting to and understanding my real feelings and that kind of stuff. She talked of my father's death and my fear of mother's death at that time, but that has nothing to do with any of this. She wants to see me again next week."

Tom studied her face. "What could Scarlotti report on you? Being ten minutes late on a ward where nothing goes on most of the time anyway?"

"I showed Dean Lyman my foundation letter before I even sat down in her office. She seemed genuinely pleased. I told her I was thinking of getting married the end of June, before the final six week elective."

Tom kissed her scar, and then the tip of each finger on that hand.

Andrea smiled at him." I was pretty nervous, but I asked her if it would be possible for me to have that week off. You see, the elective starts the last week of June, and we graduate August 7th. I plan to stay on and work at VNS."

"What did she say?"

"She turned and got my file out of her file cabinet behind her desk. She looked up my last summer's VNS rotation record. Fortunately, I'd told VNS at that time that I wanted to work there when I graduated, because I knew I needed the time and money to get my degree at Hunter. She read me the last sentence of my evaluation which said there would always be a position for this fine student nurse or something like that."

"And then?"

"She asked me, outside of vacation days, how many days I'd missed in three years of nursing school."

"I told her that I thought only the two days I took off to help Muffy in Atlanta. Then, she asked how it was going with Dr. Hillerman. I told her that Dr. Hillerman still wanted to see me."

"Dean Lyman looked across at me for a few minutes and said, 'I need to verify your days off according to your file and speak with Dr. Hillerman about your progress, but I do believe I might be able to work this out with VNS and our school requirements, Miss Deck. I will call your room a little later to verify that. And I do believe that your marriage might please Miss Scarlotti very much.'" Then, Dean Lyman smiled at me.

"You see," Andrea said, smiling at Tom, "while Miss Scarlotti was balling you out at the elevator, I had walked to the nurse's station and prepared what I was going to say to her. Luckily, I hadn't worn my engagement ring on duty since I started Monday, because I didn't want to pick up any germs. My tuberculin skin test is still negative for some strange reason. Anyway, I told her you were bothering me and trying to kiss me in the empty elevator."

"Andrea, you were whispering to me about the glories of your climax!"

"I know, but I didn't want to get into trouble, and that was really your doing."

"You'd get me trounced whi--!"

"They never bother interns. Remember, you said, you're 'slave labor.' "

"Then the funniest thing of all, and I couldn't believe Dean Lyman said this to me, but she added, 'Miss Scarlotti reports to me generally once a month about a student situation like this.' "

Tom laughed out loud. "I told you Miss Scarlotti needed some Taffy games."

Andrea smiled as she watched him laugh. "Tom, about an hour after I was back in my room, Dean Lyman called and said it would be all right to miss that last week of June. She also said that she had talked to Dr. Hillerman and I was not to miss any of my appointments with her."

"That's the best news--married in less than three months." Tom grinned. "I might make it after all!" He kissed her hand, held it to his lips with both his hands.

"Here're the lovebirds," Gerry said as she slipped into the booth next to Andrea. Dick moved in next to Tom.

"We're getting married in June!" Tom blurted out.

"Why didn't you tell me?" wailed Gerry to Andrea and kissed her cheek at the same time.

"I just this moment told Tom. Dean Lyman approved late this afternoon. Our parents and sisters don't even know. You know the date and I hope you'll be my maid of honor," Andrea said putting her arm over Gerry's shoulder.

Gerry grimaced. "Guess I'd better or you'll never get there on time."

"Let's celebrate. Sneak champagne in the dorm lounge?" Gerry said.

"No. Dancing at the Biltmore," Tom said. "My treat."

Dick ran his hand over his thick blond hair. "I didn't get lunch today. I've got to eat a couple hamburgers and coat my stomach if we're drinking tonight."

"We'll meet you at the Biltmore in one hour," Tom said. "Andrea, my parents wanted us to stop by, so let's tell them en route."

Much later in the nursing school elevator, Gerry said to Andrea, "You're going to sleep here tonight? You sure haven't been home at night much," she giggled and giggled. "How is it up there in the interns' quarters?"

"I have the 'curse' so I'm staying in. I hope I don't dream and wake you."

"Dreaming is the excuse you give for going all the way with Tom up there in the sky?" she laughed and swayed again.

"You're punchy, punchy drunk. I'm not doing 'it' till we marry. I told you." Andrea laughed out loud, "But it sure as hell is getting close."

"I can be ready in three minutes. I timed it last time I was with Dick," Gerry said leaning against her door.

"Holy Smokes, scientific to the end. Dean Lyman would be pleased, you goody, goody nursing student." Andrea bumped into her door. "I've already got the whirligigs and I'm not in bed yet."

"See ya tomorrow," Gerry said, stumbling into her room.

Chapter Nineteen

Andrea felt anxious. She looked at her bitten hang nail, sat on her bed, and dialed home one more time. "Mother, when did you get home? I've been telephoning all day."

"I walked in this minute."

"Are you weary? How was John Taylor? Were all the Macphersons there?"

"I can't answer all those questions at once! Most of my generation of relatives were there, but not as many young cousins. I was happy Louise could be there with me. I was able to spend some quiet time with Elizabeth. She almost looks like a different person."

Andrea thought of the first weeks after her father died-- running home in a panic each day to find her mother in bed. Until finally, the day came when she found the doctor and friends with her mother. She got up a skeleton of her former self – even her shoes were too big for her. They took her for the first of three electric shock treatments. Andrea felt relief all over again.

"We talked about Muffy for a long time," she heard her mother say. "Elizabeth loved her to distraction, and is now fraught with guilt and despair. Beautiful Muffy with her joyful, effervescent personality became perfection itself in Elizabeth's mind. Muffy, the princess, and my sister, the queen or goddess who produced her. I'm so glad she's going to a psychiatrist next week."

"She killed Muffy by taking her away from a psychiatrist, but now she'll go herself." Andrea's voice was laced with sarcasm and anger. "I hate that woman! She killed Muffy!"

"Andrea!" Her mother spoke sharply. "She didn't kill Muffy. A car crash did. Stop that bitter talk this minute. Where's your compassion? And you didn't tell me Muffy married Bucky the day after she got home from Atlanta."

"There's my compassion! If Aunt Elizabeth had known, she'd have busted it up, plus she'd have yelled at you, like she called me a ' nosy up-start' when I was trying to save Muffy."

"What are you talking about?" her mother demanded.

"Aunt Elizabeth called Dean Lyman at school. I had to go to her office, and have Aunt Elizabeth threaten and yell at me for helping Muffy in Atlanta."

"Oh, dear." Andrea heard her mother sigh.

"Please tell me about John Taylor, Billy, and dear Uncle Orville." Andrea said.

"They're holding up pretty well, especially in front of Elizabeth, but obviously they're bereft." Her mother paused a moment. "You know, Andrea, when you're in their elegant house, it's Muffy that's all over it--in spirit and photographs. When I walked in, I visualized Muffy running down the staircase, arms outstretched to hug me." Her mother choked and Andrea cried with her. "She . . . Muffy was such a special . . . precious child," her mother said sobbing.

Andrea felt stabbed. Her head dropped. She slumped back against the wall. *I never thought of Mother! Alone, except maybe Bill. No Tom to share with. I've engulfed myself in my own selfish grief.*

"Oh, moth - -"

"The Houston Episcopal service was beautiful," her mother interrupted in a more composed voice. Over 800 people were there--a tribute to our Muffy and a great honor for her parents. Louise and I sat with Elizabeth, Orville, and their sons, and then the very next afternoon we were at Bucky's funeral."

Andrea cried out loud over the phone, "Mother, I should have gone with you! I let you down! I'd like to come out tomorrow and see you." She sobbed out loud. "I'm sorry."

"This may have been better for you, and for Elizabeth at this time. John Taylor wanted to be especially remembered to you. He brought the most lovely woman to meet us. Her name is Helen Saros. She is striking--singularly beautiful with very dark eyes and hair. She's serene and exceptionally well poised for such a young woman. I believe it was the first time Elizabeth met her, too. Helen attended both funerals with John Taylor, and the gatherings at the respective homes afterwards."

"I'm on evenings all week, Mother, but I'll catch the 9:25 train in the morning and we can visit till we both work at 3:00."

"That will be lovely, dear. I'll fix you a good lunch, and maybe you can nap in the train so you won't be too tired for evening duty."

Andrea smiled through her tears at her mother's perpetual preoccupation with her eating and sleeping. "Want some good news?" she asked her mother.

Her mother sighed. "I could use some."

"I won the Jessie Smith Albright scholarship with a wonderful living stipend, and Tom and I've decided to be married June 24th!"

"June 24th? But, Andrea, that's not even three months away. Two years was too long, but I thought you'd at least wait until you graduated from nursing school."

Andrea heard her mother draw in her breath over the telephone. " I knew we should have had your engagement party before now. I haven't even met Tom's parents, and we have so much to do--the invitations, announcements. What if we can't get the church for that date?"

"We'll call tomorrow morning when I'm at home. It doesn't matter what time on that day, just so they can squeeze us in."

"Oh, Andrea, you'll be the death of me."

Andrea smiled at her familiar expression. "I hope not, but Mother, you're not going to beat me till I bleed, are you? "

"Andrea, stop that talk."

"That's what you used to say."

"I know, and it's awful, but you could be such a rascal. How will we get everything done by then?"

"In bits and pieces."

"What?"

"Just like all those high school years, when I was in school and sports all day, and you worked all evening. We did everything in a hurry--a little at a time. Last night we told Tom's parents about the June wedding date. They want you to come for dinner as soon as you, me, and Tom are all off on the same night."

"They should have me"

"What?"

"That's what Emily Post says--groom's parents invite bride's to first meeting."

"There you go again. Like everything else, I suppose *the* Miss Post will run my wedding. I wish she'd organize it, too."

"Etiquette is very important, Andrea."

"You'll like Tom's parents. At first I thought they were old-fashioned, and I'm still a tiny bit scared of his father, but his mother, do you know what she told me?"

"No, Andrea." She heard her mother chuckle.

"You don't have to tell your husband everything, because if he gets upset, then he upsets you. She has two cigarettes a day and Dr. Scofield doesn't know, or Tom either, for that matter. And then she told me last night, secretly in the kitchen after I told them of the stipend as well as the tuition support, 'you manage your stipend, Andrea. A woman should always keep her hard-earned money and live on her husband's income. Isn't that a riot? I'm not going to do either of those things, but that's what she said."

"I guess I'll have to borrow from the bank again for the wedding."

"We'll talk about it tomorrow. I think we can do it for about $400."

"Roddy's was $500," her mother said.

"I'll show you my figures. I want a very simple dress, but whether you borrow or not, Mother, I'll start paying back August first, when my stipend starts. I can't believe how rich we'll be. I can pay back at least $50 dollars a month and maybe more."

"We'll see, Andrea. You've given me good news. I imagine Tom's ecstatic."

"He's pretty frisky. I'll see you at 10:00 when I step off ye old New Haven."

"Andrea, let's don't forget to schedule an appointment with Dr. Copper in the morning."

"Why?"

"I had your sisters see her before they were married. She'll talk about things with you and fit you for a diaphragm."

"What sort of *things,* Mother? Oh I should have known. I'm shocked you even said 'diaphragm.' Must be because I'm a nursing student now."

"Andrea, stop that!"

"You never told me about 'the curse' but sent me off to camp with all the supplies neatly packaged in pink tissue paper-- nothing about how to use them. Nancy had to show me how to pin the sanitary belt and she laughed at me when I had the rubber pants on inside-out."

"Andrea!"

"And when you told me about the birds and bees, I asked you how the man's seed got to the woman's egg and you answered you'd tell me when I was a little older, and I'm still waiting to hear your explanation."

"Andrea, you'll be the death of me. I'll see you at the train station in the morning."

#

"It's wonderful to hear your voice, John Taylor," Andrea said later in the day on the phone in her dorm room. She looked out her window at Lexington Avenue. "I'm sorry now that I didn't go to the funeral to support you and my mother. I was just so furious with Aunt Elizabeth and still am."

"You might not, if you saw her, Andrea. It's pretty awful to watch, but she goes to therapy three times a week and says it helps."

"If she'd gone before, or just let Muffy stay in the hospital with her therapist, she wouldn't have killed her."

"We don't know that, Andrea. And she didn't kill Muffy. It was an automobile accident."

"If I hear one more person say that, I'll vomit," Andrea said bitterly.

"How many times have you heard those words?"

"Three--you, Tom, mother."

"Maybe you ought to see a psychiatrist."

"Oh, I forgot. Her, too. I am--the doctor who helped Muffy, and sent her to Dr. Ashworth, who, by the way, wrote me the most beautiful letter about Muffy."

"But you believe your version."

"I miss her so much." Andrea cried out loud and tears poured down her face. She couldn't talk for a few moments. "We've just decided to move up our wedding date to June 24th. I'm starting to plan it, and I think of Muffy all the time. I never thought she wouldn't be here with me. It's awful, and no one can understand."

"I do."

"A little, but Muffy and I played out our weddings, when little, with dolls, and then stuffed animals, summer after summer. You're far away. It's awful. I want Muffy here."

"I feel she is." John Taylor's voice was low and strong.

"How can you feel that?" Andrea wailed. "She came to me, with Bucky, in a dream the first night I learned she was gone, but she hasn't come again."

"Her spirit always included you and me," John Taylor said. "Me first, then you for many years, till Bucky came along. Initially I was jealous of him, too.

"Muffy wants us to live on with her, for her," John Taylor said gently. "I hear you sobbing. Have you cried at all?"

"A little."

"I've cried buckets--alone and with Helen."

"You have?"

"You're so angry Muffy's gone, that maybe you can't yet. If you'd been here, the funerals in the church might have helped you. Muffy's grave site is perfect for her. Momma's seen to that."

"Don't tell me about her grave!" Andrea screamed into the phone. "I don't want to know about it!"

"I wish we could cry together--in person, to face Muffy's death. Funerals make you do that," John Taylor said slowly. "You missed that."

"Yes," Andrea cried on.

"I'm going to tell mother soon, about Helen, the marriage, and the move to Boston. We're not going to elope, but get married in our church. Helen is seeing our Bishop and will be confirmed soon."

"You are? She will?"

"I think Momma will accept it, all of it. When she hears Helen tell her, that she'll definitely be disowned from her family. I hope mother will accept her as another daughter. Never to replace or be Muffy, but just another member of our bereaved, splintered family."

"Splintered?"

"Billy is acting out his grief in his way, away from the family. It hurts all of us."

"When will you tell her?"

"We're not sure."

"You'll come, won't you, John Taylor, to my wedding in June?"

"Wouldn't miss it!"

Andrea burst out crying again as she heard his voice almost shout to her.

"You sounded like Uncle Orville."

"You're hurting so, Andrea, and it makes me sad. None of us would dream of not being with you, especially Momma, Dad, and Billy. Helen's eager to meet you, too."

"Oh."

"Tom's a lucky man. Dad mentioned last night at dinner how much we all liked him when we ate at Rockefeller Center--when you and Muffy skated off for hours."

"Tom's the only reason I can work, study, smile, and laugh since Muffy died."

"You sound far away, like in a trance. Speak louder," John Taylor said.

Andrea looked up from the floor. "I've been stingy, selfish in my grief."

"We have to. To get over it, through it, past it."

"Mother says Helen is so beautiful and serene."

"She is. You'll love her. We'll both be at your wedding and may go on to Boston to look for an apartment. Will you promise me to cry?"

"I will."

"And will you repeat frequently that Muffy died in a car crash."

"I'll try."

That afternoon there was a slip in her mailbox, which meant a package for her. At the desk, the receptionist gave her an enormous box from Sak's Fifth Avenue.

Andrea banged Gerry's door on the way to her room. "Come to my room. I think I have an early wedding gift."

Gerry followed her into her room. Andrea opened the box on her bed, then stood back aghast.

"What is it, Andrea? You look ill," Gerry said.

"It's Muffy's wedding dress. And my aunt doesn't even know yet that we've moved up the wedding date."

Gerry looked in the tissue and took out a little white card. She handed it to Andrea. "Read it," Gerry said.

Andrea opened the card and read. "With love, Aunt Elizabeth and Uncle Orville. P.S. Please call Miss Heath in the bridal salon for more information."

Andrea sat in her green chair, put her head in her hands, and cried in great wrenching, heaving sobs. Gerry carefully wrapped the dress and moved the box to the floor. She opened Andrea's bed and helped her into it. Andrea lay down on her side and cried. Gerry sat at the edge of the bed and rubbed her shoulder until she got up to answer Andrea's phone.

"She can't talk now, Tom," Gerry said. "She's crying in earnest. Wait." Gerry turned to Andrea. "Can I tell him, Andrea?"

Andrea nodded.

"Her aunt and uncle sent her Muffy's wedding dress."

"Oh, God," Tom said. "But Gerry, she needs to cry lots."

"I know. I heard her scream again last night in her sleep," Gerry said.

"Tell her I'll call later. Can you stay with her?" Tom asked.

"Yes, we're both off this afternoon." Gerry hung up and bent over the box and took out the card and dialed the number on it.

Andrea watched her as she tried to stop shaking. Then she closed her eyes and listened.

"This is Andrea Deck speaking," Gerry said. "May I please speak to Miss Heath in the bridal salon?" Andrea blinked open her eyes, raised herself up on one elbow and watched Gerry.

"I just received this package sent by my aunt. Could you please tell me what she means by 'more information' written on her card? I see. Will you be there this afternoon?"

Andrea shook her head and whispered, "No."

"Wonderful. We'll be there in an hour or so. Anytime before 5:00 is convenient? I see. Thank you."

Gerry smiled at Andrea. "Isn't this exciting? You get to choose between two gorgeous dresses--this one and the one Muffy preferred."

"My aunt had said that to Miss Heath?"

"That's what she said. Now let's get ready and go down--"

"I'm not wearing that dress!" Andrea screamed. "Muffy didn't want to either. Her mean mother made her select one that she didn't even want. I'm not wearing either dress!"

"Why?"

Andrea told Gerry even more of the events than she'd told her earlier.

"But, Andrea, your aunt didn't kill Muffy."

"You too," she glared at her, and cried again.

"Your aunt sounds lovely. She loved Muffy as much if not more, than you did, and she obviously loves you, too. How would Muffy feel about your hate for her mother?"

"Oh my God," Andrea gasped. She grabbed her neck between her hands, her eyes wide open, staring ahead.

"Andrea, what is it?" Gerry alarmed at her red face.

"Strangled, smothered, suffocated by asphyxiation. That's how I *feel!* Dr. Hillerman told me to feel." She gagged. "I never thought how Muffy loved her mother. Muffy did what her mother wanted till her very life was at stake! Gerry, I need to run to the chapel." And she dashed out of the room.

In the empty chapel, Andrea sat in the same place where she sat when Muffy was married. She spoke in a soft whisper. "You're disappointed in me, Muffy, because you haven't come back to me in my dreams, like that first night. I've been waiting all this time. It's been so long. I ache to see you.

"But this is why, isn't it? I'm sorry, Muffy. It's just I miss you so, but I've been selfish and self-centered and haven't thought of Mother, or John Taylor or Aunt Elizabeth or Tom or anybody. But that's it, isn't it? Because I haven't loved your mother like you did. Oh, Muffy, I'm sorry I hated your mother. You loved her. I didn't understand. You expected me to love her, because I loved you so. I blamed her for taking you away from me."

Andrea cried as if her heart would break. Rays of sunlight through the stained glass windows graced the simple gold cross above the altar, and made it glitter. Through wet eyes, she looked up, tears streaming down her face, dripping from her nose and covering her lips. She reached for Kleenex, but her skirt pocket was empty. She sucked her tears into her mouth as Muffy appeared before her in her wedding gown on the cross. She looked like a goddess--radiant and happy like in her first dream.

"I see, Muffy. I see how you loved her. You wear before me the wedding dress she wanted. You knew to love her though she's not perfect. You loved your mother and I didn't, couldn't, understand. Aunt Elizabeth is as miserable as I am, probably worse. I'm sorry Muffy. I'll love her for you."

Andrea stretched out both arms high to the cross. "You look so beautiful. I love you," she cried. Andrea looked down and reached into her other pocket for a Kleenex. Tears streamed down her face. She looked up again. Muffy was gone, but Andrea felt at peace. She bowed her head, "Forgive me, God, for I knew not how to act. Forgive me, Muffy, Aunt Elizabeth, J.T., Mother, Tom." She lay down on the pew and slept.

Later Tom gently patted her shoulder. "Are you all right?"

"Yes," she smiled and hugged him. "How did you know I was here?"

"Gerry had me paged over the intercom. She was worried about you. She's on her way." Tom handed her his handkerchief.

"I saw her," Andrea said.

"Gerry?"

"No, you goose," and she hugged him again. "Muffy. She came back to me, because I told her I was sorry I hated her mother. You see, Muffy loved her mother very much. I promised her I wouldn't hate her mother any more."

Tom put his arms around her. "Oh, Andrea, I love you. You'll feel better now."

"You knew that was it, didn't you? Muffy was right there, Tom." Andrea pointed to the cross. "In the light there, on the right side of the cross. She was wearing the wedding dress I'm going to wear--the one Aunt Elizabeth wanted her to wear. Now I understand. It's all clear."

Gerry raced in. She carried the big box. "Oh, you're all right. I worried, because it got so late. Andrea, I'm your maid of honor, and you have to get this dress, or I'll not be able to get you down that aisle on time to marry this hunk." Gerry tipped her head toward Tom and winked at her. "We've got to run to Sak's before it closes. I brought the dress along."

#

"Do you want to try the other dress on? " Miss Heath inquired later in the elegant well-decorated bridal saloon. "The one I think your dear cousin really preferred?"

"No, thank you. I want to wear the one her mother wanted."

"Are you crazy?" Gerry said. "You vehemently screamed the opposite just two hours ago!"

"I've been a little crazy, but I'm all right now." Andrea smiled at Gerry.

"We'll keep the dress here for you, Miss Deck. We'll let it out and alter it now, but you come back four weeks before the wedding for the final fitting. And goodness, that's very soon," she said, writing on her calendar. "I'm surprised you hadn't selected a dress by now."

Gerry threw her a wink. "Do you want to hear me say, 'I told you so?' "

Chapter Twenty

Andrea lay on her side on her bed in her room. She frowned and sighed. She crumpled another piece of stationary into a ball and threw it on the floor. She started to copy her first letter over again.

March 30, 1959

Dear Uncle Orville,

I'm writing to ask if you would do me the honor of giving me away to Tom Scofield on Saturday June 24 at 3:00 in the afternoon. I can't imagine walking down the aisle with anyone but you. You and Aunt Elizabeth have always been so kind to me, and I remember happy times in your Houston home with Muffy and all of you. I loved our trips to Winter Park and the Grand Canyon.

You might enjoy knowing my favorite memory at your home was your making Sunday morning breakfasts. You were always in such high spirits, and Muffy and I giggled with glee when you'd pull out the top of Aunt Elizabeth's robe and peek down or pinch and pat her bottom. For years, Muffy and I imitated you when we played with our dolls.

I hated scrambled eggs at home and Mother was always mad at me, because I could hardly eat them. But I loved yours. Do you remember when I asked you how you made them? You said come over here and look 'my little dumplin.' No one has ever called me that, before or since.

I had never seen a daddy cook breakfasts before, and yours were the best. I watched by your side and learned. When I returned home, I never had trouble again, because mother or I cooked the eggs in butter. It was the bacon grease I disliked, and do to this day.

I hope you'll say yes, because I know I'll be so nervous, and you'll say some wonderful thing like you always do and make me laugh.

Please give my best to Aunt Elizabeth, to whom I just wrote, and to John Taylor and Billy.

Love,
Andrea

Andrea re-read the letter, and added a comma. "Mother probably would only approve the first paragraph, but off it goes, in the nick of time."

Andrea re-read her second letter. She got up and walked over to her Victrola and turned the record over. She lit a cigarette and sat on the side of her bed, re-reading her letter for the tenth time. She sighed and lay down again. She placed her stationary on her magazine, opened her fountain pen and started to copy it.

March 30, 1959

Dear Aunt Elizabeth,

I write to send you my heart felt thanks for the generous gift of Muffy's wedding gown. Your overwhelming kind gesture of love awakened in me some painful truths that I wish to share with you. These truths helped me to recover from the great shock and terror of Muffy's death.

On the Sunday night after I had learned from mother about Muffy's death, I had the most magnificent dream of Muffy with Bucky. They were radiant and happy and dressed as they were in front of your gold piano when toasts were made in your beautiful living room the night of her elegant engagement party at Christmas.

I was so happy when I awoke. I felt I'd been with her, almost touched her. Tom, at twelve, lost his little brother to whom he was devoted, and Tom told me Billy came to him in many real life-like dreams.

I waited and waited for Muffy to reappear. It pains me now, but I write you the truth. I was very angry at you, Aunt Elizabeth, because I blamed you for Muffy's death. My mother,

Tom, a psychiatrist, Dr. Hillerman, John Taylor, and a girlfriend all told me the car killed Muffy. I couldn't see or believe this.

When the dress arrived in its box, I swore to my friend that I'd never wear it, especially the one you had selected, not the one Muffy really wanted to wear. Wrought with anger and emotion, I ran to the beautiful little stained-glass chapel in the hospital.

Through my tears it dawned on me how much Muffy loved you, Aunt Elizabeth, exemplified by that very dress you sent me. Through my sobs, I apologized to Muffy for being so mean to you in my mind. I knew Muffy wanted me to love you as she had, to accept you as the wonderful mother that you were to her and to me in so many ways.

I had to rid myself of anger to accept, not deny, her loss and allow myself to grieve. I prayed to God for forgiveness for hating you. Then I looked up at the shining gold cross behind the altar. Muffy appeared with a sweet smile on her radiant face. She wore the satin wedding gown you sent me. Muffy has come to me in two dreams since then. Tom tells me they will not last, but will leave when I am over the worst of my grief. When Muffy reappeared in the chapel, I sat in the first pew where I sat at 1:00 on the Sunday Muffy was married. On that day I had visualized her in her white Chanel suit with navy trim. I kept my promise I made to you on the phone in the Dean's office. I had no involvement with Muffy's wedding. Bucky was her sole accomplice. Muffy telephoned a few hours before her marriage. She told me of their marriage plans and asked that at the time of her wedding, I repeat our secret call in the chapel. Muffy was my soul sister, John Taylor says. I loved her--her vitality, beauty, love. I know you love her as I do. My heart pours out to you in my pain and for your pain. Dr. Hillerman tells me to work on forgiving myself. I would ask for your forgiveness as I ask for God's.

I love you, Aunt Elizabeth. You and Uncle Orville provided me a second home, which became especially meaningful after we lost Daddy and our old homestead, and now, with Muffy's loss, it means more than ever. Upon the threshold of creating my new home with Tom, I think often of you in yours.

Love,
Andrea

P.S. Muffy wrote me the Wednesday following her marriage. I received her letter Monday, the day after Mother told me she had died. I send it to you in the hope it will bring you solace and further understanding of how much Muffy truly loved you.

#

"Mother, please don't worry. It'll all get done," Andrea said six weeks later at her home with her mother. We've addressed the invitations and announcements already, and they don't have to go out till June 1, says *the* Miss Emily Post, your close friend, these days." Andrea tapped the Emily Post book on the coffee table between them on the living room couch.

"Andrea--"

"The photographer, caterer, and flowers are set, and last night I wrote up an organized list of the bridal party; who goes in which car from the church to the Manor Club. We've got all the Macphersons, whom we know in advance are coming, quartered and housed so we're almost ready."

"My friend, Woodis's shower is on May 23rd, Andrea. That will give you time to get your thank you notes written before the wedding."

"Yes, Mother. Don't forget the Scofields' friend's shower is next Wednesday night, and I have my nursing school classmates' tomorrow night. Did Louise say anything about my asking Uncle Orville to give me away?"

"No. Because her husband gave Roddy away, I don't think they assumed he'd do your wedding, too. They know how close you were to Muffy. Orville's pleased to give you away. He and Elizabeth love you, as I did Muffy. Love goes up and down between younger and older generations."

"What are you talking about?"

"Some years parents love their children more than they love them back and vice versa. Just like in a marriage. Some years, I loved your father more. Other years he loved me more."

"Oh, I think I'll always love Tom more."

"I don't know that you do now." Her mother looked at her intently.

Andrea's eyebrows went up. "What?"

"You're young. I think Tom Scofield is devoted, appreciates and needs you."

"Gosh. I hope so." Andrea shook her head back and forth. "How did we get into this?" She frowned. "Do you think my sisters mind Gerry is my maid of honor?"

"Of course not. They are matrons of honor, and you could never choose between them."

"That's right. And I hope Sandra Scofield will be nice. She wrote me a sweet letter. I sent her a size fourteen dress. She must be bigger than she looks in her pictures."

"Andrea, I received a wonderful letter from Elizabeth yesterday. She wrote that you helped her feel so much better. She had a real breakthrough after she received your letter. Can you understand that?"

"Yes, I can." Andrea looked out the porch door across the room. "I'm glad I helped her. Muffy would be happy." Then she looked back to her mother. "And how are we doing financially?"

"We're all right. Wasn't it nice of Bill to offer to lend me the $500? I was going the next day to the bank, but last time it took several weeks until they approved. I'll be glad when we get it paid off. I don't like being indebted to a bank, and even less to Bill."

"I'll start sending you the checks right after August 1." Andrea frowned. "I hope Bill will keep you company when I'm gone that week in June."

"He will." Her mother smiled gently. "We play Bridge on my night off every week with Woodis and Prince, like Daddy and I played monthly with Bill and Irene all those years. And we go to dinner and the movies the second night I'm off. We're platonic friends, Andrea. Do you understand that?"

"Yes, darling."

"Andrea, stop that teasing now."

"Mother, you can't deny what I heard on the phone when you thought I was Bill calling. Anyway I'm glad he's around. I wish you'd marry him and have a double wedding with me."

"I'll never marry again. I told you that. Besides, Bill's pension stops when he dies, and he has some heart disease."

"Oh, no. You didn't tell me that before." She took her mother's hand. "You've looked into this marriage, haven't you? I'm sorry to learn about his health problem. And mother, I want you to check under your pillow for a note on the night of my wedding."

"I will. It sounds to me like you're getting teary." She patted Andrea's hand.

"I am, Mother. I love you, and I don't want you to think I'm leaving you and forgetting you."

"I know you won't. Remember when I drove you into nursing school the night before it began? We unpacked and settled your room and we cried and cried in the lobby when I left. We were only a thirty minute train ride apart. I know you love me and you know I'll always love you, Andrea."

"Yes, I know Mother." She smiled sadly. "I guess we're both emotional."

"It's probably that 'time of the month' for you, and you need to rest. Nothing will change between us, so don't get weepy, especially on your honeymoon. I'll be just fine here, and when you're married to Tom and living in New York, it'll be much like now. We'll talk on the phone, and you'll come out for church and dinner, and sometimes I'll come in and you can cook for me."

"Will you bring Bill?"

"Maybe sometimes. Not all the time."

"I'll never cook well enough. I'll get Tom to cook."

"You can't ask Tom to do that. He'll be too tired from working his residency."

"Mother, are you going to pass your sleep concerns for me over to Tom when we're married?"

#

"Meet me in thirty minutes in the lobby." Tom said excitedly on her phone that evening.

Andrea sighed. "Oh, Tom, I must study tonight."

"A furnished apartment became available at Ma Freeman's. Hank just called me."

"Goody," said Andrea. "I'll be in the lobby."

Later Andrea sat across the booth from Tom at Charlie's, where they were eating after seeing the apartment. "Ma Freeman glared at us from the door the whole time," Andrea said.

"I know and I'd planned to play with you in there for awhile--a little foreplay before we moved in and really started doing 'it.' You remember when I explained foreplay?" he grinned as he held her hand and kissed it.

"Remember? You gave me a two hour graphic example, night before last, in your bed." Andrea laughed. "Did you forget already?"

"No, I've had it on my mind every moment since then. I almost dropped a retractor in a patient's chest on the table today, and Dr. Harris made me jump. 'Are you thinking of our Pelham star or are you going to put some muscle in it?' Remember, he told me to take care of you. He's merciless now that he's learned the wedding's in five weeks."

"You saw his name on mother's invitation list, didn't you? All the Pelham doctors who work here and at New Rochelle will be there. That is, the ones who knew my father as well as mother. My parents knew all their children, too."

"But your father wasn't a doctor." Tom started on his second hamburger.

"I know, but they knew and respected both my parents. Some of them go to our church. And lots of the doctors worked with mother during the air raids in the war as well as at the hospital where mother works. Pelham's a small town where people take care of each other. I'm the prime example.

"I loved the apartment." Andrea frowned. "But do you think our landlady, Ma, will be around much? She scared me, and she'd put such a damper on things." Andrea took a sip of beer.

"Afraid she'll peep in and see us at Taffy?"

"*Toom!*" Andrea looked around at the other booths.

"I wanted to open the hide-a-bed in the one room off the kitchen and try it out, but instead, I asked the old battle ax about it."

"She said it was good," Andrea said, looking up from her salad.

"Sure," he grimaced. "It probably has cardboard for springs."

"But we don't need it. We have the double bed in the other room off the kitchen."

"I intend to make love to you everywhere in that apartment."

Andrea laughed. "You walk into the kitchen. There's a tiny room on each side. That won't be too hard."

"Plus the 'john.'"

"That's just a closet." Andrea continued looking at him.

"You'll see. And there's the wonderful tub with the board on top of it in the kitchen."

"I hope it's legal and not perverse."

"I've noticed you seem to like those illegal and perverse things."

She felt herself blushing, and looked down to wipe her mouth with her napkin. "Dr. Copper gave me a big book in her office yesterday."

"What's it called?"

"<u>The Joy and Techniques of Marriage</u> by Dr. Annette Twining."

"Good. We'll bring it on our honey moon and study it every day and every afternoon and every night." Tom took her hand in his and kissed it.

"Oh, Tom, you're so funny," Andrea said.

"You told me you loved me, because I was serious," he said, kissing her hand again.

"I do and you are. You're both. That's why I love you so much."

"Now, if you love me so much, will you please, please give up cigarettes? The apartment is five flights up. There is nowhere you can smoke in those three tiny rooms without smoking me out. It will take you so long to go up and down the flights to smoke, that you'll be lonely and I'll be utterly miserable. It will cut into our lovemaking time."

"Oh, all right. I'll try. But not until the Wednesday before we're married."

"I'm the happiest man in the world," he grinned, then took a bite of his salad.

"You could sweet talk anybody into anything."

"Baby, I'm going to sweet-talk myself right into your body every night."

"Tom! That's crude." She looked around again to make sure no one could possibly hear him.

"Oh, Andrea, I have so much to teach you. There is a difference between crude and good healthy love talk. You'll see. That will be one of our honeymoon lessons."

"One?"

"I have a huge list for my loving student."

"Do you think I'm a good student?" She smiled up at him.

"Honey, you're an A plus. I notice you're highly motivated, and your teacher likes that." Tom finished his beer.

"What's your parents' cottage on St. Simons like? It sure was nice of them to let us use it for our week."

"It's the most wonderful place in the world. I can't think of another place I'd rather take you. In fact, friends of my parents offered us a week's use of their beach front cottage in Cuba--"

"Cuba? We couldn't go there. Castro's off fighting in the woods."

"Right, and nothing compares to 'Monlochy.' Mother and Dad were touched, and I think delighted, that I had such happy memories and wanted to ravish you there on our honeymoon."

"You didn't tell them that, did you?"

"No." Tom laughed. "But I think they just may suspect we'll get into bed together." He opened the palm of her hand and kissed it.

"Why is it called Monlochy?"

"My mother named it when she and Dad bought it back in the thirties. Her ancestors are Scottish and they apparently had a cottage called Monlochy near Lake Inverness in Scotland. Monlochy is the Gaelic word for 'at the foot of the River Lochy.'

The cottage is rustic with lots of little rooms, but it's very charming. There's a Dutch kitchen door at the white stone gravel driveway that we use more than the front door.

"It's on a street named King's Way which is fitting for me, but Kings wouldn't live in our little cottage today. The street is lined with old live oaks whose branches, laden with Spanish Moss, form an arch as they touch overhead. Monlochy smells musty and woody from the fireplaces. The kitchen is old and big and yummy. My bedroom that I shared with Billy has pine-paneled walls with wooden pegs sticking out all over the entire wall across from our beds. We never opened the closet door the whole month we were there. We used the pegs for our jeans and shirts and p.j.'s

"There are black, wrought iron latches on all the pine-paneled doors, and you can hear latches singing, scraping, and clicking all the time. It's the most wonderful sound, for it means family and guests are about, and you're not alone.

"Dad's first medical bags are stored in the attic, and I'd explore and play with the stethoscopes, wooden stick tongue depressors, and blood pressure cuffs, always treating Billy. It's hard to think of Monlochy without Billy. Because he was four years younger, we always had to watch out for him--at the beach, in the boats, fishing. He loved everything and wanted to do everything I did.

"We'd get up at five in the morning and go fishing with Dad and Granddad until he passed away. Dad would prepare our peanut butter and jelly sandwiches for breakfast. We loved that. When we came back, my mother would take the fish behind the cottage and cut off their heads, because Billy and I hated that part. And Billy and I never ate the fish. We couldn't."

"What else did you do?"

"The beach was wonderful, enormous, and filled with shells, sand dollars, Pelicans, and sandpipers. We'd swim and ride in the surf for hours on end. Billy and I made sand castles, and as we got older, we learned to sail a sailfish, and the summer before Billy died, my parents let me drive our little aluminum outboard motor boat. I'd take Billy with me. Both of us wore life jackets, and my parents watched us from their beach chairs. We went round and round in circles in this one little area in a bay."

"Where was Sandra?"

"She sat next to my parents with her head in a book. She was four years older, and she lived in her books. She's still a great reader, and much smarter than I am."

"I can't believe that," Andrea said.

"She is. You'll see when you meet her."

"That's why, when we have our Billy and Deborah, I want them closer in age than I was with my sister and Billy."

"I never, ever, had a boyfriend who talked so much about having children."

"I'm always sad when I go to church, and there's a baptism. I want children. That's what makes me sad. Remember, I'm 26, and 27 in August."

"A worldly, sexually-experienced 26 is all I can say."

"We're going to have some fun, Andrea. You're such an amazing fast learner, I think you'll be teaching me soon."

"Tell me more about St. Simons. I love to hear you talk about it. I can tell you were happy there."

"The island is a bit isolated, so my parents had parties, music concerts, and readings in their home. They even had a harpist play out in the backyard one night. Dad had a beautiful rose garden. He paid Tom, this ancient, wizened, little old man, to care for it year round, when we weren't there."

"Did you go at other times of the year?"

"Sometimes the week after Christmas, sometimes Easter week when school was out--that is, before Billy died. On the cool nights, we had fires in the fireplaces, and we had game nights. Mother and Dad taught us how to play Poker and later Bridge. My parents have a maiden lady friend, Carrie Lee Ellis. She was more fun. She'd walk around the rooms of our cottage and play the accordion. She gave me the most wonderful gifts-- once a broken alarm clock that I could take apart and put together again. Then she gave me a big, blue glass piggy bank filled with pennies. I had to figure out how to get the pennies out."

"Did you?"

"No. She finally showed me. Hold the piggy bank upside down and insert a dinner knife into the slot and out they roll. Carrie Lee taught me all sorts of neat card tricks, and she came to our house on game night."

"What did you play?"

"Charades, Who am I, with the name pinned on my back, and my family asked me questions till they guessed me. I was often Eisenhower, General MacArthur or Nixon, but sometimes local people, or even people in my family.

"Carrie Lee gave us the most wonderful, unusual parties-- sometimes we'd play croquette or badminton in her yard or have sack races, or we'd play spoons on the floor in her giant sun room."

"She sounds wonderful."

"You'll love her, Andrea. She'll insist we come to some party or another."

"She's still there?"

"It's her permanent home. She's an artist. She still gives 'soirees' as she calls them, and she has a playreader's group where everyone has a part to act out. We did that at our house with her, too."

"What do I bring to wear?"

"Nothing. I'm excited just thinking about it." He put his hands under the table and rubbed her knees and moved up her skirt.

"Tom!" She blushed. "Stop. People will see you."

"I want to see you walk around the cottage naked all the time."

"You're scaring me."

Tom drew back and his face grew serious. "Have I once scared you in my bed on the 23rd floor?"

"Ah," Andrea hesitated. "Only once when you were mad at your parents."

"Oh yeah," Tom said, "I'm sorry about that, but since then have I ever frightened you?"

"Ah no. You may have shocked me at first, but I can't say you've scared me, because you usually told me or prepared me for what you were up too," she said smiling. "If you could begin to know the willpower it takes for me--love's the only explanation."

"Tom," she hesitated and flushed and she knew he saw it.

"I see you blushing. Out with it."

"Dr. Copper gave me a diaphragm. I've been practicing, but you'll have to give me time to put it in."

"Oh, my darling." He laughed, and rubbed her knees again. "I will. I promise."

"I *must* get my degree before we have babies. If I work really hard, I think I can do it in a year and a half. But I've got to go back and study now."

"We'll fly to St. Simons--actually to Atlanta. And then, we'll drive to the cottage in a rental car. We go Sunday morning."

"You didn't tell me what to take."

"Pack shorts, shirts, swim suits and maybe a dress or two. It's casual and rustic so we don't have to dress up, except to Carrie Lee's, where I always had to wear a coat and tie.

"On our wedding night, Mother and Dad are giving us a treat--a honeymoon night in the Madison Hotel. It's up on 86th and Madison. It's old and elegant with Oriental rugs and high ceiling bedrooms. You'll like it because it's filled with antiques."

"Will I have time to see them from our bed?"

He smiled at her lovingly. "Only when I'm sleeping."

"Oh, Tom, I can hardly wait."

Chapter Twenty-One

"I forgot to show you Uncle Orville's letter," Andrea said to Tom, walking home from Charlie's. They were holding hands. It was a warm spring evening and the city noises were changing as the twilight grew darker. The parade of cars lessened and the rumblings of the subway beneath the iron grids in the sidewalks grew more infrequent. "He agreed to give me away."

"Not away." Tom turned to her and stopped her. "To me, Andrea--who's here panting by your side. Let's go to my room."

"No, Tom. I told you I have to study some more, but come into the lobby so I can read you his letter."

"Let's see if there's a small date room available."

"Tom, listen to the letter here. Please?" She giggled up at him in the large well-lit lobby, then led him over to the corner wing back chairs, where they sat down and Andrea read Tom her letter.

April 17, 1959

My dearest Andrea,

You do me great honor in asking me to send you off to that brilliant doctor of yours. I assume this great responsibility with respectful solemnity and dignity, but I will have a parcel full of jokes to get my beautiful niece down to her panting handsome doctor. I believe this would please Muffy, as much as it pleases us. We'll laugh and smile all the way down that aisle, my little dumplin.

Elizabeth has cried over your letter many times. Your compassion is rare, and you have helped her, and thus all of us who care for her here in residence on River Oaks Boulevard. She is composing a letter to you, but she keeps crying, the ink blurs, and she has to start all over.

Copious tears have spilled here since our Muffy was taken from us, but each day gentle soothing winds blow over our bleeding hearts and quench the flow as we heal, grow and come to cherish what we have--our families, our church, our larger Macpherson clan and all our fine friends.

We find great solace in the prayer our aged great Uncle John Taylor says annually at our final breakfast in North Carolina, concluding our Macpherson reunions.

It is the tragedies in our families as well as the joys that bring us together in a circle, like a boat's rescue ring. Make this family a circle of strength, love, and acceptance as each birth and marriage increases our joy of sharing. Make us remindful that each crisis faced together as a family strengthens our family circle. Amen.

We look forward to your wedding with great anticipation, and eagerly welcome Tom into the Macpherson clan. My best wishes to you both.

Love,
Your devoted Uncle Orville

"You see, he knows I'm panting," Tom said.

"Uncle Orville is such fun. He's always peeping down Aunt Elizabeth's blouses. He pulls them right out straight and peeks down. Then he pinches her bottom. Muffy and I used to laugh at them all the time."

"That's what I'm going to do, 'my little dumplin,'" Tom said. "Is that really what he calls you?"

"For as long as I can remember, and Muffy was 'my little miss muffin.'"

"I hope Elizabeth feels better soon so Uncle Orville's happy, boisterous ways return. He delights in his continuous risqué relish of Aunt Elizabeth."

"And I'm ravishing for you. I'll time it. Honestly. Five minutes in the date room," Tom said and he took her hand and led her toward the lounge.

"Oh, all right Tom, but I have an exam at 4 tomorrow afternoon and I work 7:00 to 3:00, so we must keep it to 5 minutes. Are you listening?"

After work the next afternoon Andrea saw a thick envelope in her mailbox with Aunt Elizabeth's return address. Andrea took it to her dorm room and read it several times.

May 3, 1959

My dearest Andrea,

I have taken some time before putting my thoughts on paper for you. Your letter helped me break through some barriers, my psychiatrist said. Yes, I go to a psychiatrist, something I didn't even have the courage or dignity to allow for my own beloved Muffy.

It has been a horrendous, deep, bottomless hole where I've lived without the sunny sunshine of beautiful Muffy in my life.

But before I even started to climb out, I was furious with you for encouraging Muffy to go to Atlanta for treatment. I blamed you for her death, because she subsequently married and had the accident with wonderful Bucky. Like you, I heard it was a car that killed her, not Andrea, but I lay in bed day and night knowing the real truth. It was me.

I'm far from out of that well, but your letter helped me to understand Muffy loved me and thought I was a good mother even with my imperfections. Her illness occurred for a myriad of reasons, including her own genes, parental and society's expectations, and her own drive for perfection.

John Taylor told me of his proposal of marriage to Helen Saros and his new career choice. He told me you knew of this.

I was horrified. Like my mother before me, I've hated Catholics all my life. Greek Orthodox believers were worse than Catholics   my mother, then I, believed from childhood.

The afternoon John Taylor told me his news, your letter arrived. I read it over and over and over, and also the letter Muffy had written you after her marriage. That night, I had a dream.

Before I tell you the dream, I will share with you an event that occurred many years ago. I've revealed this to no one except Orville.

One afternoon I was gardening in the back yard of our first Houston home. Our maid was in the kitchen. Muffy appeared by my side. She was almost two. I was shocked she'd managed the stairs without the maid seeing her or injuring herself.

She pulled at me. Then she took my hand and pulled harder and started to cry. She said, "JaJa," which was her name for John Taylor. I finally got up and Muffy toddled me upstairs to John Taylor's nursery. John Taylor sat in his crib eating pills from a big bottle of baby aspirin. Thirty minutes later, his stomach was pumped out--his life saved. I told no one, other than Orville, Andrea. Not even your mother, because I was ashamed I'd been a careless mother.

The night I received your letter, I dreamed first of you and Muffy playing in the sandbox near my flower garden where I had been weeding that day long ago. Then I dreamed of Muffy pulling me and saying "Ja Ja." Muffy adored John Taylor, just eighteen months older. She toddled everywhere after him. Never a good napper herself, she'd sit on the floor of his nursery, watch him sleep and wait for him to wake up so she could play with him.

When I awakened from my dream, I clearly understood Muffy wanted me to accept John Taylor and Helen. This may be difficult for you to understand, but it took me many more days before I could give John Taylor my blessing. I asked him to bring Helen to the house for dinner.

When Helen told what she was willing to give up to be John Taylor's wife, I hugged her and asked her if she would allow us to provide a wedding for her. That beautiful self-possessed girl cried. She has been terribly close to her family.

That night, Muffy was in my dream smiling in her wedding dress. Now you know what your letter means to me.

Our generation has been rigid and puritanical in its religious thought and prejudices, deeply ingrained during our youth. It's not only religion, but also some of society's rules and mores of the time.

Someday after time passes, I hope to be able to have Helen's family here in our home.

Helen vows that it will never happen, because she's heard her father preach in the pulpit of their church all her life. I pledge, and this may take many years, to try, if he's a High Holy Priest, or King, to help him accept his own daughter and our fine son, and who knows, maybe a group of grandchildren someday.

Finally, I ask your forgiveness for calling you an upstart.

You provided Muffy with invaluable help. As a result, she died happy with Bucky, optimistic of recovery. I've talked with Dr. Hillerman and met with Dr. Ashworth in Atlanta, both of whom have the utmost respect for you and Muffy. I return forthwith the letter Muffy wrote you after her marriage. I know her sharing her joy has precious meaning for you.

I send you my love and forgiveness, and ask only for yours in return.

We all look forward to your wedding, and it will give Orville and me special joy to see you in Muffy's wedding dress.

We enjoyed talking with Tom when you and Muffy sailed away on ice skates last February. From your wedding, we travel with John Taylor and Helen to Boston where they want to share with us a preview of their new life.

With kind regards to your mother, I remain

Your devoted Aunt Elizabeth

#

Andrea heard a lone robin singing on the morning of her wedding day. She opened her eyes and hugged her pillow in her twin bed in her childhood home where she had lived since she was thirteen. She studied the pink nubbly stucco walls that she and her mother had planned to wallpaper. They had never had the time nor the money. She looked at the picture across the wall that her mother had brought back from her own Bermuda honeymoon.

Andrea looked out her small, paned, casement window and saw the next door beige triplex just like theirs. 'Squeezed in like sardines,' mother had said when we first came to look, 'but this nice place will feel cozy,' and she had bought it, and made a new home. The very next day she started working as an evening nurse at the nearby hospital. It had been 23 years since she had nursed in Chicago, but she had met the challenge to support her daughters and herself.

I wonder if Tom's awake or what he's thinking. No, I just wonder if he's awake. *I know he's thinking about sex.* I wonder if he'll always be so sex-starved. *I hope so.* She giggled and rolled over with her pillow. 'Horny,' she thought, was the word he'd used. *What a funny word. I must ask him its derivation. Surely he'll know, for he seems to know everything.*

Andrea heard the pipes shudder and rumble. She knew her mother was taking a bath. She'd have to wait now until the water heated up again. No showers here, like at nursing school, she thought. But I've loved this tiny home, without a laundry, modern kitchen appliances, or even a t.v.

Andrea turned on her back and hugged her pillow. Wonder what it will feel like with Tom inside me. *Will it be as wonderful as he says?* Her buttocks tingled with pleasure and she thought about their farewell night to Tom's intern room two nights ago. *His new room will be with me in Ma Freeman's five flight walk-up. I never had much time to clean or make it ready.*

If I miss smoking too much, maybe I'll smoke with Mrs. Scofield some time. It's not been too bad since Wednesday, but then I've been busy at school until yesterday.

I'm going to save lots of money each month, she thought. We'll need a bigger place after I get my degree--for the babies. *I can work right up to delivery, then stay home and just take care of the baby. It'll be like a vacation for me, after working and going to school for so long.*

She remembered her bedroom before her daddy died. The wonderful light blue wallpaper with puffs of white, fluffy clouds clustered between bouquets of red, yellow and blue balloons braided together in a ribbon tie. Her big three-tiered blue shelf held her <u>Book Trails</u>, her favorite collection of miniature china dogs, a tiny gold tea set, a few little maroon Mexican plates with white trim, and a blue Shirley Temple glass on the bottom shelf. She thought with a smile of her special, little, light brown doggie--the one she'd bought at the dime store on Main Street in New Rochelle with her 10 cents allowance. It was so like Taffy.

Her window paned door had opened onto a silver tin-roofed porch. In the summer, her mother would open the door and just before she went to sleep, she'd watch the rain. Its drops danced up and down like little tin soldiers tinkling out the most delightful tunes as they marched in their band. Sometimes she looked between fluffy, white organdy tie-back curtains for her bird's nest, always built in the same spot early each spring, but later in the summer it seemed hidden behind gigantic, light, green leaves that also covered the peeling light bark from the birch tree.

Across the bedroom had been her little, brown wood desk with an ink well, but there was no ink bottle in it. The top of the desk lifted up, and there she had kept all her secret letters from Muffy. Her dresser was dark brown. Daddy had sanded and stained it for her, but it had big grooves across the top. Daddy, she guessed, had been better as an editor than as a refinisher of furniture.

The maid they had before Evelyn had had this furniture first--all but the desk. Daddy had bought that especially for her. Louise had matching mahogany and Roddy matching maple furniture. She didn't tell them, but she really liked hers better.

One of her doors opened right into her parents' bedroom. When she was little, she sometimes crept into her mother's twin bed, to the right just inside her door. It always had a nice warm smell. Her mother had big breasts that hung down almost to her waist under her nightie. Her mother told her this was because, when she grew up, it wasn't fashionable to have breasts, and she had bound hers with strips of white sheets. Now they were flatten down, sort of like big brown pancakes. Andrea chuckled at her own memory.

"Andrea, are you wool-gathering or sleeping in there?" Andrea heard her mother's footsteps coming up the stairs. "It's time to get up. You can't keep your groom waiting at the altar. Come on now. It's your wedding day." Her mother opened the door carrying a tray of cinnamon toast, flowers, and two coffee cups.

"That was a lovely rehearsal dinner last night at the Pelham Country Club," her mother said, sitting on the edge of her bed. She handed a coffee cup to Andrea. "You looked radiant in your blue silk print. The toasts were magnificent and the food superb. You could rest longer if you'd decided earlier to have this wedding. Then we could have had it at 4:00 or 5:00 p.m."

"Mother, if you say that one more time--3:00 is proper and fine. Tom says he's getting me to the hotel by 4:00."

"He most certainly is not. You and Tom are to circulate at your wedding, and say hello to everyone. I want you to take Tom around to talk a little more with your Macpherson relatives. They made a long trip to be here for your wedding."

Andrea smiled at her mother. "You've sounded more like Aunt Elizabeth these past three harried months."

"Andrea, did you hear me about mingling?"

"Yes, Mother."

"That's better." Her mother's shoulders relaxed.

"You always calm down when I say, 'yes mother.' "

"Because I'm always afraid you won't!" she exclaimed, and they laughed at each other and hugged. "It's been fine, Mother, really fine." She squeezed her tightly.

"It has, dear, dear, Andrea. It hasn't always been easy these last seven years, but we've had some fun along the way and we made it. But we must stop, or you'll have red eyes for your wedding."

"Emily Post probably wouldn't allow it!" Andrea laughed out loud. "How would you live without her, Mother?"

"Oh, Andrea, you'll be the death of me."

Andrea smiled and gave her standard answer. "I hope not."

"There's the first door bell, probably the bridal bouquets. I'll get it. The water must be hot by now. Take your bath right away." Her mother stood up. "I hear your sisters' voices at the front door. I'm going down to fix our little bridal luncheon."

"Mother," Andrea smiled at her lovingly, but teased. "I thought you'd want me to get some more rest."

Her mother looked back at her in exasperation. "Andrea, do get up now. This minute."

Andrea lay back in bed as she heard her mother's footsteps on the stairs. She took the letter she had written the night before, from under her pillow. She read it once more.

On the eve of my wedding

Dear Mother,

Tomorrow is a day of excitement, love, commitment, sharing, and families. It starts a new beginning and an ending for you and me.

For it will never be quite the same. It's a bit sad to leave the old, you and me together for so many years in this house on Monroe Street.

How lucky we were to find it. Remember all those awful places we looked at together? Then going to the closing, and you forgot your checkbook, and we had to run home for the checkbook and then to the bank?

We've had fun and trying times--staying afloat of the bills, the snow banks in the winter, shoveled by whomever was home first from work or school, the boiler tank leak causing the basement to flood, then the car accident, and those many rushed shopping expeditions.

This part of our lives is over, but I'll not say good-bye.

Even the thought of a good-bye between us makes me shiver and shake with tears streaming down my face. Tom seems to have a big crush on you for which I'm thankful. I understand it. He loves your dinners, too. So tomorrow it's a new beginning--a future, with Tom along with us.

You made tomorrow possible. Not just the effort, work and bills of the last three months, but a lifetime of work—raising me, watching me, sacrificing for me, and especially since Daddy died.

You've been a wonderful mother. The strict upbringing I hated when little, provided me the discipline to obey your house rules when alone here so much through my high school years. I never, ever, felt alone because you were such a huge presence in my mind. I never felt poor or sorry for myself because I had you--the most wonderful mother in the world, who worked for and with me. On the contrary, I always felt richer than my rich friends with two parents and big houses, because I had you.

You have been my strength, my bulwark for any challenge.

They've been incredible years, with great highs and lows that taught me to appreciate life and its gifts to its fullest, for tomorrow they could be gone. Many of my friends haven't had that opportunity. I'm the lucky one. We learned some of those things together, didn't we? To 'make-do,' be self-sufficient, strong, appreciate what we did have.

It's now as I marry, I think more of Daddy, and what a fine father he was. He loved me and spent so much time with me that if it had to be God's plan, thirteen years was more than enough.

I feel fortunate snuggled in close between you and Tom--two such wonderful people. Thank you again for everything, Mother. I love you now and always,

Andrea

#

Andrea stood later that day in the gray stone slate vestibule of the Huguenot Memorial Church. Surrounded by her sisters, and Gerry, she studied her Mother. She looked handsome in her beige, lace, and satin dress. She sure was a proud Presbyterian. She had always wanted the church to be called the Huguenot Memorial *Presbyterian* Church. *I wonder how Mother and her Episcopalian sister handle this.*

I'll ask Uncle Orville when we go down the aisle. Where is he? She looked around again. It was almost 3:00, and all the guests seemed to be in the church.

The mint green taffeta dresses looked perfect with the purple violets and white baby's breath bouquets. Mother would have preferred another color for her attendants, but Andrea had insisted. She hadn't wanted them to wear any hats, but mother won that one. The tiny veils with 'do-das' were as little as she could get away with.

She looked down at her veil. She had used lace from her mother's wedding gown to make a stunning mantilla that framed her face. She'd refused to have a veil over her face. She wanted to watch Tom on her long walk down the aisle.

She looked down and touched the lace with her fingers. She had longed to wear something of her mother's. Her mother had lovingly removed the lace from her own wedding gown, and Andrea had held her breath as her mother carefully, gingerly stirred it in the kitchen sink with just a little Chlorox in the water--too much Chlorox and it would disintegrate. But it had worked. The yellowing from long years folded in a box disappeared. They celebrated that night with a bourbon and water.

"Where's my uncle?" Her sisters came to her. "Don't worry. Everyone will get here. It'll be all right," Louise said.

"There's Sandra. Finally," Andrea said to them. "Gerry. I hardly know her and didn't get to say but two words to her last night, but I'm relieved she's finally here. Tom says she's very intelligent. I thought maybe she was so brainy that she'd forget the time."

Sandra came immediately to Andrea. "Well, I made it." She smiled at Andrea. "This is a special treat for me, and I love meeting you and being in your wedding, though we hardly know each other. Sure hope you can keep up with my brother. He was a rake, if you know what I mean. The good thing about that is that, if you ever want something..." she leaned over and whispered in a loud voice in Andrea's ear, "just hold out a little sex and you'll get it *immediately*. Remember, keep Tom horny when you want something. It always works in my house," she laughed with a wicked wink at Andrea. Andrea was so taken aback she didn't know what to say.

But Gerry had heard Sandra and she laughed out loud. "Thanks for the good advice."

Andrea knew Sandra saw her look about, hoping no late guests were coming into the church vestibule and could hear her.

Sandra said to her," Good for their staid Presbyterian ears."

Then, Andrea broke into laughter with Gerry and her sisters.

"Our moments together are brief," Sandra said more seriously to Andrea, "but I hope not our future times together. I want you to come visit us in New Hampshire. Tom loves to ski and go back to Dartmouth where he was a total hell raiser as well as a brilliant student--a fact he tries to hide. Do you ski, Andrea?"

"No."

"I don't either. We could sit home--talk, read, relax, and drink, but Tom will have you out on skis as much as you'll allow." Sandra took her hand and kissed her lightly on the cheek. "Please do promise to come stay with us, dear sister. Philip, our 3 year old Michael, and the secret little bundle in here," she said patting her stomach, "will love your visits. Come any time. We live very close to a ski area. It'll be cheap for you, and as my illustrious brother plans to be poor for six more years to get his hands and brains ready to be a surgeon, you'll need cheap accommodations."

"How's my little dumplin this morning? You look ravishing and entertained" Uncle Orville boomed, coming up behind her.

"Oh, I'm so glad you're here, Uncle Orville." Andrea grabbed his hand in hers. She thought of Muffy, but vowed not to cry for all the Davidsons, as well as Tom, her mother, and Muffy herself.

"We'll sail down this aisle and maybe even perk up the ears of those sedate Presbyterian guests of your mother's."

The musical strains of Lohengrin's wedding march brought then to order. The Scofields kissed her forehead as they passed her and went down the aisle. Andrea blew a kiss to her mother as she took her son-in-law's arm to go sit next to Aunt Elizabeth who was already seated in the first pew. She wished she'd seen John Taylor and Helen when they went into the church.

Emily Post and her mother wouldn't have approved of the vestibule talk. Even Andrea was a bit shocked, especially by Sandra. But Sandra was starting the walk down the aisle already, then her sisters, and Gerry.

Andrea almost stepped backward when she saw all the people standing ahead in the filled church. She loved this church and looked for the spot where she had always sat for the children's sermon, right near her mother. But she was afraid she'd cry if she caught her mother's eye. She looked at the familiar altar and the beautiful, stained glass Rosette window in the chancel. She thought of her hospital chapel and again of Muffy. She looked down at her dress and winked at it for Muffy and her aunt, for truly it was the most delicate, beaded satin wedding dress she'd ever seen.

Andrea peered down the aisle to see Tom.

"He's there, yearning for you, my little dumplin," she heard her uncle say. "We'd better get up there before he races up this aisle and carries you off to fairyland."

"Oh, Uncle Orville. I'm so glad you're here with me."

"If you cry now, my little dumplin, both your mother and Aunt Elizabeth will put me out in the dog house tonight."

Andrea chuckled. A little closer, Andrea saw Tom standing tall and straight. She looked for his smiling brown eyes and white sprinkly hairs at the temples of the face that she so loved to kiss. She looked quickly for portly five foot Dr. Smith and felt relieved. He had talked a long time to them, on two different occasions, and Andrea remembered the afternoon he kneeled down on the floor and prayed right in the middle of their living room, at the big house when Daddy had died. She'd been so surprised when he did that, but they had all copied him and held hands in a circle.

She gripped Uncle Orville's arm.

He squeezed her hand in response. "I'm not letting those guests get near you. You're safe by me. That man down there at the altar, the one named Tom, has a big grin on his face. You'd think he were in your bed already."

"Uncle Orville, I can't laugh. Mother told me just to smile."

"Then I'll just lightly humor you."

Andrea saw her mother and her throat tightened. She thought she was going to cry, but her mother stuck her hand out from her hips and just out from her pew, looked around to make sure no one was watching her, and then she waved her hand downwards over and over.

Andrea's taut throat relaxed into a beaming smile. "Emily Post and Mother want us to slow down, Uncle Orville."

"Yes, Mistress Andrea, Mrs. Deck and Miss Post. Our march will slow to a turtle's pace. There, your mother's stopped waving at us, so I guess we're doing it right," Uncle Orville said.

But Andrea didn't hear him, though she walked very slowly in unison with his step. She saw only Tom and could not remove her eyes from his.

"Who gives this woman to this man?" Dr. Smith said a few moments later.

She heard her mother's voice, "Her mother, Marie Deck." Then she heard Uncle Orville's booming voice. "Her aunt and uncle, Elizabeth and Orville Hamilton."

Uncle Orville was a little behind her, as well as to her left. She felt his pat on her behind before he moved to his seat. She hoped her mother hadn't seen that, but Andrea smiled and thought of Muffy.

Andrea looked at Tom and then up at the gold cross behind the altar. She blinked her eyes once and then again. "Tom, it's Muffy, in my dress, on the cross. See her?" Andrea raised her left arm high, and pointed to the cross with her hand.

"Ictaminigoalagosectobingolady, yoo hoo!" Tom said slowly in a hushed voice. Andrea felt Tom's eyes on her. She whispered softly with him. "Ictaminigoalagosecto-bingolady, yoo hoo." But she kept her eyes on Muffy, until she disappeared. *Good-bye Muffy. I love you. Thank you for coming to me. This will keep Mother from crying, for she'll worry through the service if Emily Post would approve.* Andrea slowly lowered her arm.

"The bride and groom have now completed their private benediction," Dr. Smith's sonorous voice rang out, "and we will commence." Tom winked at her as Andrea turned her radiant face to him.

THE END

ABOUT THE AUTHOR

For 20 years, first as a nurse and then as a Realtor, BARBARA ROTHE observed the loving fabric of family life ravaged by children's and parents' deaths, divorce, illnesses, accidents, and estrangements. Now retired with her husband in South Carolina, she writes about the importance of families.

The author has completed <u>RESCUE</u> <u>RING</u> the sequel to <u>PASSIONATE</u> <u>VISIONS</u>, and she is currently writing the final novel of the Rescue Ring Trilogy. The author's royalties are donated to family organizations.